I STEPPED BACK, PULLING MY HAND FROM HIS. "I don't understand," I said, my voice mistrustful. "What's wrong with you?"

He looked resigned. "I'm sorry I ever got you mixed up in this. It was selfish. But I didn't think it would turn out this way. I didn't think . . . at all. Obviously."

My feeling of general alarm was replaced by a creeping sensation of fear of what would come next. I couldn't imagine what sort of revelation he was going to come out with. But a little voice inside me said, *You knew.* And I realized that I had.

I had known that there was something different about Vincent. I had felt it, even before I saw his photo in the obituaries. It was something just a little east of normal, but too obscure for me to put my finger on. So I had ignored it. But now I was going to find out.

Also by Amy Plum

Until I Die

DIE FOR ME

AMY PLUM

An Imprint of HarperCollinsPublishers

HarperTeen is an imprint of HarperCollins Publishers.

Die for Me
HarperCollins Children's Books, a division of HarperCollins Publishers,
10 East 53rd Street, New York, NY 10022.
www.epicreads.com

Library of Congress Cataloging-in-Publication Data
Plum, Amy.
    Die for me / Amy Plum. — 1st ed.
        p.   cm.
    Summary: After their parents are killed in a car accident, sixteen-year-old Kate Mercier and her older sister, Georgia, each grieving in her own way, move to Paris to live with their grandparents, and Kate finds herself powerfully drawn to the handsome but elusive Vincent who seems to harbor a mysterious and dangerous secret.
    ISBN 978-0-06-200402-4
    [1. Grief—Fiction.   2. Dead—Fiction.   3. Supernatural—Fiction.
4. Love—Fiction.   5. Sisters—Fiction.   6. Paris (France)—Fiction.
7. France—Fiction.]   I. Title.
PZ7.P7287Di 2011   2010030785
[Fic]—dc22   CIP
                                                                  AC

Typography by Ray Shappell
12 13 14 15 16 CG/RRDH 10 9 8 7 6 5 4 3 2 1
❖
First paperback edition, 2012

This is for you, Mom. I miss you every day.

Unable are the loved to die. For love is immortality.
—*Emily Dickinson*

PROLOGUE

THE FIRST TIME I HAD SEEN THE STATUE IN THE fountain, I had no idea what Vincent was. Now, when I looked at the ethereal beauty of the two connected figures—the handsome angel, with his hard, darkened features focused on the woman cradled in his outstretched arms, who was all softness and light—I couldn't miss the symbolism. The angel's expression seemed desperate. Obsessed, even. But also tender. As if he was looking to her to save him, and not vice versa. And all of a sudden, Vincent's name for me popped into my mind: *mon ange*. My angel. I shivered, but not from the cold.

Jeanne had said that meeting me had transformed Vincent. I had given him "new life." But was he expecting me to save his soul?

ONE

MOST SIXTEEN-YEAR-OLDS I KNOW WOULD DREAM of living in a foreign city. But moving from Brooklyn to Paris after my parents' death was anything but a dream come true. It was more like a nightmare.

I could have been anywhere, really, and it wouldn't have mattered—I was blind to my surroundings. I lived in the past, desperately clinging to every scrap of memory from my former life. It was a life I had taken for granted, thinking it would last forever.

My parents had died in a car accident just ten days after I got my driver's license. A week later, on Christmas Day, my sister, Georgia, decided that the two of us would leave America to live with our father's parents in France. I was still too shell-shocked to put up a fight.

We moved in January. No one expected us to go back to school right away. So we just passed the days trying to cope in our own desperate ways. My sister frantically blocked her sorrow by going out every night with the friends she had made during our summer visits. I turned into an agoraphobic mess.

Some days I would get as far as walking out of the apartment and down the street. Then I found myself sprinting back to the protection of our home and out of the oppressive outdoors, where it felt like the sky was closing in on me. Other days I would wake up with barely enough energy to walk to the breakfast table and then back to my bed, where I would spend the rest of the day in a stupor of grief.

Finally our grandparents decided we should spend a few months in their country house. "For a change of air," Mamie said, which made me point out that no difference in air quality could be as dramatic as that between New York and Paris.

But as usual, Mamie was right. Spending the springtime outdoors did us a world of good, and by the end of June we were, if only mere reflections of our previous selves, functional enough to return to Paris and "real life." That is, if life could ever be called "real" again. At least I was starting over in a place that I love.

There's nowhere I'd rather be than Paris in June. Even though I've spent every summer there since I was a baby, I never fail to get that "Paris buzz" as I walk down its summer streets. The light is different from anywhere else. As if pulled straight out of a fairy tale, the wand-waving brilliance makes you feel like absolutely anything could happen to you at any moment and you wouldn't even be surprised.

But this time was different. Paris was the same as it had always been, but I had changed. Even the city's sparkling, glowing air couldn't penetrate the shroud of darkness that felt superglued to my skin. Paris is called the City of Light. Well, for me it had become the City of Night.

I spent the summer pretty much alone, falling quickly into a solitary routine: eat breakfast in Papy and Mamie's dark, antique-filled apartment and spend the morning entrenched in one of the small dark Parisian cinemas that project classic films round-the-clock, or haunt one of my favorite museums. Then return home and read the rest of the day, eat dinner, and lie in bed staring at the ceiling, my occasional sleep jam-packed with nightmares. Get up. Repeat.

The only intrusions on my solitude were emails from my friends back home. "How's life in France?" they all started.

What could I say? *Depressing? Empty? I want my parents back?* Instead I lied. I told them I was really happy living in Paris. That it was a good thing Georgia's and my French was fluent because we were meeting so many people. That I couldn't wait to start my new school.

My lies weren't meant to impress them. I knew they felt sorry for me, and I only wanted to reassure them that I was okay. But each time I pressed send and then read back over my email, I realized how vast the gulf was between my real life and the fictional one I created for them. And that made me even more depressed.

Finally I realized that I didn't actually want to talk to anyone. One night I sat for fifteen minutes with my hands poised above the keyboard, searching desperately for something even slightly positive to say to my friend Claudia. I clicked out of the message and, after taking a deep breath, completely deleted my email address from the internet. Gmail asked me if I was sure. "Oh yeah," I said as I clicked the red button. A huge burden lifted from my shoulders. After that I shoved my laptop into a drawer and didn't open it again until school started.

Mamie and Georgia encouraged me to get out and meet people. My sister invited me along with her and her group of friends to sunbathe on the artificial beach set up next to the river, or to bars to hear live music, or to the clubs where they danced the weekend nights away. After a while they gave up asking.

"How can you dance, after what happened?" I finally asked Georgia one night as she sat on her bedroom floor, putting on makeup before a gilt rococo mirror she had pulled off her wall and propped up against a bookcase.

My sister was painfully beautiful. Her strawberry blond hair was in a short pixie cut that only a face with her strikingly high cheekbones could carry off. Her peaches-and-cream skin was sprinkled with tiny freckles. And like me, she was tall. Unlike me, she had a knockout figure. I would kill for her curves. She looked twenty-one instead of a few weeks shy of eighteen.

She turned to face me. "It helps me forget," she said, applying a fresh coat of mascara. "It helps me feel alive. I'm just as sad as you are, Katie-Bean. But this is the only way I know of dealing with it."

I knew she was being honest. I heard her in her bedroom the

nights she stayed in, sobbing like her heart had been shattered to bits.

"It doesn't do you any good to mope," she continued softly. "You should spend more time with people. To distract you. Look at you," she said, putting her mascara down and pulling me toward her. She turned my head to face the mirror next to hers.

To see us together, you would never guess we were sisters. My long brown hair was lifeless; my skin, which thanks to my mother's genes never tans, was paler than usual.

And my blue-green eyes were so unlike my sister's sultry, heavy-lidded "bedroom eyes." "Almond eyes" my mom called mine, much to my chagrin. I would rather have an eye shape that evoked steamy encounters than one described by a nut.

"You're gorgeous," Georgia concluded. My sister . . . my only fan.

"Yeah, tell that to the crowd of boys lined up outside the door," I said with a grimace, pulling away from her.

"Well, you're not going to find a boyfriend by spending all your time alone. And if you don't stop hanging out in museums and cinemas, you're going to start looking like one of those nineteenth-century women in your books who were always dying of consumption or dropsy or whatever." She turned to me. "Listen. I won't bug you about going out with me if you will grant me one wish."

"Just call me Fairy Godmother," I said, trying to grin.

"Take your frickin' books and go outside and sit at a café. In the sunlight. Or the moonlight, I don't care which. Just get out-doors and suck some good pollution-ridden air into those wasted, consumptive, nineteenth-century lungs of yours. Surround yourself with people, for God's sake."

"But I *do* see people," I began.

"Leonardo da Vinci and Quentin Tarantino don't count," she interrupted.

I shut up.

Georgia got up and laced the strap to her tiny, chic handbag over her arm. "It's not *you* who is dead," she said. "Mom and Dad are. And *they* would want you to live."

TWO

"WHERE ARE YOU GOING?" MAMIE ASKED, STICK-ing her head out of the kitchen as I unlocked the front door.

"Georgia said my lungs were in need of Paris pollution," I responded, slinging my bag across my shoulder.

"She's right," she said, coming to stand in front of me. Her forehead barely reached my chin, but her perfect posture and regulation three-inch heels made her seem much taller. Only a couple of years from seventy, Mamie's youthful appearance sub-tracted at least a decade from her age.

When she was an art student, she had met my grandfather, a successful antiques dealer who fawned over her like she was one of his priceless ancient statues. Now she spent her days restoring old paintings in her glass-roofed studio on the top floor of their apartment building.

"Allez, file!" she said, standing before me in all her compactly

packaged glory. "Get going. This town could use a little Katya to brighten it up."

I gave my grandmother a kiss on her soft, rose-scented cheek and, grabbing my set of keys off the hall table, made my way through the heavy wooden doors and down the spiral marble staircase, to the street below.

Paris is divided into twenty neighborhoods, or arrondissements, and each one is called by its number. Ours, the seventh, is an old, wealthy neighborhood. If you wanted to live in the trendiest part of Paris, you would not move to the seventh. But since my grandparents live within walking distance of the boulevard Saint-Germain, which is packed with cafés and shops, and only a fifteen-minute wander to the river Seine's edge, I was certainly not complaining.

I stepped out the door into the bright sunlight and skirted past the park in front of my grandparents' building. It is filled with ancient trees and scattered with green wooden park benches, giving the impression, for the couple of seconds it takes to pass it, that Paris is a small town instead of France's capital city.

Walking down the rue du Bac, I passed a handful of way-too-expensive clothes, interior decor, and antiques stores. I didn't even pause as I walked past Papy's café: the one he had taken us to since we were babies, where we sat and drank mint-flavored water while Papy chatted with anything that moved. Sitting next to a group of his friends, or even across the terrace from

Papy himself, was the last thing I wanted. I was forced to find my own café.

I had been weighing the idea of two other local spots. The first was on a corner, with a dark interior and a row of tables wrapped around the outside of the building on the sidewalk. It was probably quieter than my other option. But when I stepped inside I saw a line of old men sitting silently on their stools along the bar counter with glasses of red wine in front of them. Their heads slowly pivoted to check out the newcomer, and when they saw me they looked as shocked as if I were wearing a giant chicken costume. *They might as well have an "Old Men Only" sign on the door,* I thought, and hurried on to my second option: a bustling café a few blocks farther down the *rue*.

Because of its glass facade, the Café Sainte-Lucie's sunlit interior felt spacious. Its sunny outdoor terrace held a good twenty-five tables, which were usually full. As I made my way toward an empty table in the far corner, I knew this was my café. I already felt like I belonged here. I stuck my book bag under the table and sat down with my back to the building, securing a view of the entire terrace as well as the street and sidewalk beyond.

Once seated, I called to the waiter that I wanted a lemonade, and then pulled out a paperback copy of *The Age of Innocence*, which I had chosen from the summer reading list for the school I'd be starting in September. Enveloped by the smell of strong coffee wafting up from all sides, I drifted off into my book's distant universe.

"Another lemonade?" The French voice came floating through the streets of nineteenth-century New York in my mind's eye, jerking me rudely back to the Parisian café. My waiter stood beside me, holding his round tray stiffly above his shoulder and looking every bit like a constipated grasshopper.

"Oh, of course. Um . . . I think I'll take a tea, actually," I said, realizing that his intrusion meant I had been reading for about an hour. There is an unspoken rule in French cafés that a person can sit at their table all day if they want, as long as they order one drink per hour. It's kind of like renting a table.

I halfheartedly glanced around before looking back down at the page, but did a double take when I noticed someone staring at me from across the terrace. And the world around me froze when our eyes met.

I had the strangest feeling that I knew the guy. I'd felt that way with strangers before, where it seemed like I'd spent hours, weeks, even years with the person. But in my experience, it had always been a one-way phenomenon: The other person didn't even notice me.

This was not the case now. I could swear he felt the same.

From the way his gaze held steady, I knew he had been staring at me for a while. He was breathtaking, with longish black hair waving up and back from a broad forehead. His olive skin made me guess that he either spent a lot of time outside or came from somewhere more southern and sunbaked than Paris. And the eyes that stared back into my own were as blue as the sea, lined with thick black lashes. My heart lurched within my chest, and it felt like someone had squeezed all the air out of my lungs. In spite of myself, I couldn't break our gaze.

A couple of seconds passed, and then he turned back to his two friends, who were laughing rowdily. The three of them were young and beautiful and glowing with the kind of charisma that justified the fact that every woman in the place was under their spell. If they noticed it, they didn't let on.

Sitting next to the first boy was a strikingly handsome guy, built like a boulder, with short, cropped hair and dark chocolate skin. As I watched him, he turned and flashed me a knowing smile, as if he understood how I couldn't resist checking him out. Shaken out of my voyeuristic trance, my eyes darted down to my book for a few seconds, and by the time I dared peer back up he had looked away.

Next to him, facing away from me, was a wiry-built boy with slightly sunburned skin, sideburns, and curly brown hair, animatedly telling a story that sent the other two into peals of laughter.

I studied the one who had first caught my attention. Although he was probably a couple of years older than me, I guessed he wasn't yet twenty. He leaned back in his chair in that suave Frenchman manner. But something slightly cold and hard about the set of his face suggested that the easygoing pose was only a facade. It wasn't that he looked cruel. It was more that he seemed . . . dangerous.

Although he intrigued me, I consciously erased the black-haired boy's face from my mind, convinced that perfect looks plus danger probably equaled bad news. I picked up my book and turned my attention back to the more reliable charms of

Newland Archer. But I couldn't help myself from taking another peek when the waiter returned with my tea. Annoyingly, I wasn't able to get back into the rhythm of my book.

When his table stood up a half hour later, it caught my attention. You could feel concentrated feminine tension in the air as the three guys walked past the terrace. As if a team of Armani underwear models had walked straight up to the café and, in unison, ripped off all their clothes.

The elderly woman next to me leaned in to her coffee companion and said, "It's suddenly feeling unseasonably *hot*, don't you agree?" Her lady friend giggled in agreement, fanning herself with the plastic-coated menu and ogling the boys. I shook my head in disgust—there was no way those guys couldn't feel the dozens of eyes shooting darts of lust into their backs as they walked away.

Suddenly, proving my theory, the black-haired one glanced back at me and, confirming that I was watching him, smiled smugly. Feeling the blood rush to my cheeks, I hid my face in my book so he wouldn't have the satisfaction of seeing me blush.

I tried to read the words on the page for a few minutes before giving up. My concentration broken, I paid for my drinks, and leaving a tip on the table, I made my way back to the rue du Bac.

THREE

LIFE WITHOUT PARENTS WAS NOT GETTING ANY easier.

I had begun to feel like I was encased in a layer of ice. I was cold inside. But I clung to the coldness for dear life: Who knew what would happen if I let the ice thaw and actually began to feel things again? I would probably melt into a blubbering idiot and return to being completely nonfunctional like I had been for the first few months after my parents died.

I missed my dad. His disappearance from my life felt unbearable. That handsome Frenchman who everyone liked the moment they looked into his laughing green eyes. When he saw me and his face lit up with an expression of pure adoration, I knew that no matter what stupid things I might do in life, I would always have one fan in this world, cheering me on from the sidelines.

As for Mom, her death ripped my heart out, like she had been a physical part of me that was dug out with a scalpel. She was a soul mate, a "kindred spirit," as she used to say. Not that we always got along. But now that she was gone, I had to learn to live with the big, burning hole that her absence left inside me.

If I could have escaped reality for just a few hours at night, maybe my waking hours would have been more bearable. But sleep was my own personal nightmare. I would lie in bed until I finally felt its velvety fingers sweeping my face with numbness and I would think, *Finally!* Then a half hour later I was awake again.

One night I was at my wit's end, head on my pillow and eyes open, staring at the ceiling. My alarm clock read one a.m. I thought about the long night ahead and crawled out of bed, fishing for the clothes I had worn the day before and slipping them on. Stepping out into the hallway, I saw a light coming from under Georgia's door. I tapped on it and turned the doorknob.

"Hey," Georgia whispered at me from upside down. She was lying fully clothed on her bed, her head at its foot. "Just got home," she added.

"You can't sleep either," I commented. It wasn't a question. We knew each other too well. "Why don't you come out for a walk with me?" I asked. "I can't stand lying awake in my room all night. It's only July and I've read every book that I possess. Twice."

"Are you crazy?" Georgia said, rolling over to her stomach. "It's the middle of the night."

"Actually it's kind of the beginning of the night. It's just one o'clock. People are still out on the streets. And, besides, Paris is the safest—"

"—city on earth." Georgia finished my sentence. "Papy's favorite saying. He should get a job with the board of tourism. Okay. Why not? I won't sleep anytime soon either."

We tiptoed to the front hall and, with a quiet click, eased the door open and shut behind us. Once down in the vestibule, we paused to slip on our shoes and then walked out into the night.

A full moon was hanging over Paris, painting the streets with a silver glow. Without a word, Georgia and I headed toward the river. It had been the center of all our activities since we began coming here as children, and our feet knew the way.

At the river's edge, we went down the stone steps to the walkway that stretches miles through Paris along the water and set off east over the rough cobblestones. The massive squatting presence of the Louvre Museum was just visible on the opposite bank.

No one else was in sight, either down on the quay or up at street level. The city was silent except for the lapping of the waves and the sound of the occasional car. We walked a few minutes without speaking before Georgia stopped abruptly and grabbed my arm.

"Look," she whispered, pointing toward the Carrousel Bridge crossing high over our walkway some fifty feet ahead. A girl who looked to be about our age balanced on the wide stone handrail, leaning perilously over the water. "Oh my God, she's going to jump!" breathed Georgia.

My mind raced as I gauged the distance. "The bridge isn't high enough for her to kill herself."

"It depends what's under the water—how deep it is. She's near the edge," Georgia responded.

We were too far away to see the girl's expression, but her arms were wrapped around her stomach as she looked down into the cold, dark waves.

Our focus quickly shifted to the tunnel under the bridge. Even during the day it was creepy. Street people slept under it when the weather was cold. I had never actually seen anyone in it as I speed-walked through its putrid dampness to the sunlight on the other side. But the old soiled mattresses and dividers made out of cardboard boxes made it clear that, for a few unfortunate souls, the tunnel was a prime spot of Paris real estate. And now, from its otherworldly darkness came sounds of a scuffle.

There was a movement from the top of the bridge. The girl still stood motionless on the rail, but now a man approached her. He walked slowly, carefully, as if not to alarm her. When he got a stone's throw away he stretched out an arm, offering the girl his hand. I could hear a low voice—he was trying to talk her down.

The girl whipped around to look at him, and the man held up his other hand, stretching both arms toward her, entreating her to back away from the edge. She shook her head. He took another step toward her. She wrapped her arms tighter across her torso and jumped.

It wasn't really a jump. It was more of a fall. As if she was offering her body up as a sacrifice to gravity and letting it do what it would with her. She arced forward, her head hitting the water seconds later.

I felt something tug my arm and realized that Georgia and I

were clutching each other as we watched the horrific scene. "Oh my God, oh my God, oh my God," Georgia chanted rhythmically under her breath.

A motion at the top of the bridge drew my eyes up from the water's moonlit surface, where I had been watching for any trace of the girl. The man who had been trying to coax her down was now standing on the edge of the bridge, his widespread arms transforming his body into the shape of a cross as he threw himself powerfully forward. Time seemed to stop as he hovered in midair like a giant bird of prey between the bridge and the black surface of the water.

And in that split second, a streetlight by the water's edge flashed across his face. Recognition jolted through me. It was the boy from the Café Sainte-Lucie.

What in the world was he doing here, trying to talk a teenage girl out of a suicide attempt? Did he know her? Or was he just a passerby who decided to get involved?

His body sliced cleanly through the surface of the water and disappeared from view.

A shout erupted from underneath the bridge, and crouching silhouettes appeared in the murky blackness of the tunnel. "What the—!" Georgia exclaimed. She was interrupted by a flash of light and a sharp clanging of metal as two figures began to emerge from the darkness. Swords. They were sword fighting.

Georgia and I seemed to remember at the same moment that we had legs, and began sprinting back toward the stairway we had come from. Before we could reach it, a man's form materialized from the darkness. I didn't have time to scream before he caught me by the shoulders to stop me from mowing him down. Georgia froze in her tracks.

"Good evening, ladies," came a smooth baritone voice.

My eyes tried to refocus from their goal—the stairway—onto the person keeping me from getting there. "Let go," I managed to sputter in my fear, and he immediately dropped his hold. Stepping back, I found myself inches away from another familiar face. His hair was hidden beneath a tightly fitted black cap, but I would have recognized him anywhere. It was the muscular friend of the boy who had just dived into the Seine.

"You shouldn't be down here by yourselves this late at night," he said.

"There's something going on back there," Georgia gasped. "A fight."

"Police procedure," he said, turning, and applied light force to our backs, steering us rapidly toward the stairway.

"Police procedure with *swords*?" I asked, incredulous, as we jogged up to street level.

"Gang activity," he said briefly, already turning to head back down the stairway. "I would get as far away from here as you can," he called over his shoulder as he took the stairs a few at a time. He sprinted toward the tunnel just as two heads surfaced from the river near the bank. I felt a surge of relief when I saw them alive.

The guy who had steered us away arrived just as they reached land and pulled the jumper up to safety.

A howl of pain shattered the night air, and Georgia grabbed

my arm. "Let's get out of here."

"Wait." I hesitated. "Shouldn't we do something?"

"Like what?"

"Like call the police?"

"They *are* the police," she said uncertainly.

"Yeah, right. They sure don't look like police. I could swear I recognized those two guys from our neighborhood." We stood looking helplessly at each other for a second, trying to make sense out of what we had just seen.

"Well, maybe our neighborhood's under the surveillance of a special undercover SWAT team," Georgia said. "You know, Catherine Deneuve lives right down the street."

"Yeah, right, like Catherine Deneuve has her own hot-guy SWAT team trolling the neighborhood for celebrity stalkers with swords."

Unable to contain ourselves, we burst out laughing.

"We should not be laughing. This is serious!" Georgia giggled, wiping a stray tear from her cheek.

"I know," I sniffed, composing myself.

Down by the river the girl and her savior had vanished, and the fighting sounded farther away. "See, it's over anyway," Georgia said. "It's too late to do anything even if we wanted to."

We turned toward the crosswalk just as two figures sprinted up the stairs behind us. Out of my peripheral vision, I saw them approaching at full-speed and grabbed Georgia's arm to pull her out of the way. They ran past, missing us by mere inches—two huge men dressed in dark clothes with caps pulled down low around their faces. A glint of metal flashed from beneath one of their long dusters. Leaping into a car, they started the engine with a roar. But before they drove off, they pulled up beside my sister and me and slowed to a snail's pace. I could feel them staring at us through the darkened windows.

"Whatcha looking at?" Georgia yelled, and they peeled off down the road. We stood there for a moment, stunned. The crosswalk light turned green, and Georgia hooked her arm through mine as we stepped out into the street.

"Weird night," she said finally, breaking our silence.

"Understatement of the year," I replied. "Should we tell Mamie and Papy about it?"

"What?" Georgia laughed. "And spoil Papy's 'Paris is safe' delusion? They'd never let us out of the house again."

FOUR

WHEN I STEPPED OUTSIDE INTO THE COMFORT-
ing security of daylight the next morning, the events of the
previous night seemed unreal. There had been nothing about
what we had seen on the news. But Georgia and I couldn't let it
go that easily.

We discussed it more than a few times, although we got no
closer to understanding what had taken place. Our theories
ran from things as mundane as Dungeons & Dragons fanatics
playacting outdoors to the more dramatic (and laugh-inducing)
scenario of time-traveling damsels and knights.

Although I continued to do all my reading at the Café Sainte-
Lucie, I hadn't seen the mysterious group of gorgeous guys again.
After a couple of weeks, I knew all the waiters as well as the owners, and many of the regular clients became familiar faces: Little
old ladies with their teacup Yorkshire terriers, which they carried
around in their handbags and fed from their plates. Businessmen

with expensive-looking suits talking endlessly on cell phones and ogling every pretty girl who walked by. Couples of all ages holding hands under the tables.

One Saturday afternoon I was squeezed into my regular table in the terrace's far left corner, reading *To Kill a Mockingbird*. Although this was my third time through it, some passages still brought tears to my eyes. As one was doing now.

I used my dig-fingernails-into-palm trick, which, if it hurt enough, could keep me from crying in public. Unfortunately, today it wasn't working. I could tell my eyes were getting red and glassy. *This is all I need—to cry in front of my regular café crowd just as I'm getting to know them,* I thought, peering up to see if anyone had noticed me.

And there he was. Sitting a few tables away, watching me as intensely as he had the first time. It was the boy with the black hair. The scene from the river, with him leaping off a bridge to save someone's life, felt like it had been nothing but a surreal dream. Here he was, in broad daylight, drinking coffee with one of his friends.

Why? I almost said it out loud. Why did I have to get all teary about a book while this too-cute-to-be-true French guy was staring at me from a mere ten feet away?

I snapped my book closed and laid some money on the table. But just as I started toward the exit, the elderly women at the table next to mine stood and began fiddling with their massive pile of shopping bags. I fidgeted impatiently until finally one of them turned around. "So sorry, dear, but we'll be another minute.

24

Just go around us." And she practically shoved me toward where the guys were sitting.

I had hardly gotten a step beyond their table when I heard a low voice coming from behind me.

"Aren't you forgetting something?" someone asked in French.

I turned to see the boy standing inches away from me. He was even more handsome than he had seemed from afar, though his looks were sharpened by that same flinty coldness I had noticed the first time I had seen him. I ignored the sudden jolt in my chest.

"Your bag," he said, holding my book bag out toward me, balancing the strap on two fingers.

"Um," I said, thrown off by his proximity. Then, seeing his wry expression, I pulled myself together. *He thinks I'm a total idiot for leaving my bag behind.* "How kind of you," I said stiffly, reaching for the bag, as I tried to salvage any remaining scrap of confidence left in me.

He pulled his arm back, leaving me grasping air. "What?" he asked, amused. "Why be angry at *me*? It's not like I swiped it."

"No, of course not," I huffed, waiting.

"So . . . ," he said.

"So . . . if it's okay with you, I'll just take my bag now," I said, reaching out and catching the straps in my hand this time. He didn't let go.

"How about an exchange?" he offered, a smile twitching the corners of his mouth. "I'll give you the bag if you tell me your name."

I gawped at him, incredulous, and then gave the bag a hard tug—just as he let go. Its contents spilled in a heap across the sidewalk. I shook my head in disbelief. "Great! Thanks a lot!"

As gracefully as I could, I got down on my knees and began cramming my lipstick, mascara, wallet, phone, and what seemed like a million pens and tiny scraps of paper into my bag. I looked back up to see him inspecting my book.

"*To Kill a Mockingbird. En anglais!*" he commented, his voice tinged with surprise. And then, in slightly accented but perfect English, he said, "Great book—have you ever seen the film . . . Kate?"

My mouth fell open. "But . . . how do you know my name?" I managed to utter.

He raised his other hand and showed me my driver's license, which featured an exceptionally bad head shot. By this point my humiliation was so great that I couldn't even look him in the eyes, although I felt his gaze burning into me.

"Listen," he said, leaning closer. "I'm really sorry. I didn't mean to make you drop your bag."

"Stop flaunting your impeccable language skills, Vincent, help the girl to her feet, and let her take her leave," came another voice in French. I turned to see my tormentor's friend—the guy with the curly hair—holding out my hairbrush, with an expression of mild amusement creasing his razor-stubbled face.

Ignoring the hand "Vincent" was extending to help me up, I staggered to my feet and brushed myself off. "Here you go," he said, handing me my book.

I took it with an embarrassed nod. "Thanks," I replied curtly, trying not to run as I made the quickest possible exit out of the café and onto the street. As I waited for the crosswalk light to change, I made the mistake of glancing back. Both of the boys were staring my way. Vincent's friend said something to him and shook his head. *I can't even imagine what they're saying about me,* I thought, and groaned.

Turning as red as the stoplight, I crossed the street without looking their way again.

For the next few days I saw Vincent's face everywhere. In the corner grocery store, coming up the steps from the Métro, sitting at every café terrace I passed. Of course, when I got a better look at each of these guys, it was never actually him. Much to my annoyance, I couldn't stop thinking about him, and even more annoyingly, my feelings were equally divided between self-protective cautiousness and unabashed crush.

To be honest, I wasn't ungrateful for the diversion. For once I had something else to think about besides fatal car crashes and what the hell I was going to do for the rest of my life. I'd thought I had it pretty much figured out before the accident, but now my future stretched before me like a mile-long question mark. It struck me that my fixation on this "mystery guy" might just be my mind's way of giving me a breather from my confusion and grief. And I finally decided, if that were the case, I didn't mind.

* * *

Almost a week had passed since my standoff with Vincent at the Café Sainte-Lucie, and though I had made my reading sessions there a daily habit, I hadn't seen a trace of him or his friends. I was ensconced in what I now considered my private corner table, finishing off yet another Wharton novel from the school syllabus (my future English teacher was obviously a big fan), when I noticed a couple of teenagers sitting across the terrace from me. The girl had short-cropped blond hair and a shy laugh, and the natural way she kept leaning in toward the boy next to her made me think they were a couple. But upon turning my scrutiny to him, I realized how similar their features were, though his hair was golden red. They had to be brother and sister. And once that idea popped into my mind, I knew I was right.

The girl suddenly held up her hand to stop her brother from talking and began scanning the terrace, as if searching for someone. Her eyes settled on me. For a second she hesitated, and then waved urgently at me. I pointed to myself with a questioning look. She nodded and then gestured, beckoning me to come over.

Wondering what she could possibly want, I stood and slowly made my way toward their table. She rose to her feet, alarmed, and motioned for me to hurry.

Just as I left my safe little nook against the wall and stepped around my table, a huge crash came from behind me, and I was knocked flat onto the ground. I could feel my knee stinging and lifted my head to see blood on the ground beneath my face.

"Mon Dieu!" yelled one of the waiters, and scrambled over the

toppled tables and chairs to help me to my feet. Tears of shock and pain welled in my eyes.

He ripped a towel from his waist apron and dabbed my face with it. "You just have a little cut on your eyebrow. Don't worry." I looked down at my burning leg and saw that my jeans had been torn open and my knee completely skinned.

As I checked myself over for injuries, it dawned on me that the terrace had gone completely silent. But instead of focusing on me, the astonished faces of the café-goers were looking *behind* me.

The waiter stopped swabbing my eyebrow to glance over my shoulder, and his eyes widened in alarm. Following his gaze, I saw that my table had been demolished by a huge piece of carved masonry that had fallen from the building's facade. My purse was lying to one side, but my copy of *House of Mirth* stuck out from where it was pinned under the enormous stone, exactly where I had been sitting.

If I hadn't moved, I would be dead, I thought, and my heart raced so fast that my chest hurt. I turned back to the table where the brother and sister had been sitting. Except for a bottle of Perrier and two full glasses sitting in the middle of a handful of change, it was empty. My saviors were gone.

FIVE

I WAS SO SHAKEN THAT I COULDN'T LEAVE FOR A while. Finally, after allowing the café staff to use half their first-aid kit on me, I insisted that I could make it home on my own and wobbled back, my legs feeling like rubber bands. Mamie was coming out the front door as I arrived.

"Oh, my dear Katya!" she shrieked after I explained what had happened, and dropping her beloved Hermès purse to the ground, she threw her arms around me. Then, scooping up our things and leading me back into the house, she tucked me into bed and insisted on treating me like I was a quadriplegic instead of her slightly scraped-up granddaughter.

"Now, Katya, are you sure you're comfortable? I can bring you more pillows if you want."

"Mamie, I'm fine, really."

"Does your knee still hurt? I can put something else on it. Maybe it should be elevated."

"Mamie, they treated it with a million things from their first-aid box at the café. It's just a scrape, really."

"Oh, my darling child. To think what could have happened." She pressed my head to her chest and petted my hair until something in me broke and I started crying.

Mamie cooed and held me while I bawled. "I'm just crying because I'm shaky," I protested through my tears, but the truth was that she was treating me just like my mom would have.

When Georgia got home, I heard Mamie telling her about my "near-death experience." My door opened a minute later, and my sister raced in looking as white as a ghost. She sat silently on the edge of my bed, staring at me with wide eyes.

"It's okay, Georgia. I'm just a little scraped up."

"Oh my God, Katie-Bean, if anything had happened to you . . . You are all I have left. Remember that."

"I'm fine. And nothing's going to happen to me. I'll keep far away from disintegrating buildings from now on. Promise."

She forced a smile and reached out her hand to touch my own, but the haunted look stayed.

The next day Mamie refused to let me leave the house, insisting that I relax and "recover from my injuries." I obeyed, to humor her, and spent half the evening reading in the bathtub. It wasn't until I had lost myself in the warm water and a book that my nerves got the best of me, and I sat there trembling like a leaf.

I hadn't realized how scared the near miss with the crumbling building had left me until it took topping the tub up several times with scalding hot water to calm me down. Ultimately, I fell asleep with little plumes of steam rising up from the water around me.

When I passed the café the next day, it was closed, and the sidewalk outside the building was roped off with yellow plastic police tape. Workers in electric blue overalls were erecting scaffolding for builders to come stabilize the facade. I would have to find another location for my al fresco reading. I felt a pang of disappointment as I realized that this was the only place that I had a chance of seeing my recent obsession. Who knew how long it would be before I ran into Vincent again?

My mother began taking me to museums when I was a tiny child. When we went to Paris, she and Mamie and I would set off in the morning for "a little taste of beauty," as my mother called it. Georgia, who was bored by the time we reached the first painting, usually opted to stay behind with my father and grandfather, who sat in cafés and chatted with friends, business associates, and whoever else happened to wander by. But together, Mamie, Mom, and I combed the museums and galleries of Paris.

So it was no great shock when Georgia gave me a vague excuse of "previous plans" when I asked her to come museum trolling with me a few days later. "Georgia, you've been complaining that I never do anything with you. This is a valid invite!"

"Yeah, about as valid as me inviting you to a monster truck rally. Ask again if you plan on doing something actually interesting." To show her goodwill, she gave my arm a friendly squeeze before shutting her bedroom door in my face. *Touché.*

I set off alone to Le Marais, a neighborhood across town from my grandparents' home. Weaving my way through its tiny medieval streets, I finally arrived at my destination: the palacelike building housing the Picasso Museum.

Besides the alternate universe offered by a book, the quiet space of a museum was my favorite place to go. My mom said I was an escapist at heart . . . that I preferred imaginary worlds to the real one. It's true that I've always been able to yank myself out of this world and plunge myself into another. And I felt ready for a calming session of art-hypnosis.

As I walked through the gigantic doors of the Musée Picasso into its sterile white rooms, I felt my heart rate slow. I let the warmth and peace of the place cover me like a soft blanket. And as was my habit, I walked until I found the first painting that really grabbed my attention, and sat down on a bench to face it.

I let the colors absorb into my skin. The composition's convoluted, twisted shapes reminded me of how I felt inside, and my breathing slowed as I began zoning out. The other paintings in the room, the guard standing near the door, the fresh-paint smell in the air around me, even the passing tourists, faded into a gray background surrounding this one square of color and light.

I don't know how long I sat there before my mind slowly emerged from its self-imposed trance, and I heard low voices coming from behind me.

"Come over here. Just look at the colors."

Long pause. "What colors?"

"Exactly. It's just as I told you. He goes from the bright, bold palette of something like *Les Demoiselles d'Avignon* to this gray and brown monotone jigsaw puzzle in a mere four years. What a show-off! Pablo always had to be the best at everything he put his hand to, and as I was saying to Gaspard the other day, what really ticks me off is . . ."

I turned, curious to see the origin of this fountain of knowledge, and froze. Standing just fifteen feet away from me was Vincent's curly-haired friend.

Now that I saw him straight on, I was struck by how attractive he was. There was something rugged about him—unkempt, scruffy hair, bristly razor stubble, and large rough hands that gesticulated passionately toward the painting. By the condition of his clothes, which were smudged with paint, I guessed he might be an artist.

That came to me in a split second. Because after that, all I could see was the person standing with him. The raven-haired boy. The boy who had taken up permanent residence in the dark corners of my mind since the first moment I saw him. Vincent.

Why do you have to fall for the most improbable, inaccessible boy in Paris? He was too beautiful—and too aloof—to ever really notice me. I tore my gaze away, leaned forward, and rested my forehead in my hands. It didn't do any good. Vincent's image was burned indelibly into my mind.

I realized that whatever it was about him that made him seem a bit cold, almost dangerous, actually heightened my interest instead of scaring me off. What was wrong with me? I had never gone for bad boys before—that was Georgia's specialty! My stomach tightened as I wondered if I had the courage to go up and talk to him.

But I didn't have the chance to put myself to the test. When I raised my head, they were gone. I walked quickly to the entrance of the next room and peered in. It was empty. And then I just about jumped out of my skin as a low voice from behind me said, "Hi, Kate."

Vincent loomed over me, his face a good six inches above mine. My hand flew to my chest in alarm. "Thanks for the heart attack!" I gasped.

"So is this a habit of yours, leaving your bag behind in order to strike up a conversation?" He grinned and nodded at the bench where I had been sitting. Lying beneath it was my book bag. "Wouldn't it be easier to just walk up to a guy and say hello?"

The slight trace of mockery in his voice evaporated my nervousness. It was replaced by a fiery indignation that surprised us both. "Fine! Hello," I growled, my throat tight with fury. Marching over to the bench, I picked up my bag and stalked out of the room.

"Wait!" he called, jogging over to me and matching my pace. "I didn't mean it like that. What I meant . . ."

I came to a stop and stared at him, waiting.

"I'm sorry," he said, exhaling deeply. "I've never been known for my sparkling conversation."

"Then why even make the effort?" I challenged.

"Because. You're—I don't know—amusing."

"Amusing?" I pronounced each syllable slowly and shot him

my *You're a complete weirdo* look. My clenched fists rose automatically to rest on my hips. "So, Vincent, did you come over with the express purpose of offending me, or is there something else you want?"

Vincent put his palm to his forehead. "Listen, I'm sorry. I'm an idiot. Can we . . . can we just start over from scratch?"

"Start *what* over from scratch?" I asked doubtfully.

He hesitated for a second and then held out his hand. "Hi. I'm Vincent."

I felt my eyes narrow as I weighed his sincerity. I gripped his hand in mine, shaking it a bit rougher than I meant to. "I'm Kate."

"Nice to meet you, Kate," Vincent said, bemused. There was a four-second silence, during which I continued to glare at him. "So. Do you come here often?" he murmured, unsure.

I couldn't help but burst out laughing. He smiled, obviously relieved.

"Um, yes, actually. I've kind of got a thing for museums, not just for Picasso."

"A 'thing'?"

Vincent's English was so good that it was easy to forget it wasn't his first language. "It means I like museums. A lot," I explained.

"Okay. Got it. You like museums but not Picasso in particular. So . . . you just come here when you want to meditate?"

I smiled at him, mentally giving him points for trying so hard. "Where'd your friend go?" I asked.

"He took off. Jules doesn't really like to meet new people."

"Charming."

"So, are you British? American?" he said, changing the subject.

"American," I responded.

"And the girl I've seen you around the neighborhood with would be your . . ."

"Sister," I said slowly. "Have you been spying on me?"

"Two cute girls move to the area—what am I supposed to do?"

A wave of delight rippled through my body at his words. So he thought I was cute. But he also thought Georgia was cute, I reminded myself. The wave disappeared.

"Hey, the museum café has an espresso machine. Want to get some coffee while you tell me what other things you've got a 'thing' for?" He touched me on the arm. The wave was officially back.

We sat at a tiny table in front of steaming cappuccinos. "So, now that I've revealed my name and nationality to a complete stranger, what else do you want to know?" I asked, stirring the foam into my coffee.

"Oh, I don't know . . . shoe size, favorite film, athletic prowess, most embarrassing moment, hit me."

I laughed. "Um, shoe size ten, *Breakfast at Tiffany's*, absolutely no athletic ability whatsoever, and way too many embarrassing moments to list before the museum closes."

"That's it? That's all I get?" he teased.

I felt my defensiveness melting away at this surprisingly charming and decidedly not-dangerous side of him. With Vincent's encouragement I told him about my old life in Brooklyn, with

Georgia and my parents. Of our summers in Paris, of my friends back home, with whom I had, by now, lost all contact. Of my boundless love for art, and my despair at discovering I possessed absolutely no talent for creating it.

He prodded me for more information, and I filled in the blanks for him on bands, food, film, books, and everything else under the sun. And unlike most boys my age I had known back home, he seemed genuinely interested in every detail.

What I didn't tell him was that my parents were dead. I referred to them in the present tense and said that my sister and I had moved in with our grandparents to study in France. It wasn't a total lie. But I didn't feel like telling him the whole truth. I didn't want his pity. I wanted to seem like just any other normal girl who hadn't spent the last seven months isolating herself in an inner world of grief.

His rapid-fire questions made it impossible for me to ask him anything in return. So when we finally left I reproached him for it. "Okay, now I feel completely exposed—you know pretty much everything about me and I know nothing about you."

"Aha, that is part of my nefarious plan." He smiled, as the museum guard locked the doors behind us. "How else could I expect you to say yes to meeting up again if I laid everything out on the table the first time we talked?"

"This isn't the first time we talked," I corrected him, trying to coolly ignore the fact that he seemed to be asking me out.

"Okay, the first time we talked without my unintentionally insulting you," he revised.

We walked across the museum's garden toward the reflecting pools, where screaming children were celebrating the fact that it was still hot and sunny at six p.m. by splashing around ecstatically in the water.

Vincent walked slightly hunched over with his hands in his pockets. For the first time I sensed in him a tiny hint of vulnerability. I took advantage of it. "I don't even know how old you are."

"Nineteen," he said.

"What do you do?"

"Student."

"Really? Because your friend said something about your being in the police force." I couldn't help the trace of sarcasm in my voice.

"What?" he exclaimed, coming to a complete stop.

"My sister and I saw you rescue that girl."

Vincent stared at me blankly.

"The girl who jumped off the Carrousel Bridge during that gang fight. Your friend escorted us away and told us it was a police procedure."

"Oh, he did?" Vincent muttered, his expression assuming the hardened look it'd had the first time I met him. He thrust his hands back into his pockets and continued walking. We were getting closer to the Métro stop. I slowed my pace to buy a little more time.

"So what are you guys, undercover cops?" I didn't believe it for a second, but tried to sound sincere. His sudden change in mood had intrigued me.

"Something like that."

"What, kind of like a SWAT team?"

He didn't respond.

"That was really brave, by the way," I insisted. "Your diving into the river. What did the girl have to do with the gang fighting under the bridge, anyhow?" I asked, digging further.

"Um, I'm not supposed to talk about it," Vincent said, studying the concrete a few inches in front of his feet.

"Oh yeah. Of course," I said lightly. "You just look really young to be a cop." I couldn't stop a facetious smile from spreading across my lips.

"I told you . . . I'm a student," he said, giving me an uncertain grin. He could tell I didn't buy it.

"Yeah. Okay. I didn't *see* anything. I didn't *hear* anything," I said dramatically.

Vincent laughed, his good mood returning. "So . . . Kate, what are you doing this weekend?"

"Um . . . no plans," I said, silently cursing my reddening cheeks.

"Do you want to do something?" he asked, with a smile so charming that my heart forgot to beat.

I nodded, since I couldn't speak.

Taking my silence as hesitation, he added quickly, "Not like a formal date or anything. Just hanging out. We can . . . take a walk. Wander around the Marais."

I nodded again, and then managed to get out, "That would be great."

"Okay, how about Saturday afternoon? Daylight. In public. A

perfectly safe thing to do with a guy you barely know." He held up his hands as if showing he wasn't hiding anything.

I laughed. "Don't worry. Even if you *are* on a SWAT team, I'm not afraid of you." As soon as it was out of my mouth I realized that I *was* afraid. Just a little bit. I wondered once more if that was his pull on me. Maybe my parents' deaths had left me with a lack of self-preservation and it was the hint of danger that I was going for. Or maybe I was attracted to the vague aura of untouchable aloofness that he exuded. Maybe all he was to me was a challenge. Whatever the reason, it was effective. I really liked this guy. And I wanted to see him again. Night, day, I didn't care. I'd be there.

He lifted an eyebrow and chuckled. "Not afraid of me. How . . . amusing." I couldn't help myself from laughing along.

Nodding the other direction down the boulevard, he said, "Jules is probably waiting for me. See you Saturday. Meet you outside the rue du Bac Métro station at three?"

"Saturday, three o'clock," I confirmed as he turned and walked away. I don't think it would be exaggerating much to say that my feet didn't touch the ground the whole way home.

SIX

VINCENT WAS WAITING FOR ME BY THE MÉTRO entrance. My heart caught in my throat as I wondered (not for the first time) why this too-gorgeous-to-be-true guy had any interest whatsoever in plain old . . . okay, maybe slightly pretty, but by no means beautiful on his level . . . me. My insecurity crumbled when I saw his face light up as I approached.

"You came," he said as he leaned in to give me the *bises*, those double-cheeked air-kisses that Europeans are famous for. Though I shivered when his skin touched mine, my cheeks were warm for a good five minutes afterward.

"Of course," I said, drawing on every drop of my "cool and confident" reserve, since, to tell the truth, I was feeling a bit nervous. "So, where are we off to?"

We began walking down the steps to the subway tracks. "Have you been to the Village Saint-Paul?" he asked.

I shook my head. "Doesn't ring a bell."

"Perfect," he said, seeming pleased with himself but giving no further explanation.

We barely talked on the train, but it wasn't for lack of conversation. I don't know if it is just a cultural thing, or because the trains themselves are so quiet, but as soon as people step into the car from the platform they shut up.

Vincent and I stood facing each other, holding on to the central steel pole for balance, and checked out the other passengers, who were busy checking us out. Have I mentioned that checking people out is the French national pastime?

As we turned a corner and the train jerked to one side, he put an arm around my shoulders to steady me.

"We haven't even gotten there and you're already making a move?" I laughed.

"Of course not. I'm a gentleman through and through," he responded in a quiet voice. "I would throw my coat over a puddle for you any day."

"I'm no damsel in distress," I retorted as the train pulled to a stop.

"Whew—well, that's a good thing," he said, breathing a fake sigh of relief. "How about opening the door for me, then?"

I grinned as I flipped up the metal door-release lever and stepped onto the platform.

We emerged from the Saint-Paul stop directly in front of the massive classical church called the Église Saint-Paul. "I used to come here when I was a kid," I said to Vincent as I peered up at the decorative facade.

"Really?"

"Yeah. When I came to visit my grandparents during the summer, there was a girl I used to play with who lived just there." I pointed to a building a few doors away. "Her dad told us that this street was used for jousts in the Middle Ages. Sandrine and I used to sit on the church steps and pretend we were in the middle of a medieval tournament." I closed my eyes and I was back, ten years ago, reliving the sounds and colors of our imaginary tourney. "You know, I always thought that if the centuries and centuries of Paris's ghosts could materialize all at once, you would find yourself surrounded by the most fascinating people." I stopped, suddenly embarrassed that I was spouting off to this guy I barely knew with details about one of my several dreamworlds.

Vincent smiled. "If I were riding to the challenge, would you give me your favor to display on my arm, fair lady?"

I pretended to dig through my bag. "I can't seem to find my lace kerchief. How about a Kleenex?"

Laughing, Vincent threw an arm around my shoulders and squeezed me tightly. "You're amazing," he said.

"That's a definite step up from 'amusing,'" I reminded him, unable to prevent my cheeks from reddening with pleasure.

We headed to a side road leading down toward the river. Halfway there, Vincent stepped through the large wooden doorway of a four-story building, pulling me behind him.

Like many Parisian apartment blocks, this one had been constructed around an internal courtyard sheltered from the street. The most modest courtyards are barely as big as a king-size bed, with only enough space to hold the building's trash bins. Others are large, some even having trees and benches, forming a quiet haven for residents away from the busy street.

This courtyard was massive and had little shops, and even an outdoor café, scattered among the ground-floor apartments, something I had never seen before. "What is this place?" I asked.

Vincent smiled and touched my arm, pointing to another open doorway on the far side of the courtyard. "This is just the beginning," he said. "There are about five of these courtyards all linked together off the street, so you can wander for as long as you want without seeing or hearing the outside world. It's all art galleries and antique shops. I thought you'd like it."

"Like it? I love it! This is incredible!" I said. "I can't believe I haven't been here before."

"It's off the beaten path." Vincent seemed proud of his knowledge of Paris's out-of-the-way spots. And I was just happy that he wanted me along to explore them with him.

"I'll say," I agreed. "It's almost completely hidden from the outside. So . . . you've been here before. Where do we start?"

We strolled through stores and galleries packed with everything from old posters to ancient Buddha heads. For a city heaving with summer tourists, the shops had surprisingly few visitors, and we wandered through the spaces as if they were our own private treasure troves.

As we browsed through an antique clothes store, Vincent stopped in front of a glass case that held jewelry. "Hey, Kate, maybe you can help me. I need to get a gift for someone."

"Sure," I said, peering into the case as the shopkeeper lifted the cover for us. I fingered a pretty silver ring with a cluster of flowers curving outward from its surface.

"What would someone your age like?" he said, touching a vintage jeweled cross pendant.

"My *age*?" I laughed. "I'm only three years younger than you. Maybe less, depending on your birthday."

"June," he said.

"Okay, then two and a half."

He laughed. "All right, you got me there. It's just that I'm not sure what she'd like. And her birthday's coming up."

I felt like someone had punched me in the stomach. What an idiot I had been: totally misreading his intentions. He obviously just saw me as a friend . . . a friend with good enough taste to help him choose a present for his girlfriend.

"Hmm," I said, closing my eyes and trying to hide my dismay. I forced them back open and stared at the case. "I guess it depends on her taste. Does she wear more feminine, flowery clothes, or is she more into . . . um . . . jeans and T-shirts like me?"

"Definitely not flowery," he said, stifling a laugh.

"Well, I think this is really pretty," I said, pointing to a leather cord with a single teardrop-shaped silver pendant hanging from it. My voice wavered as I tried, unsuccessfully, to swallow the lump in my throat.

Vincent leaned closer to the piece. "I think you're right. It's perfect. You're a genius, Kate." He lifted the necklace from the case and handed it to the shopkeeper.

"I'm just going to wait for you outside," I said, and left as he fished through his pockets for his wallet.

Get a grip, I chided myself. It had seemed too good to be true, and it *had* been. He was only a really friendly guy. Who said I was cute. But who must just like to hang out with cute girls while buying vintage jewelry for his girlfriend. *I wonder what she looks like.* My hands were clenched so tightly that my fingernails dug little trenches into my palms. The pain felt good. It relieved some of the stinging in my chest.

Vincent came out of the shop, tucking a little envelope into his jeans pocket as he closed the door behind him. Seeing my face, he came to an abrupt stop. "What's wrong?" he asked.

"Nothing," I said, shaking my head. "I just needed some air."

"No," he insisted. "Something's bothering you."

I shook my head resolutely.

"Okay, Kate," he said, linking his arm through mine. "I won't force you to talk." The pressure of his arm against my own filled me with warmth, but I mentally pushed it away. I was so used to self-protection by now that it was almost a reflex.

We wandered out of that courtyard and into another, walking in silence for a few minutes as we paused to look into shop windows. "So," I said finally. I knew I shouldn't say it, but I couldn't help myself. "Who's your girlfriend?"

"Sorry?" he asked.

"Your girlfriend. Who you bought the necklace for."

He stopped and faced me. "Kate, the necklace is for a friend . . . who happens to be a girl. A very good friend." He sounded uncomfortable. I wondered for a second if it was the truth, then decided to give him the benefit of the doubt.

Vincent studied my face. "You thought I was asking you to help me choose a present for my girlfriend? And that made you feel . . ." From the smile stretching across his lips I could tell he was about to say something that would embarrass me, so I began walking away.

"Wait, Kate!" he said, catching up to me and lacing his arm back through mine. "I'm sorry."

I decided to play nonchalant about it. "You told me this wasn't a formal date when you invited me to come. Why should I care if you have a girlfriend?"

"Absolutely," he said, giving me a fake-serious look. "Yeah, you and I are just friends . . . out for a friendly walk. Nothing more, nothing less."

"Exactly!" I agreed, my heart giving a little painful twist.

He broke into a large grin and, leaning over, kissed me on the cheek. "Kate," he whispered, "you are way too gullible."

SEVEN

I WAS ABLE TO BASK IN THE MEANING OF HIS words for exactly three seconds before he put a firm arm around my shoulders and began steering me toward an exit. "What—" I began, but his steely expression quieted me and I followed his lead—walking steadily, but not quite running, toward a doorway.

Once on the street, he headed back toward the subway. "Where are we going?" I asked, breathless from the brisk pace.

"I saw someone I didn't want to run into." He slipped his cell phone from his pocket and speed-dialed a number. Getting no response, he hung up and tried another.

"Do you mind telling me what's going on?" I asked, confused by his sudden personality change. In an instant Prince Charming had morphed into Secret Agent Guy.

"We have to find Jules," Vincent said, talking more to himself than to me. "His painting studio's right around the corner."

I stopped, and since he had ahold of my arm, I pulled him

backward. "Who are we running away from?"

It took a lot of effort for Vincent to compose himself. "Kate. Please let me explain later. It's really important that we find one of my . . . friends."

The wonderful feeling from five minutes ago had disappeared. Now I felt like telling him to go ahead without me. But remembering what my days had consisted of lately, I decided to throw caution (and boredom) to the wind and follow him.

He led me to an apartment building that practically oozed with old-Paris charm next to the Église Saint-Paul. We climbed a tightly winding wood staircase to the second-floor landing. Vincent knocked once before pushing the door open.

The studio's walls were hung with paintings all the way up to the high ceiling. Reclining nudes hung alongside geometric-looking townscapes. The visual overload of color and form was as overwhelming as the strong smell of paint thinner.

In the far corner of the room a stunningly beautiful woman was draped across an emerald green couch. Dressed in a tiny bathrobe that barely covered her, she might as well have been naked. "Hi, Vincent," she called across the room with a low, smoky voice that couldn't have matched her seductive looks better if she had bought them as a paired set.

Vincent's friend, Jules, walked out of a tiny bathroom just beyond the couch. Wiping some dripping paintbrushes on a rag, he said without looking up, "Vince, man. Just getting started with Valerie here. Did you get Jean-Baptiste's call?"

"Jules, we have to talk," Vincent said with a sense of urgency that made Jules jerk his head up. He looked at me in surprise and then, seeing Vincent's face, his own darkened. "What's going on?"

Vincent cleared his throat, staring expressionlessly at Jules. He pronounced his words with care. "Kate and I were walking around the Village Saint-Paul and I saw *someone* there."

The code word meant something to Jules. His eyes narrowed. "Outside," he said, looking sideways at me, and strode out the door.

"Be right back, Kate," Vincent said. "Oh, and this is Valerie, one of Jules's models." And having made that introduction, he followed Jules into the staircase, the door slamming behind him.

A gentleman even during a crisis, I thought, amazed at Vincent's sangfroid in making sure I was introduced to Naked Girl before leaving us alone together. "Hi," I said. *"Bonjour,"* she replied, bored. Picking up a paperback, she settled back to read. I lingered near the door, looking at the paintings while trying to hear what was going on outside.

Their voices were hushed, but I could pick up a few words. " . . . couldn't do anything without backup," Vincent was saying, bitter regret in his voice.

"I'm with you now. Ambrose can be our third," Jules responded.

There was silence, and then Vincent was speaking to someone on the phone. He hung up and said, "He's on his way."

"Why the hell did you bring her with you?" Jules sounded incredulous.

"I'm not on duty twenty-four/seven. She's with me because we had a date." Vincent's low voice traveled through the thin wood door easily.

He called it a date, I thought with as much pleasure as I could derive under the circumstances.

"That is exactly why she should not be here," Jules continued.

"JB only said we couldn't bring people *home.* . . . I don't see why she can't come here." Their voices were getting lower. I scooted closer to the door, keeping an eye on Valerie, who glanced at me and back down at her book. She obviously couldn't care less if I was eavesdropping.

"Dude. Anywhere we have a permanent address is off-limits for . . . 'dates.' Or whatever. You know the rules. In any case, date's over!"

There was a pregnant silence, which I imagined was taken up by lots of boy-to-boy stare-down action, and then the door opened and Vincent walked in, looking apologetic. "Kate. I'm sorry, I have to take care of something. I'll walk you to the Métro." I waited for him to give an explanation, but none came.

"That's okay," I said, trying to sound like I didn't mind. "But don't worry about seeing me to the Métro. I'll do some wandering on my own. Walk up to rue des Rosiers for some shopping or something."

He looked relieved, as if that was the response he had hoped for. "I'll at least come downstairs with you."

"No, really, that's okay," I said, feeling a little cloud of anger form inside me. Something was obviously going on that I didn't know about. But it was still rude of Jules to demand that I leave. Not to mention cowardly of Vincent to give in.

"I insist," he said, and opening the door for me, he followed me out into the hallway. Jules stood, arms crossed over his chest, glowering at us.

Vincent walked me down the stairs and into the courtyard. "I'm sorry," he said. "There's something going on. Something I have to take care of."

"Like police business, you mean?" I said, unable to hide my sarcasm.

"Yeah, something like that," he said evasively.

"And you can't talk about it."

"No."

"Okay. Well, I guess I'll see you around our neighborhood . . . ," I said, attempting to mask my disappointment with a smile.

"I'll see you soon," he said, and reached out his hand for mine. Though I wasn't very happy with him, his touch warmed me to my toes. "Promise," he added, looking like he wanted to say more. Then, giving my hand a squeeze, he turned to walk back into the building. My bad mood eased a little with his gesture, and I wandered through the gate feeling not quite ditched but not very pleased with how things had turned out, either.

I started walking north, trying to decide whether to visit the shops on the rue des Rosiers or stroll under the shady arcades surrounding the seventeenth-century square called Place des Vosges. I wasn't even halfway up the block when I decided my heart wasn't in it. I wanted to know what was going on with Vincent. Curiosity was killing me, and if I wasn't going to get any answers, I just wanted to go home.

I stopped at the crepe stand outside the Dome café and waited as the vendor spread the batter on the piping hot circular grill. I couldn't help but wish that Vincent were here getting a crepe with me as I watched people come and go from the Métro stop across the street. As if prompted by my wish, I spotted Vincent approaching the entrance with Jules. They began making their way down the stairs.

This is my chance to find out what's going on with the policeman charade, I thought. Vincent had said that there was something he had to take care of. Based on his behavior at the Village Saint-Paul, it seemed more like some*one* he had to take care of. I wanted to know who it was. I reasoned that if I was going to keep seeing Vincent, or whatever it was we were doing, I should be aware of any mysterious activities he was involved in.

"Et voilà, mademoiselle," said the vendor, handing me a paper-towel-wrapped crepe. I pointed to the change I had left on the counter and called, *"Merci,"* as I sprinted toward the subway entrance.

Once through the turnstile, I spotted the boys heading down the tunnel to the train. When I reached the bottom of the steps, I saw them standing halfway down the track. Before they could notice me, I slipped onto one of the plastic benches lining the wall.

It was then that I saw the man.

Just a stone's throw away from Vincent and Jules, a clean-cut thirtysomething man wearing a dark suit stood at the edge of the platform, holding a briefcase in one hand and pressing the other against his lowered forehead. It looked like he was crying.

In all my years of riding the Paris Métro, I had seen some weird things: Street people peeing in the corners. Madmen ranting about government persecution. Bands of children offering to help tourists with their luggage and then taking off with it. But I had never seen a grown man cry in public.

The whoosh of air that precedes the train came gusting through the tunnel, and the man looked up. Calmly placing his briefcase on the ground, he crouched down, and using one hand to steady himself on the edge of the platform, he jumped down onto the tracks. "Oh my God!" I felt the words coming out of my mouth in a scream, and looked around frantically to see if anyone else had noticed.

Jules and Vincent turned my way, not even glancing at the man on the tracks, though I was wildly pointing at him with both hands. Without speaking, they nodded at each other before each moving rapidly in a different direction. Vincent approached me and, taking me by the shoulders, tried to turn me away from the track.

Fighting him, I whipped my head around to see Jules jump down off the platform onto the tracks and push the now sobbing man out of the way. With the oncoming train just feet away, he looked up at Vincent and, giving a slight nod, touched his index finger to his forehead in a casual salute.

The sound was terrible. There was the earsplitting screech of the train's brakes, way too late to avoid the disaster, and then the loud thud of metal hitting flesh and bone. Vincent had prevented me from seeing the actual crash, but a snapshot of the penultimate second lodged in my mind: Jules's calm face nodding to Vincent as the train rushed up behind him.

I felt my knees give way and slumped forward with only Vincent's arms to hold me from falling. Screams came from all sides, and the sound of a man's loud wailing drifted from the direction of the tracks. I felt someone lift me and begin to run. And then everything was as silent and black as a tomb.

EIGHT

I AWOKE TO THE SMELL OF STRONG COFFEE AND lifted my head from between my bent knees. I was outside, sitting on the sidewalk, with my back against the wall of a building. Vincent crouched in front of me, holding a tiny steaming cup of espresso a few inches away from my face, waving it around like smelling salts.

"Vincent," I said, without thinking. His name felt natural coming from my mouth, like I had been saying it all my life.

"So you followed me," he said, looking grim.

My head began to spin as a throbbing headache materialized just above the nape of my neck. "Ow," I groaned, reaching back and massaging it with my hand.

"Drink this, then put your head back between your knees," Vincent instructed. He placed the cup to my lips, and I threw it back in one gulp.

"That's better. I'm just taking this cup back to the café next door. Don't move, I'll be right back," he said as I closed my eyes.

I couldn't have moved if I had wanted to. I couldn't even feel my legs. *What happened? How did I get here?* And then the memory came back to me, crushing me with its horror.

"Do you feel strong enough to take a taxi?" Vincent was back, squatting down to bring his face level with mine. "You've had quite a shock."

"But . . . your friend! Jules!" I said, incredulous.

"Yes, I know." He furrowed his brows. "But we can't do anything about that now. We need to get you away from here." He stood up and signaled a taxi. Lifting me to my feet and supporting me with a strong arm across my shoulders, he picked up my bag and walked me to the waiting car.

Vincent helped me inside, and scooting in beside me, he gave the driver an address on a street not far from my own.

"Where are we going?" I asked, suddenly concerned. My rational mind tapped me on the shoulder to remind me that I was in a car with someone who had not only just watched his friend die in front of a speeding train, but looked as calm as if it happened every day.

"I could take you to your house, but I'd rather take you to mine until you calm down. It's just a few streets away."

I can probably "calm down" better at my own house than at yours. My thought was interrupted as the meaning of his words clicked in. "You know where I live?" I gasped.

"I've already confessed to following around our neighborhood's new American imports. Remember?" He flashed me a disarming smile. "Besides, who followed who into the Métro today?"

I blushed as I wondered how many times he had seen me as I wandered, oblivious that I was being watched.

And then the memory of Jules in the Métro returned and a tremor shook me. "Just don't think. Don't think," Vincent whispered. At that moment, my emotions felt tugged in two opposite directions. I was frightened and confused by Vincent's indifference to Jules's death, but I desperately wanted him to comfort me.

His hand lay casually on his knee, and I had the strongest desire to grab it and press it to my cold face. To hold on to him and avoid slipping deeper under the wave of fear that threatened to engulf me. Jules's fate echoed too loudly of my own parents' accident. I felt like death had followed me across the Atlantic. It was trailing along in my wake, threatening to take everyone I knew.

And as if Vincent had heard my thoughts, his hand slid across the seat and pulled my fingers from where they were wedged between my knees. As he folded my hand inside his own, I was instantly enveloped in a feeling of safety. I leaned my head back against the headrest and closed my eyes for the rest of the drive.

The taxi came to a stop in front of a ten-foot-high stone wall set with massive iron gates. Their bars were fitted from behind with black metal sheets that tastefully blocked any view of what was inside. Thick wisteria vines draped over the edges of the wall, and a couple of stately trees were visible behind the barrier.

Vincent paid the taxi driver, then came around to my side and opened the door for me. He walked me up to a column embedded with a high-tech audiovisual security system.

The lock clicked after he typed the security code into a keypad. He pressed the gate open with one hand and pulled me gently behind him with the other. I gasped as I took in our surroundings.

I was standing in the cobblestone courtyard of a *hôtel particulier*, one of those in-town castles that wealthy Parisians built as their city dwellings in the seventeenth and eighteenth centuries. This one was built of massive honey-colored stones and peaked with a black slate roof with dormer windows spaced evenly along its length. The only time I had actually seen one of these buildings up close was when Mom and Mamie took me with them on a guided tour.

In the middle of the courtyard stood a circular fountain carved in granite, its dark gray basin big enough to swim a few strokes across. Over the splashing water stood a life-size stone figure of an angel carrying a sleeping woman in his arms. Her body was visible through the fabric of her dress, which was worked so finely by the sculptor that the heavy stone was transformed into the finest gauze. The woman's fragile loveliness was offset by the strength of the male angel carrying her, his massive wings curving protectively over the two figures. It was a symbol combining beauty and danger, and it cast a sinister aura across the courtyard.

"You live here?"

"I don't own the house, but yes, I live here," Vincent said, walking me across the courtyard to the front door. "Let's get you inside."

Remembering the reason we were there, the sound of Jules's body being crushed by a ton of metal resonated in my ears. The tears I had been holding back began to flow.

Vincent opened the ornately carved door and led me into an enormous entrance hall with a double staircase winding up either wall to a balcony overlooking the room. A crystal chandelier the size of a Volkswagen Beetle hung over our heads, and Persian rugs littered a marble floor inlaid with stone flowers and vines. *What is this place?* I thought.

I followed him through another door into a small, high-ceilinged room that looked like it hadn't been touched since the seventeenth century, and sat down on an ancient stiff-backed couch. Holding my head in my hands, I leaned forward and closed my eyes. "I'll be right back," Vincent said, and I heard the door close as he left the room.

After a few minutes I felt stronger. Resting my head against the couch, I studied the imposing room. Heavy drapes at the window blocked the daylight. A delicate chandelier, which looked like it had originally been set with candles instead of the flame-shaped electric bulbs it now held, threw out just enough light to illuminate walls that were crowded with paintings. A dozen faces of bad-tempered, centuries-old French aristocrats frowned down at me.

A servants' door hidden in the back wall swung open, and

Vincent walked through. He set a massive porcelain teapot in the shape of a dragon and a matching cup onto the table in front of me next to a plate of paper-thin cookies. The fragrance of strong tea and almonds wafted up from the silver tray.

"Sugar and caffeine. Best medicine in the world," Vincent said as he sat down in an upholstered armchair a few feet away.

I tried to pick up the heavy teapot, but my hands were shaking so hard I only succeeded in making it clatter against the cup. "Here, let me do that," he said as he leaned over and poured. "Jeanne, our housekeeper, makes the best tea. Or so I've heard. I'm more a coffee man myself."

I blanched at his small talk. "Okay, stop. Just stop right there." My teeth were chattering: I couldn't tell if it was my shattered nerves or the dawning fear that something was very wrong. "Vincent . . . whoever you are." *I'm in his house and I don't even know his last name,* I realized in a flash before continuing. "Your friend just died a little while ago, and you are talking to me about"—my voice broke—"about coffee?"

A defensive expression registered on his face, but he remained silent.

"Oh my God," I said softly, and began crying again. "What is wrong with you?"

The room was silent. I could hear the seconds ticking away on an enormous grandfather clock in the corner. My breathing calmed, and I wiped my eyes, attempting to compose myself.

"It's true. I'm not very good at showing my emotions," Vincent conceded finally.

"Not showing your emotions is one thing. But running off after your friend is demolished by a subway train?"

In a low, carefully measured tone he said, "If we had stayed, we would have had to talk to the police. They would have questioned both of us, as they must have done with the witnesses who stayed. I wanted to avoid that"—he paused—"at all costs."

Vincent's cold shell was back, or else I had just begun noticing it again. Numbness spread up my arms and throughout my body as I realized what he was saying. "So you're"—I choked—"you're what? A criminal?"

His dark, brooding eyes were drawing me toward him while my mind was telling me to run away. Far away.

"What are you? Wanted? Wanted for what? Did you steal all the paintings in this room?" I realized I was yelling and lowered my voice. "Or is it something worse?"

Vincent cleared his throat to buy time. "Let's just say that I'm not the kind of guy your mother would want you hanging around with."

"My mom's dead. My dad, too." The words escaped my lips before I could stop them.

Vincent closed his eyes and pressed his hands to his forehead as if he were in pain. "Recently?"

"Yes."

He nodded solemnly, as if it all made sense.

"I'm sorry, Kate."

However bad a person he is, he cares about me. The thought crossed my mind so abruptly that I couldn't stop it from triggering a reaction. My eyes filled with tears. I picked up the cup of tea and raised it to my lips.

The hot liquid slid from my throat to my stomach, and its calming effect was immediate. My thoughts felt clearer. And weirdly enough, I felt more in control of the situation. *He knows who I am now, even if I don't know the first thing about him.*

My revelation seemed to have shaken him. *Vincent's either struggling to hold himself together*, I thought, *or to hold something back*. I decided to take advantage of this apparent moment of weakness to figure something out. "Vincent, if you're in such a . . . dangerous situation, why in the world would you try to be friends with me?"

"I told you, Kate, I had seen you around the neighborhood"— he weighed his words carefully—"and you seemed like someone I would want to know. It was probably a bad idea. But I obviously wasn't thinking."

As he spoke, his voice turned from warm to icicle cold. I couldn't tell if he was angry with himself for getting me involved in whatever mess he was in—or with me for bringing it up. It didn't matter. The effect of his sudden frostiness was the same: I shuddered, feeling like someone had walked over my grave. "I'm ready to go," I said, standing suddenly.

He rose to his feet and nodded. "Yes, I'll take you home."

"No, that's okay. I know the way. I'd . . . rather you not." The words came from the rational part of me. The part that was urging me to get out of the house as fast as possible. But another part of me regretted it as soon as I spoke them.

"As you wish," he said, and leading me back through the grand entrance hall, he opened the door to the courtyard.

"Are you sure you'll be all right?" he insisted as he blocked the doorway, waiting for an answer before he would let me leave. I ducked under his arm to squeeze by, passing inches from his skin.

My mistake was inhaling as I did. He smelled like oak and grass and wood fires. He smelled like memories. Like years and years of memories.

"You look weak again." His hard shell cracked open just enough to show a glimpse of concern.

"I'm fine," I replied, attempting to sound sure of myself, and then seeing him standing there, calm and composed, I rephrased my answer. "I'm fine, but you shouldn't be. You just lost a friend in a horrible accident and you're standing there like nothing happened. I don't care who you are or what you've done to make you run away like that. But for it not to affect you . . . you've got to be seriously messed up."

A surge of emotion crossed Vincent's dark face. He looked upset. Well, good.

"I don't understand you. And I don't want to." My eyes narrowed in disgust. "I hope I never see you again," I said, and began walking toward the gate.

I felt a strong hand grip my arm, and whipped my head around to see that Vincent stood inches behind me. He leaned over until his mouth was next to my ear. "Things aren't always as they appear, Kate," he whispered, and carefully released my arm.

I ran toward the front gate, which was already swinging open to let me through. Once I was outside, it began to close. A loud crash that sounded like porcelain being smashed against marble came from somewhere inside the house.

I stood motionless, looking back at the massive metal gates. My intuition told me that I had done something wrong. That I had misjudged Vincent's character. But all signs pointed to the fact that he was some sort of criminal. And from the smashing sounds still emanating from the house, maybe even a violent one. I shook my head, wondering how I could have lost my capacity for reason just because of a handsome face.

NINE

OVER THE NEXT FEW WEEKS, I COULDN'T STOP replaying the events of that day in my mind, over and over again like a broken record. From the outside I must have looked the same. I got up, did my reading at an alternate café, went to the occasional movie, and attempted to join Georgia's and my grandparents' dinner-table conversations. Even so, they seemed to know that I was troubled. But they had no reason to attribute my dark mood to anything new.

Every time Vincent pushed his way into my mind I tried to push him back out. How could I have been so mistaken? The fact that he was a part of some sort of criminal network made more sense now that I thought back to that night at the river. There must have been some kind of underworld gang war going on. *Even if he's a bad guy, at least he saved that girl's life,* my conscience nagged.

But whatever his past contained, I couldn't justify his cold detachment after Jules was hit by the train. How could anyone leave the scene of a friend's death to insure his own safety from the law? The whole thing chilled me to the bone. Especially knowing that I had already started to feel something for him.

The flirty way he had teased me at the Picasso Museum. His intense expression as he grasped my hand in Jules's courtyard. The comfort I'd felt when he placed his hand over mine in the taxi. These instants kept flashing up in my memory, reminding me of why I had liked him. I shoved them aside again and again, disgusted with myself for having been so naive.

Finally Georgia cornered me one night in my room. "What is wrong with you?" she asked with her usual tact. She threw herself onto my rug and leaned roughly back against a priceless Empire dresser that I never used because I was afraid I would break the handles.

"What do you mean?" I responded, avoiding her eyes.

"I mean, what the hell is wrong with you? I'm your sister. I know when there's something wrong."

I had been yearning to talk to Georgia but couldn't even imagine where to start. How could I tell her the guy that we saw leap off the bridge was actually a criminal I had been hanging out with—that is, until I saw him walk away from his friend's death without shedding a tear?

"Okay, if you don't want to talk I can just start guessing, but I *will* get it out of you. Are you worried about starting a new school?"

"No."

"Is it about friends?"

"What friends?"

"Exactly!"

"No."

"Boys?"

Something on my face must have given me away, because she immediately leaned toward me, crossing her legs in a tell-me-more pose. "Kate, why didn't you tell me about . . . whoever he is . . . before it got to this?"

"You don't talk to me about your boyfriends."

"That's because there are too many of them." She laughed and then, remembering my low spirits, added, "Plus, none of them are serious enough to mention. *Yet*." She waited.

There was no way I was getting off the hook. "Okay, there's this guy who lives in the neighborhood, and we kind of hung out a few times until I found out he was bad news."

"Like how bad is the bad news? Married?"

I couldn't help but laugh. "No!"

"Druggie?"

"No. I mean, I don't think so. It's more like . . ." I watched for Georgia's reaction. "It's more like he's in trouble with the law. Like a criminal or something."

"Yeah. I'd say that's bad news," she admitted pensively. "Sounds more like someone I'd go for, actually."

"Georgia!" I yelled, throwing a pillow at her.

"Sorry, sorry. I shouldn't joke about it. You're right. He doesn't sound like good boyfriend material, Katie-Bean. So why don't you just pat yourself on the back for not getting in too deep before you found out, and be on your merry way back to Guyland?"

"I just can't believe that I was so mistaken about him. He seemed so perfect. And so interesting. And—"

"Handsome?" my sister interrupted.

I fell back on my bed and stared at the ceiling. "Oh, Georgia. Not handsome. Gorgeous. Like heart-stoppingly amazing. Not that it matters now."

Georgia stood and looked down at me. "I'm sorry it didn't work. It would have been nice seeing you out and about enjoying yourself with some hot Frenchman. I won't keep bugging you about it, but as soon as you're ready to start living again, let me know. There are parties nearly every night."

"Thanks, Georgia," I said, reaching out to touch her hand.

"Anything for my little sister."

And then, without me even noticing, summer was officially over and it was time to start school.

Georgia and I speak French fluently. Dad always spoke it with us, and we spent so much time in Paris during our vacations that French comes as easily for us as English. So we could have gone to a French high school. But the French system is so different from the American that we would have had to make up all sorts of missing credits to graduate.

The American School of Paris is one of those strange places in foreign cities where expatriates huddle together in a defensive circle and try to pretend they're still back at home. I saw it as a place for lost souls. My sister saw it as an opportunity to make more international friends who she could visit in their native countries during school breaks. Georgia treats friends like outfits, happily trading one for another when it's convenient—not in a mean way, but she just doesn't get too attached.

As for me, being a junior, I knew I had two short years with these people, some of whom would be leaving to go back to their home country before the school year was even out.

So after walking through the massive front doors on the first day of school, I headed directly to the office to get my schedule and Georgia walked straight up to a group of intimidating-looking girls and began chatting away like she had known them all her life. Our social dice were cast within our first five minutes.

I hadn't been to a museum since I had seen Vincent at the Musée Picasso, so it was with a sense of trepidation that I approached the Centre Pompidou one afternoon after school. My history teacher had assigned us projects on twentieth-century events happening in Paris, and I had chosen the riots of 1968.

Say "May '68" and any French person will immediately think of the countrywide general strike that brought France's economy to a halt. I was focusing on the weeks-long violent fighting between the police and university students at the Sorbonne. We were supposed to write our papers in the first person, as if we had experienced the events ourselves. So instead of looking through history books, I decided to search contemporary newspapers to find personal accounts.

The materials I needed were in the large library located on the Centre Pompidou's second and third floors. But, since the other floors housed Paris's National Museum of Modern Art, I planned on following my schoolwork with some well-deserved art gazing.

Once settled in at one of the library's viewing booths, I flipped through microfilm spools from the riots' most eventful days. Having read that May 10 was a day of heated fighting between police and students, I scanned that day's front page, took some notes, and then flipped past the headlines to read the editorials. It was hard to imagine that kind of violence happening just across the river in the Latin Quarter, a fifteen-minute walk from where I was sitting.

I ejected the spool and replaced it with another. The riots had flared back up on July 14, France's Independence Day. Many students, as well as tourists visiting Paris for the festivities, were taken to nearby hospitals. I took notes from the first few pages, and then flipped back to the two-page spread of obituaries and their accompanying black-and-white photos. And there he was.

Halfway down the first page. It was Vincent. He had longer hair, but he looked exactly like he had a month ago. My body turned to ice as I read the text.

Firefighter Jacques Dupont, nineteen years old, born in La Baule, Pays de la Loire, was killed in duty last night in a building fire believed to have been sparked by a Molotov cocktail thrown by student rioters. The residential building at 18 rue Champollion was in flames when Dupont and his colleague, Thierry Simon (obit., section S), rushed into the building and began pulling out its inhabitants, who had taken cover from the fighting at the adjacent Sorbonne. Trapped under burning timbers, Dupont expired before he could be evacuated to the hospital, and his body was received by the morgue. Twelve citizens, including four children, owe their lives to these local heroes.

It can't be him, I thought. *Unless he is the spitting image of his dad, who happened to sire a son before he died at* . . . (I glanced back at the obituary) *nineteen. Which* isn't *impossible* . . .

As my reasoning foundered, I forwarded to the next page and scanned the *S*s for "Simon." There he was: Thierry Simon. The muscle-bound guy who had turned Georgia and me away from the fight at the river. Thierry had a voluminous Afro in the photo but wore the same confident grin that he had flashed me with that day across the café terrace. It was definitely the same guy. But more than forty years ago.

I closed my eyes in disbelief, and then opened them again to read the paragraph under Thierry's head shot. It read the same as Jacques's, except it gave his age as twenty-two and place of birth as Paris.

"I don't get it," I whispered, as I numbly pressed a button on the machine to print both pages. After returning the micro-film spools to the front desk, I left the library in a daze and hesitated before stepping on the escalator going to the next floor. I would sit in the museum until I figured out what to do next.

My thoughts were being yanked around in ten different directions as I drifted through the turnstile and into an enormous high-ceilinged gallery with benches positioned in the middle of the room. Sitting down, I put my head in my hands as I tried to clear my mind.

Finally I looked up. I was in the room dedicated to the art of Fernand Léger, one of my favorite early- to mid-twentieth-century French painters. I studied the two-dimensional surfaces filled with bright primary colors and geometric shapes and felt a sense of normalcy return. I glanced over to the corner where my favorite Léger painting hung: one with robotic-looking World War I soldiers sitting around a table, smoking pipes and playing cards.

A young man stood in front of it, his back to me as he leaned in closer to inspect something in the composition. He was of medium height with short-cropped brown hair and messy clothes. *Where have I seen him before?* I thought, wondering if it was someone from school.

And then he turned, and my mouth dropped open in disbelief. The man standing across the gallery from me was Jules.

TEN

MY BODY NO LONGER FELT CONNECTED TO MY mind. I stood and walked toward the phantom. *Either I'm having a mental breakdown that started in the library,* I thought, *or the guy standing in front of me is a ghost.* Both explanations seemed more probable than the alternative: that Jules had actually survived a head-on collision with a subway train, not only in one piece but apparently uninjured.

When I was a few feet away, he saw me coming, and for a split second, he hesitated. Then he turned to me with a completely blank look on his face.

"Jules!" I said urgently.

"Hello," he said calmly. "Do I know you?"

"Jules, it's me, Kate. I visited your studio with Vincent, remember? And I saw you at the Métro station that day of . . . the crash."

His expression changed from blank to amused. "I am afraid that you have me confused with someone else. My name is

Thomas, and I don't know anyone called Vincent."

Thomas, my foot, I thought, wanting to shake him. "Jules. I know it's you. You were in that horrible accident when . . . just over a month ago?"

He shook his head and shrugged, as if to say, *Sorry.*

"Jules, you have to tell me what's going on."

"Listen, um, Kate? I have no idea what you're talking about, but let me help you over to that bench. You must be overexcited. Or overwrought." He took me by my elbow and began leading me back to the benches.

I jerked my arm away and stood facing him with fists clenched. "I know it's you. I'm not crazy. And I don't know what's going on. But I accused Vincent of being heartless for running away from your death. And now it turns out you're alive."

I realized that my voice had been rising as I saw a security guard head our way. I flashed Jules a furious look as the uniformed man walked up to us and asked, "Is there a problem here?"

Jules calmly looked the guard in the eyes and said, "No problem, sir. She seems to have mistaken me for someone else."

"I have not!" I hissed under my breath, then left, walking quickly toward the exit. Turning to see Jules and the guard staring my way, I strode out of the museum and ran down the escalators.

There was only one place I could go.

The subway ride back to my neighborhood seemed interminable, but finally I found myself sprinting up the Métro steps into the fading sunlight and heading toward the rue de Grenelle. Standing before the massive vine-draped wall, I rang the doorbell. A light went on above my head, and I looked up into a video surveillance camera.

"*Oui?*" a voice asked after a few seconds.

"It's Kate. I'm . . ." I paused, momentarily losing my courage. But remembering the cruelty of my last words to Vincent, I spoke with renewed resolve. "I'm a friend of Vincent's."

"He's not in." The male voice crackled metallically through the tiny speaker on the bottom of the keypad.

"I need to talk to him. Can't I leave a message?"

"Don't you have his phone number?"

"No."

"And you're a friend?" The voice sounded skeptical.

"Yes, I mean no. But I need to talk to him. Please."

There was a moment of silence, and then I heard the click that meant the gate had been unlocked. It swung slowly inward. Across the courtyard, a man stood in the open doorway. My heart dropped an inch when I saw that it wasn't Vincent.

I walked quickly across the cobblestones to face the man, trying to come up with something to say that wouldn't make me sound like a crazy person. But when I reached him, all words escaped me. Although he seemed to be in his sixties, his faded green eyes looked centuries-old.

His longish gray hair was smoothed back with pomade, and his face was punctuated by a long, hooked, noble-looking nose. I immediately recognized in his face and dress the mark of French aristocracy.

If I hadn't already met his type as clients of Papy's antiques business, I would have recognized his features from the portraits of nobility hanging in every French castle and museum. Old family. Old money. This palace of a house must be his.

His voice cut me off midthought. "You're here to see Vincent?"

"Yes . . . I mean yes, *monsieur*."

He nodded approvingly as I corrected my manners to befit his age and station. "Well, I am sorry to inform you that, as I said before, he is not here."

"Do you know when he'll be back?"

"In a few days, I would think."

I didn't know what to say. He turned to leave, and feeling completely awkward, I blurted, "Well, could I at least leave him a message?"

"And what message would that be?" he asked dryly, adjusting the silk ascot tied at the neck of his impeccable white cotton shirt.

"Could . . . could I write it?" I stammered, fighting the urge to just walk away. "I'm sorry to impose on your time, sir, but would you mind if I wrote him a message?"

He lifted his eyebrows and studied my face for a moment. And then, opening the door behind him for me to pass through, he said, "Very well."

I walked into the magnificent foyer and waited as he closed the door behind us. "Follow me," he said, leading me through a side door into the same room where Vincent had brought me tea. He gestured to a desk and chair and said, "You will find writing paper and pens in the drawer."

"I have some with me, thanks," I said, patting my book bag.

"Do you wish me to send for some tea?"

I nodded, thinking that would win me a few minutes to think of what to write. "Yes, thank you."

"Then Jeanne will bring you your tea and show you out. You can give the note for Vincent to her. *Au revoir, mademoiselle.*" He gave me a curt nod, and then closed the door behind him. I breathed a sigh of relief.

Pulling a pen and notebook out of my bag, I tore off a piece of paper and stared at it for a full minute before starting to write. *Vincent,* I began.

> *I'm starting to understand what you meant when you said*
> *that things aren't always as they seem. I found your photo,*
> *and that of your friend, in the 1968 obituary pages. And then,*
> *right afterward, I saw Jules. Alive.*
>
> *I can't imagine what all this means, but I want to apologize*
> *for the mean things I said—after you treated me so kindly.*
> *I told you I never wanted to see you again. I take it back.*
>
> *At least help me understand what's going on, so I won't end up*
> *in a loony bin somewhere, blabbering about dead people for*
> *the rest of my days.*
>
> *Your move.*
> *Kate*

I folded the note and waited. Jeanne never came. I watched the minutes tick away on the grandfather clock, growing more nervous with each passing second. Finally I began to worry that perhaps I was supposed to go find Jeanne. Maybe she was waiting in the kitchen with my tea. I walked into the foyer. The house was silent.

I noticed, however, that a door across from me was ajar. Walking slowly over to it, I peeked inside. "Jeanne?" I called softly. There was no response. I pushed the door open and walked into a room that was almost identical to the one I had come from. It had the same small door in the corner as the one that Vincent had brought my tea through. *The servants' entrance,* I thought.

Opening it, I saw a long, dark passageway. My heart in my throat, I walked toward a windowed door at the end, with light illuminating its panes. It swung open onto a large, cavernous kitchen. No one was there. I breathed a sigh of relief, and realized that I had been afraid of running into the master of the house once more.

Deciding to leave the note in the mailbox on the way out, I hurried back down the tunnel-like space. Now that the kitchen's light was at my back, I saw several doors punctuating the long hallway and noticed that one was slightly ajar. A warm light was glowing from inside. Maybe this was the housekeeper's room. "Jeanne?" I called in a low voice. There was no response.

I stood motionless an instant before feeling myself driven forward by an irresistible impulse. *What am I doing?* I thought as I stepped through the doorway. Heavy curtains blocked the outside light, like in the other rooms. The only illumination came from a few small lamps scattered around on low tables.

I stepped into the room and softly closed the door behind me. I knew it was insane. But the rational part of my brain had lost the battle, and I was now on autopilot, trespassing in someone's house in order to satisfy my curiosity. My skin felt like it was being pricked by a million tiny adrenaline darts as I began to look around.

To my right, bookcases surrounded a gray marble fireplace. Above its mantel hung two enormous swords, crossed above the hilts. The other walls were hung with framed photographs, some in black-and-white and others in color. They were all portraits.

There seemed to be no sense to the collection. Some of the people in them were old, some young. A few pictures looked as if they were taken fifty years ago, and others looked contemporary. The only thing tying them together was that they were all candid: The subjects didn't know their picture was being taken. *Weird collection,* I thought, shifting my gaze to the other side of the room.

In one corner stood a massive four-poster bed hung with translucent white cloth. I walked toward it to take a closer look. Through the gauzy fabric I could see the shape of a man lying on the bed. My heart froze.

Not daring to breathe, I pulled the curtain aside.

It was Vincent. He was lying above the covers, fully clothed, on his back with his arms to his sides. And he didn't look like he was sleeping. He looked like he was dead.

I lifted a hand and touched his arm. It was as cold and hard as a store mannequin's. Recoiling, I cried, "Vincent?" He didn't move. "Oh my God," I whispered, horrified, and then my eyes fixed on a framed photo sitting on the table next to his bed. It was of me.

My heart stopped in my chest, and holding my hand to my throat, I backed away until my shoulders hit the marble chimney and I let out a terrified scream. Just then, the door burst open and an overhead light switched on. Jules stood in the doorway. "Hi, Kate," he said ominously, and then, turning the light back off, he nodded and said, "Looks like the game's up, Vince."

ELEVEN

"YOU'LL HAVE TO COME WITH ME." JULES WORE A grim expression. When he realized that I was incapable of movement, he took my arm and led me toward the door.

"But Jules," I said, my shock worn off enough to allow me to speak, "Vincent's dead!"

Jules turned to me and stared. I must have looked like a trauma victim. I know I sounded like one, my voice coming out all quivery.

"No, he's not. He's fine." He took my hand and pulled me into the hallway. I jerked it back.

"Listen to me, Jules," I said, starting to sound hysterical, "I touched him. His skin is cold and hard. He's dead!"

"Kate," he said, sounding almost annoyed, "I can't talk to you about this right now. But you have to come with me." He took a gentle hold of my wrist and began leading me down the hallway.

"Where are you taking me?"

"Where should I take her?" he asked himself. It wasn't in a pondering tone, like people use when they ask a question they already know the answer to. It sounded like he didn't know and expected someone else to answer.

My eyes widened. Jules was crazy. Maybe he had been brain-damaged in the subway wreck, I thought. Maybe he was criminally insane and had murdered Vincent and left him on his bed, and now he was taking me somewhere to kill me, too. My thoughts were spinning out of control: I was now in slasher-film mode. Terrified, I tried to yank my hand from his grasp, but his grip tightened.

"I'm taking you to Charlotte's room," he said, answering his own question.

"Who's Charlotte?" I asked, my voice wavering.

"I'm *not* trying to scare her!" Jules said, coming to a stop. He turned to me, looking exasperated. "Listen, Kate. I know you had a shock in there, but your being in that room is completely your own fault. Not mine. Now I'm going to take you somewhere to calm down, and I'm not going to hurt you."

"Can I just leave?"

"No."

A tear rolled down my cheek. I couldn't help myself. I was too confused and frightened to be calm, and too horrified that I was crying to look at him: Looking weak or fragile was the last thing I wanted. I stared at the floor.

"What now?" he said, dropping my hand. "Kate? Kate?" His rough manner softened. "Kate."

I met his eyes as I wiped my tears away with shaking fingers.

"Oh my God, I've terrified you," he said, taking his first good look at me. He stepped backward. "I've done this all wrong. I'm such an idiot." *Be careful,* I told myself, *he might just be acting. But he's sure doing a believable job with the remorse.*

"Okay, let me explain"—he hesitated—"as much as I can. I'm not going to hurt you. I swear, Kate. And I promise Vincent will be fine. It's not what it seems. But I just need to talk to the others—the other people who live here—before I can let you leave."

I nodded. Jules was acting a lot saner than he had a few minutes before. And he was looking so apologetic that I almost (but not quite) felt sorry for him. *Even if I want to run,* I thought, *I can't get past the security gate outside.*

He reached his hand toward me, this time in a peaceful way, as if he wanted to place it comfortingly on my forearm, but I recoiled.

"Okay. It's okay," he soothed, raising his hands in the air in an *I surrender* gesture. "I won't touch you again."

He looked really upset now. "I know," he said, speaking to the air, "I'm a total moron," and began walking down the hallway toward the foyer. "Please follow me, Kate," he said in a downcast voice.

I followed him. What other choice did I have?

He led me up the winding double staircase to the second floor and down a hallway. Opening a door to a darkened room, he flicked on the lights and stayed in the hallway as I walked in.

"Make yourself comfortable. I might be a while," he said, avoiding my eyes. He pulled the door closed behind me. The lock clicked.

"Hey!" I yelled, grabbing the handle and twisting it. It was definitely locked.

"I *had* to lock it. We can't just have her wandering around the house." Jules was talking to himself again, as his footsteps grew faint.

There was nothing more that I could do, besides leaping out the second-floor window and scaling the front gate. *That's just not going to happen,* I thought, and resigned myself to the fact that I was powerless to do anything else until someone unlocked the door.

You could have done worse for a prison, I thought, looking around. The walls were lined with a patterned rose-colored silk, and heavy mint green drapes were tied back on either side of the windows, which had upper panes in the shape of hearts. Delicate painted bedroom furniture was arranged around the edges of the room. I sat down on a silk-upholstered daybed.

My shaking calmed, and after a long while I let myself stretch out and put my head on a cushion, drawing my legs up off the floor. I shut my eyes, just for a second, and the effects of the stress and fear had their way with my brain. I was out like a light.

It must have been hours later when I awoke. I could see a night sky approaching dawn through the window, and for one delirious moment I thought I was back in my Brooklyn bedroom.

Then my eyes flicked upward to a large chandelier with arms ending in impossibly delicate glass flowers. The ceiling was painted to look like a cloudy sky edged with fat baby angels carrying armloads of ribbons and flowers.

For a second, I didn't know where I was. Then, remembering, I sat up.

"You're awake," said a voice from across the room. I looked over to find its source. It was the girl from the café with the cropped blond hair, the one who had saved me from being crushed by the falling stone. *What is she doing here?* I thought.

She sat curled up in an armchair next to an ornate stone fireplace. Slowly and hesitantly she unfolded herself and walked carefully toward me.

The light from the chandelier shone through her hair, making it glow like burnished bronze. Her cheeks and lips were the color of the velvety pink roses in Mamie's country garden. High cheekbones set off her beautiful eyes, their irises a bewitching green.

The girl stood next to me now, and timidly held out a hand to take my own. "Kate," she said with a shy voice, squeezing my hand and letting it go. "I'm Charlotte." I sat on the edge of the daybed, looking up at her in awe.

"You're the one who saved my life," I murmured.

Laughing, she pulled up a chair to sit in front of me. "That wasn't really me." She smiled. "I mean, it was me, but I'm not responsible for saving your life. It's kind of complicated," she said, crossing her legs impishly. Around her neck hung a leather cord with a silver teardrop-shaped pendant.

So this is the girl Vincent was so close to, I thought with dismay, my eyes traveling from the necklace back to her elegant face. She was around my age, but a bit younger. Vincent had said she was just a friend. I couldn't help wondering how close they had been.

"Welcome to my room," she said.

My heart fell. *She lives in his house?*

"It's stunning," I managed to eke out.

"I like to surround myself with beauty," she said, flashing me an embarrassed smile.

Her boyish haircut and long, thin figure, dressed in tight black jeans and faded striped T-shirt, couldn't disguise her striking feminine beauty. Although it looked like she was attempting to do just that. *She doesn't even have to try, and she's breathtaking,* I thought, mentally surrendering as I realized I would never have been able to compete with Charlotte.

I couldn't speak, my throat was closed so tightly with jealousy over the thought of this girl getting to see Vincent every day. Of her waking up in this beautiful room and knowing that Vincent was there, in the same house as her.

And then I remembered how he had looked in the bed downstairs, and I tried to shake myself out of my pettiness. Even though Jules said he wasn't dead, he had sure seemed dead to me. I didn't know what to think anymore. But being jealous of this girl wasn't going to help anything.

"What happened to Vincent?" I asked.

"Ah. The million-euro question," she said softly. "And the one I've been specifically requested not to answer. Apparently the boys don't trust me. Discretion and tact are not among my strong points. However, they asked me to stay here with you, in case you freaked out and tried to run away once you woke up." She hesitated, waiting. "So . . . are you going to freak and run?"

"No," I said, rubbing my forehead. "I mean, I don't think so." And then, alarmed, I blurted, "My grandparents! They'll be panicking! I've been gone all night!"

"No, they won't," she said, smiling. "We texted them from your phone that you were spending the night with a friend."

My relief was replaced by a chilling thought. "So I can't leave? Are you keeping me prisoner?"

"That makes it sound a bit melodramatic," she said.

Her eyes looked as if they were used to taking much in, while giving little away. The eyes of an older woman reflecting the spirit of a little girl. "You saw things you shouldn't have. Now we have to decide how to handle the situation. You know . . . like damage control. You're the one who took the bite out of the apple, Kate. Although with a serpent that handsome, I can't say I blame you."

"You're not going to hurt me?" I asked.

"You answer that question," she said, and placed her fingertips on my arm. A warm rivulet of peace seemed to flow from her touch, and I was suffused with tranquillity.

"What are you doing?" I asked, looking at the spot where her skin touched mine. If I wasn't feeling so relaxed, I'm sure I would have leaped to my feet in dismay at the weirdness of her gesture. She didn't say a thing, but the corners of her mouth curved up slightly and she removed her hand.

I looked her steadily in the eye and asked, "No one else is going to hurt me either?"

"I'll make sure they don't."

There was a knock at the door. Charlotte rose. "It's time."

She held out her arm for me to link mine through. I couldn't help but glance at the pendant again, and hesitated.

"What's wrong?" she asked, and touched the silver teardrop.

Something on my face must have told her, because her expression changed as she said, "Vincent told me you picked out my necklace. I'm glad he had you there—I never know what the boys are going to come up with." She smiled and pressed my hand in a friendly gesture. "Vincent's like my brother, Kate. There is absolutely nothing between us . . . except a long history of boring birthday presents. You broke my losing streak. It's the first time in years he's given me something besides *his* favorite recent CD."

She laughed, and the jealousy that had been pricking me like needles eased a little. She certainly spoke of him like someone would a brother. I took her arm.

As we made our way to the door, I noticed that her walls were hung with the same jumble of photographs that I had seen in Vincent's room. But this collection was set in pretty painted wood-and-enamel frames and attached to the wall with ribbons.

"Who are those people?" I asked.

Her eyes flicked casually in the direction I was looking, and leading me through the door, she said, "Them? Well, Kate, though I can't take credit for saving your life, those are the people I *did* save."

TWELVE

CHARLOTTE LED ME DOWNSTAIRS AND THROUGH the servants' passageway into Vincent's room. She tapped on the door and, without waiting for a response, led me directly to Vincent's bed. My steps faltered when I saw him sitting up, propped against pillows. He looked very weak and as pale as a sheet. But he was alive. My heart leaped in my chest—as much with excitement at seeing him alive as with fear. How was it possible?

"Vincent?" I asked cautiously. "Is that you?" Which sounded a bit stupid. It looked like him, but maybe he had been possessed by . . . I don't know, some kind of alien being or something. At this point, things were strange enough for me to believe almost anything.

He smiled, and I knew it was really him.

"You're not . . . but you were dead!" I had to force the irrational words out of my mouth.

"What if I told you I'm just a deep sleeper?" his low voice came, slow and with great effort.

"Vincent, you were dead. I saw you. I touched you. I know. . . ." My eyes filled with tears as I had a flashback to the Brooklyn morgue and my parents' bodies laid out on stretchers. "I know what 'dead' looks like."

"Come here," he said. I inched my way toward him, not knowing what to expect. He lifted his arm, slowly, and touched my hand. He wasn't as cold as before, but he didn't feel quite human, either.

"See?" he said, the corners of his lips curving upward. "Alive."

I stepped back, pulling my hand from his. "I don't understand," I said, my voice mistrustful. "What's wrong with you?"

He looked resigned. "I'm sorry I ever got you mixed up in this. It was selfish. But I didn't think it would turn out this way. I didn't think . . . at all. Obviously."

My feeling of general alarm was replaced by a creeping sensation of fear of what would come next. I couldn't imagine what sort of revelation he was going to come out with. But a little voice inside me said, *You knew*. And I realized that I had.

I had known that there was something different about Vincent. I had felt it, even before I saw his photo in the obituaries. It was something just a little east of normal, but too obscure for me to put my finger on. So I had ignored it. But now I was going to find out. A frisson of expectancy caused me to shudder. Vincent saw me tremble and frowned regretfully.

We were interrupted by a tapping at the door. Charlotte rose to open it and moved aside as, one by one, people stepped into the room.

Jules walked up to me first and, gently touching my shoulder, asked, "Are you feeling better?"

I nodded.

"I am so, so sorry for how I handled things before," he said with remorse. "It was a knee-jerk reaction, trying to get you away from Vince as soon as possible. I was rough with you. I wasn't thinking."

"Really. It's okay."

A familiar figure walked up behind him and jokingly pushed him aside. The muscular guy from the river turned to Jules and said, "Trying to hog her for yourself?" and then, bending down to my height, he held out his hand. "Kate, enchanted to meet you. I'm Ambrose," he said in a baritone voice that was as thick as molasses. Then, switching into a perfectly American-accented English, he said, "Ambrose Bates from Oxford, Mississippi. It's nice to meet a fellow countryman in this land of crazy French people!"

Clearly enjoying the fact that he had surprised me, Ambrose laughed deeply and clapped me on the arm before sitting down next to Jules on a couch and giving me a friendly wink.

A man I had never seen before stepped toward me and gave a nervous little bow. "Gaspard," he introduced himself simply. He was older than the others, in his late thirties or early forties. Tall and gaunt, he had deep-set eyes and a shock of badly cut black hair sticking up in all directions. He turned and walked away toward the others.

"This is my twin brother, Charles," said Charlotte, who had stayed by my side as presentations were made. She pulled forward the redhead copy of herself. Bowing and giving my hand a mock kiss, he said sarcastically, "Nice to see you again, now that it's not raining masonry." I smiled unsurely at him.

I don't know if it was my imagination, or if everyone actually took a step backward, but all of a sudden it seemed like the only people in the room were me and the man I was facing. It was the aristocratic gentleman from yesterday—the owner of the house. Though everyone else had greeted me in a somewhat friendly manner, my host was not smiling.

Standing before me, he bowed stiffly from the waist. "Jean-Baptiste Grimod de la Reynière," he said, looking stonily into my eyes. "Although the rest of my kindred may reside here, this is *my* house and I, for one, feel that your presence here is very unwise."

"Jean-Baptiste," came Vincent's voice from behind me. "None of this was intentional." He lay back on the pillow and closed his eyes, seeming to have used all his energy with those six words.

"You, young man . . . you were the one who broke the rules by bringing her into our house in the first place. I have never permitted any of you to bring your human lovers here, and you flaunted my injunction most egregiously."

I felt my cheeks flame at his words, but wasn't sure which I was responding to: the "human" part or the "lovers" part. Nothing made sense anymore.

"What was I supposed to do?" Vincent argued. "She had just seen Jules die! She was in shock."

"That was your own problem to solve. You shouldn't have got ten involved with her in the first place. And now you are going to have to clean up your own mess."

"Ah, lighten up, JB," said Ambrose, leaning back and casually draping his arms along the entire length of the couch back. "It's not the end of the world. We've checked her out, and she's definitely not a spy. Plus, she's not exactly the first human to know what we are."

The older man shot him a withering look.

The one who'd introduced himself as Gaspard spoke up in a timorous voice. "If I may be permitted to clarify . . . the difference here is that every other human interacting with us was . . . ah . . . was individually chosen from families who have served Jean-Baptiste for generations."

Generations? I thought with dismay. An icy finger brushed its way up my spine.

"Whereas you," Jean-Baptiste continued with undisguised distaste, "I have known for less than a day, and already you are intruding on my kindred's privacy. You are most unwelcome."

"Sheesh!" exclaimed Jules. "Don't hold back your true feelings, Grimod. You old-timers really need to learn to open up and express yourselves." Jean-Baptiste acted like he hadn't heard.

"Well, what are we supposed to do then?" Charlotte said, addressing our host.

"Okay, stop. Everyone," Vincent said with a shallow breath. "You are my kindred. Who votes that we tell Kate?"

Ambrose, Charlotte, Charles, and Jules raised their hands.

"And what would you have us do?" Vincent directed his question toward Jean-Baptiste and Gaspard.

"That's your problem," Jean-Baptiste said. He stared me down for another few seconds and then, turning on his heel, strode rapidly out of the room, slamming the door behind him.

THIRTEEN

"SO," SAID AMBROSE WITH A CHUCKLE, RUBBING his hands together. "Majority rules. Let's get this party started."

"Here," said Charlotte, pulling a couple of big cushions from the couch to the floor. Sitting down Indian-style on one, she smiled at me and patted the other invitingly.

"It's okay," Vincent reassured me when I hesitated, and relinquished my hand.

"Kate," Jules said, "you realize that what we talk about here doesn't go outside these walls."

Vincent's words were slow and precise: "Jules is right. Our lives are in your hands once you know, Kate. I hate to force that type of responsibility on anyone, but the situation's gone too far. Do you promise to keep our secret? Even if you"—it sounded like he was running out of breath—"even if you leave today and decide never to return."

I nodded. Everyone waited. "I promise," I whispered, which

was the best I could do with a lump in my throat the size of a grapefruit. Something extremely bizarre was going on here, and I had too few clues to guess what it was. But with Jean-Baptiste's flippant use of the word "human" and Vincent and Jules both apparently having been resurrected, I knew I had gotten myself in deep. It was not knowing what I was deep *in* that was scaring the pee out of me.

"Jules . . . you start," Vincent said, closing his eyes and looking more dead than alive.

Jules measured up the situation and decided to have pity. "Maybe it would be easier if we let Kate ask us what she wants."

Where to even start? I thought, and then remembered what had set everything into such a downward spiral in the first place. "I saw a picture of you and Vincent in a 1968 newspaper that said you died in a fire," I said, turning to Ambrose.

He nodded at me with a little smile, urging me on.

"So how can you be here now?"

"Well, I'm glad we're starting with the easy questions," he said, stretching his powerful arms and then leaning toward me. "The answer would be . . . because we're zombies!" and he let out a horrible groan, stretching his mouth open and baring his teeth as he curled his hands into claws.

Seeing my terrified expression, Ambrose began cracking up and slapping his knee with his hand. "Just kidding," he cackled, and then, calming down, looked at me sedately. "But no, seriously. We're zombies."

"We are *not* zombies," said Charlotte, her voice rising with annoyance.

"The correct term, I believe, would be, ah, undead," said Gaspard in a wavering voice.

"Ghosts," said Charles, grinning mischievously.

"Stop scaring her, you guys," said Vincent. "Jules?"

"Kate, it's a lot more complicated than that. We call ourselves *revenants*."

I looked around at them, one by one.

"Ruh-vuh-nahnt," Jules pronounced slowly, obviously thinking I didn't understand.

"I know the word. It means 'ghost' in French." My voice shook. *I am sitting in a room of monsters,* I thought. *Defenseless.* But I couldn't afford to freak out now. What would they do to me if I did? What would they do to me even if I didn't? Unless they were the kind of monsters who could erase people's memories, I was in on their secret now.

"If you go back to the root of the word, it actually means 'one who returns' or 'one who comes back,'" offered Gaspard pedantically.

Though the room was warm, I found myself shivering. They all stared at me expectantly, as if I were their group science project: Would I blow up or just kind of fizzle out? Charles hissed, "She's going to freak and run away, like I said."

"She's *not* going to freak and run away," argued Charlotte.

"Okay, everybody out," came Vincent's voice, more forceful

than it had been so far. "No offense, but I'd rather talk to Kate myself. You guys are making a mess of the whole thing. Thank you for your votes of confidence, but please . . . go."

"Impossible." The room fell silent as everyone stared at Gaspard. His voice lost its authority and he began picking at his fingernail. "I mean to say, if I may," he stuttered self-consciously, "Vincent, you cannot take over the task of informing the human, I mean Kate, yourself. We are all affected by this breach. We all need to be aware of what information she has . . . and doesn't have. And I will have to give a full account to Jean-Baptiste afterward. Before she is allowed to leave."

My tenseness eased just a fraction. *They're going to let me leave.* That knowledge became my light at the end of the terrifyingly dark tunnel.

"I might, ah, also point out that you're too weak to even sit up," Gaspard continued. "In your condition, how can you be expected to handle the explanation of something of such importance to us all?"

The silence lasted a full minute while everyone watched Vincent. Finally he sighed. "Okay. I understand. But for God's sake, try to behave yourselves." He looked over to me and said, "Kate, please come sit with me. At least it will give me an illusion of having some control over the situation."

Getting up, I walked to the bed and watched as Vincent effortfully lifted his arm and grasped my hand in his. The instant our skin touched, I felt the same peace that I had when Charlotte touched me in her room. I was awash in a tide of calm and safety, as if nothing bad could happen so long as Vincent held my hand. This time I knew it had to be some kind of supernatural trick.

I sat down gingerly on the side of the bed, watching Vincent's face as I did. "I'm not in pain," he reassured me, keeping hold of my hand as I sat next to him.

"Okay, Kate, first of all, you're touching me," Vincent said for the room to hear. "So I'm not a ghost."

"And we're not *true* zombies," Charles said with a grin, "or he would have already eaten your face off."

Vincent ignored him. "We're not vampires or werewolves or anything else that you should be afraid of. We're revenants. We aren't human"—he paused, summoning his strength—"but we're not going to hurt you."

I tried to compose myself before saying to the room in as steady a voice as I could muster, "So you're all . . . dead. But you look alive. Except for you," I said, hesitating as I glanced at Vincent. "Although you look better than you did last night," I conceded.

Vincent was grave. "Jules, could you tell Kate your story? It's probably the best way to explain. Gaspard is right: I can't manage it myself."

Jules caught my gaze and didn't let go. "Okay, Kate. I know this is going to sound incredible, but I was born in 1897. In a small village not far from Paris. My dad was a doctor, and my mom a midwife. I showed artistic talent, so at age sixteen they sent me to study painting in Paris. My schooling was cut short when I was drafted into the war in 1914. I fought the Germans for two years, until, in September 1916, I was killed in action. Battle of Verdun.

"And that would be the end of my story . . . if I hadn't woken up three days later."

The room was silent while I tried to wrap my mind around what he had said. "You woke up?" I finally managed. The boy I faced looked no older than twenty, but was claiming to be over a hundred years old.

"Technically he 'animated,'" offered Gaspard, holding up a thin finger to make his point, "not 'woke up.'"

"I came back to life," Jules clarified.

"But how?" I asked in disbelief. Vincent's grasp on my hand bolstered my courage. "How could you just come back to life, unless you weren't really dead in the first place?"

"Oh, I was dead. No question about that. You can't be in that many pieces and live through it." Jules's grin turned to a look of regret as he saw me blanch.

"Give the lady a break," said Ambrose. "We're laying this on her all at once." He looked at me. "There's this special . . . what should I call it? Not to sound too *Twilight Zone*, but 'law of the universe,' right? It says that if, under certain circumstances, you die in the place of someone else, you will subsequently come back to life. You're dead for three days. Then you wake up."

"Animate," corrected Gaspard.

"You *wake up*," insisted Ambrose, "and, except for being as hungry as hell, you're just like you were before."

"Except that after that you don't sleep," added Charles.

"Have you ever heard of TMI, Chucky?" Ambrose asked, clenching his hands in exasperation.

"Kate," Charlotte said softly, "dying and animating are really hard on the human body. It kind of kicks us into a different life cycle. 'Animated' is a good way to put it, actually. We are so animated when we wake up that we go for more than three weeks without stopping. Then our body shuts down and we 'sleep like the dead' for three days. Like Vincent just did."

"You mean, we *are* dead for three—" Charles began, correcting her.

Charlotte interrupted him. "We're not dead. We call it 'being dormant.' Our body is just kind of hibernating, but our mind is still active. And once our body awakes, we go back to a few more weeks of absolute, but sleepless, normalcy."

Charles mumbled, "Yeah, right."

"Well, one could say that that gives the bare bones of the story," Gaspard said helpfully.

"You were . . . dormant yesterday?" I asked Vincent.

He nodded. "The end of the three days," he said. "Now I'll be fine for almost a month."

"You don't look very fine to me," I responded, staring at his skin's waxy pallor.

"It takes several hours to recover from dormancy," Vincent said with a weak smile. "For a human it would be like having open-heart surgery. You don't just pop out of the hospital bed as soon as the anesthesia wears off."

That made sense. If he kept going with the human analogies,

I might be able to stomach this whole bizarre scenario a bit better. From the way they were arguing, they clearly weren't used to having to explain their situation. It was up to me to figure things out.

I turned to Jules. "You're over a hundred years old."

"I'm nineteen," he said.

"So you never age?" I asked.

"Oh yeah, we age all right. Look at Jean-Baptiste—he died at thirty-six, but he's in his sixties!" said Charles.

"And how old would Jean-Baptiste be if he hadn't . . . you know?" I fumbled for words.

"Two hundred thirty-five," answered Gaspard without hesitation and, looking at the others, continued, "May I?"

Charles nodded, and the rest stayed quiet.

"After we animate, we age at the same rate as anyone else. However, each time we die, we subsequently reanimate at the same age that we died the very first time. Jules died when he was nineteen, therefore each time he dies, he starts again at nineteen. Vincent was eighteen when he died, but hasn't died for, what's it been now? A bit over a year?" He directed his question to Vincent, but I cut him off.

"What do you mean, 'each time you die'?" I asked. The spine-chilling icy finger was making another appearance. Vincent tightened his hold on my hand.

"Let's just say there are a lot of people who need to be saved," said Jules, winking.

I stared at him, struggling to understand what he was inferring.

Then my eyes widened. "The man in the subway!" I gasped. "You saved his life!"

He nodded.

"But how—I mean, didn't—" I burst out, not able to form one single thought as a dozen flooded my mind simultaneously. I remembered Vincent diving after the girl, and Charlotte saving me from death-by-crushing.

"You died saving someone, and you keep doing it after death," I said finally. Maybe I was stating the obvious, but the lightbulb had finally flicked on above my head.

"It's the whole reason for our being," Vincent said. "We're bound to that one mission for the rest of our existence."

I stared at him. I didn't even know how to react. My mind was a blank.

"I think it's time to wind down this Q and A session," Vincent said to the others. "Kate's getting to the information-overload stage. And I'm too tired to continue."

"You can't tell her—" began Gaspard.

"Gaspard!" Vincent yelled, and then closed his eyes from the effort. "I . . . swear I will not tell Kate anything else . . . of importance . . . without consulting you first. Cross my heart." Vincent drew an *X* across his chest and glared at the man.

"Well, then," Ambrose said, getting up. "Now that we're done scaring the human—I mean, Katie-Lou here"—he paced over and clapped me on the shoulder affectionately—"it's time for some grub," and he walked through the doorway.

Charlotte touched my arm softly as the others left. "Come

have breakfast with us. You probably won't be allowed to"—she glanced at Vincent—"leave right away anyway."

"What time is it?" I asked, realizing I had no clue how long I had slept.

Charlotte looked at her watch. "Almost seven."

"Seven a.m.?" I asked, astonished that I had fallen asleep in a strange house under such disturbing circumstances. "Thanks, but I think I'll stay and talk to Vincent."

"You should eat," said Vincent softly. "Jean-Baptiste's going to come storming through that door in a few minutes anyway, after Gaspard gives him his update."

"Let me stay with you till then," I asked. "I'll come find you when Jean-Baptiste kicks me out," I told Charlotte.

"'kay!" she said with an encouraging smile, and shut the door behind her.

I turned to Vincent. But before I could open my mouth to speak, he stole my words. "I know," he said. "We need to talk."

FOURTEEN

WE WERE ON OUR OWN. FINALLY. AND WHAT
should have been a terrifying situation—me . . . alone in an old
castle . . . sitting next to someone I had just discovered was a monster—well, it wasn't terrifying at all. Incredibly, it seemed more
awkward than anything.

I sat facing him on his bed, this boy who seemed to be on the
verge of death. Even in his feeble state he was beautiful. I had
every reason to be afraid, but instead I was gripped by the strangest emotion. I felt like protecting him.

"So . . . ," Vincent said.

"So . . . you're immortal?"

"'fraid so."

He looked tired and worried, and for the first time, very vulnerable. I suddenly felt like I held all the power in my hands.
Which, concerning *us*, I suppose I did.

"How's that make you feel?" he asked.

"Um. It's a lot to take in all at once. But it definitely explains things." I felt his fingers clutch my own. "Is the reason I'm not afraid right now because you're holding my hand?"

"What do you mean?" he said with an uneven smile.

"It's one of your superpowers, isn't it? What is it? The Tranquilizing Touch or something?"

"Superpowers!" He chuckled. "Um. Yeah, Miss Perceptive. How did you figure that one out?"

"Charlotte used it on me earlier. And I doubt I could have gotten through this informational meeting without the few hits you gave me."

The corners of his mouth curved slightly. His fingers loosened and then curved back around my hand. "I see. And no, even though I'm touching you, I'm not doing the 'Tranquilizing Touch' as you call it. It doesn't happen every time I touch you. I have to will it. But at the moment, you seem to be managing fine on your own."

I glanced at his bedside table and saw that my photo had been placed downward. Resting on top of it was the letter I had written to him the day before. It already seemed like years ago.

"You got my note," I said.

"Yeah. It helped explain why you went all stalker on me." He laughed. "I still can't believe that Jean-Baptiste let you in. It's just as much his fault that you found me as my own for bringing you here the first time. I'm definitely not letting him hold that one over my head. How you managed to convince him to let you past the front door, I will never understand."

Vincent's laugh was edged with something that sounded like victory. "You're amazing," he said, his eyes radiating warmth. I sat there basking in it, until he closed them and laid his head back against the pillow.

"Are you okay?" I asked, worried.

"Yeah, I'm fine. I'm just feeling really weak. Do you mind giving me something from that table?" He nodded toward a folding tray set up next to the head of his bed, holding an array of fruits and nuts.

I picked up a plate of dates and then sat back down next to him with it.

"Thanks," he said, touching my hand again before picking up a fruit and popping it into his mouth.

"So the necklace was for Charlotte," I said, watching his face carefully.

He grinned. "See? Girl *friend*. Not girlfriend. Just someone I've known for what . . . the last half century?"

"Not that it matters," I said quickly, embarrassed.

"Of course not," Vincent said, faking a serious look and nodding solemnly.

I looked down at my hands. "You said it takes a while to recover from . . . whatever. When will you be up and about?"

"It depends on what condition you're in when you become dormant. I wasn't injured or anything, so by tonight I'll be as good as new. Better, actually."

I could tell he was trying to lighten the mood, but he looked so exhausted I couldn't help but feel sorry for him. "Oh, Vincent."

"It's not bad, really, Kate. It's actually good to have some downtime . . . to recharge a little, since after this I won't sleep again for weeks."

My frown made him stop. "We don't need to talk about this now. Don't worry about me, though. I'm the one who's worried about you. How—how are you?"

I rolled my eyes and laughed. "Well, if you're not doing the calming thing and I haven't freaked out and run screaming from your house, I guess I'm doing pretty well."

"Amazing," he said again.

"Okay, stop it with the flattery," I teased. "Save it for the next victim you draw helplessly into your lair."

Vincent's laugh was cut short by the sound of the door opening. I turned to see Jean-Baptiste striding into the room, with Gaspard trailing along in his wake.

"Kate, go find Charlotte and the others," Vincent said softly, "but once you're told you can go, don't leave without coming back to see me. Please."

Gaspard walked me to the open door. "They're in the kitchen," he said, indicating the far end of the corridor. Then, leaving me in the hallway, he closed the door behind him.

I followed the delicious smell of fresh bread toward the kitchen, but hesitated in front of the swinging door. Taking a nervous breath, I pushed it open and stepped inside. The whole crew was sitting around a huge oak table. As one, they looked up and waited for me to do something.

Ambrose broke the ice. "Enter, human!" he said in a *Star Trek* voice, muffled slightly by a full mouth.

Charlotte and Charles laughed, and Jules waved me over to an empty chair next to him. "So you survived the wrath of Jean-Baptiste," he said. "Very brave."

"Very stupid for coming here," Charles added, not looking up from his plate.

"Charles!" Charlotte scolded.

"Well, it was!" Charles said defensively.

"What would you like, dear?" interrupted a motherly voice from above my shoulder.

I turned to see a plump middle-aged woman wearing an apron. She had soft rosy cheeks, and her graying blond hair was tied up in a bun.

"Jeanne?" I asked.

"Yes, dear Kate," she answered. "That's me. I've been hearing all about your eventful evening from the others. I'm sorry I didn't get to meet you before, but unlike the rest here, I need a good night's sleep."

"Then you're not . . ." I hesitated.

"No, she's not one of us," Jules responded. "But Jeanne's family has been in the service of Jean-Baptiste for . . ."

"Over two hundred years," Jeanne said, finishing his sentence as she shoveled a mountain of scrambled eggs onto Ambrose's plate. He gave her a ravishing smile, and said, "Marry me, Jeanne," leaning over to kiss the hand holding the serving spoon. "In your dreams," she laughed, and tapped him playfully on the hand with the spoon.

Putting a fist on her hip, she looked up at the ceiling as if trying to remember a poem she had memorized. "My great-great-great-grandfather (plus a few) was Monsieur Grimod de La Reynière's valet, and went to war with him when he fought under Napoleon. It was that ancestor, only fifteen at the time, whom Monsieur Grimod saved, pushing him from the path of a cannonball that took his own life. It's a good thing the boy was determined to bring Monsieur's body back from Russia for burial, because he was there three days later when Monsieur woke up and was able to care for him. And my family's been with Monsieur ever since."

She recounted this incredible story like she would describe her trip to the market that morning. It must seem natural to her, having been raised by a mother and grandmother who told her the same story. But I felt overwhelmed as my mind tried to twist its way around the repercussions.

"Thanks, Jeanne. Kate looked almost normal again until you started talking," Jules said.

"I'm fine," I responded, smiling at her. "I'll just have some bread and coffee, thank you."

Jeanne pushed a coffee capsule into a high-tech coffee machine and turned it on before bustling over to the oven and taking a tray of croissants out.

"I'm off," Charles said, pushing his chair under the table, and after coolly bumping fists with Jules and Ambrose, he marched out of the kitchen without a second glance at me.

I looked at the others. "Was it something I said?"

"Kate," Ambrose said, chuckling, "you've got to remember—

even though Charles's body should be eighty-two, his maturity level is stuck at fifteen."

"I'll go with him," Charlotte chirped, seemingly embarrassed by her twin's rudeness. "Bye, Kate." She leaned over to kiss me on both cheeks. "I'm sure we'll be seeing you soon."

"So what happens now?" I asked as the door closed behind her. I felt oddly torn between the urge to go back to my grandparents' house and see my real, living, breathing family and the desire to stay here, among these people who, after just a few hours of knowing me, already seemed to accept me. Or at least most of them did. Never mind that they weren't human.

Before anyone could answer, Gaspard stuck his porcupine hair through the door. "You can go, Kate. But Vincent asked to see you on your way out." He disappeared back into the passageway.

As I rose to my feet, Jules stood and said, "Do you want me to walk you home?"

Ambrose nodded, and with a full mouth said, "Walk her home."

"No, that's okay, I can get home on my own."

"I'll walk you to the door, then," Jules said, pushing his chair under the table.

"Good-bye, Jeanne. Thanks for the breakfast. Bye, Ambrose," I called as Jules politely opened the door for me to pass through first, and walked with me down the long hallway to Vincent's door. I went in and he closed the door behind me, waiting in the hallway.

"So what did they say?" I asked, approaching the bed. Vincent was whiter and weaker-looking than before, but smiled consolingly.

"It's okay. I've promised to take full responsibility for you."

Though I didn't know what that meant, I felt torn between thinking I didn't need a babysitter on the one hand, and rather liking the idea of being Vincent's ward on the other.

"You can go home now," he continued, "but as Jean-Baptiste said before, you can't talk about us to anybody. Not that they would believe you anyway, but we try to stay as under the radar as possible."

I looked at him quizzically.

"You've heard of vampires?" he asked, smiling mysteriously.

I nodded.

"You've heard of werewolves?"

"Of course."

"Had you ever heard of us?"

I shook my head.

"That's called 'staying under the radar,' dear Kate. It's what we're good at."

"Gotcha." I took his outstretched hand.

"Can I see you again in a few days?" he asked.

I nodded, suddenly uncertain when I thought of what the future could hold. Pausing at the door, I called, "Take care," and then immediately felt stupid. He was immortal. He didn't have to *take care*. "I mean rest up," I corrected myself.

He smiled, amused by my confusion, and saluted me.

"Milady." Jules stepped forward, bowing like a doorman in

a Merchant-Ivory film, and placed my hand on his arm. "Shall we?" I couldn't help but laugh. He was going all out to make up for upsetting me.

Back in the grand foyer, I picked up my book bag. As I stepped outside, he touched my arm and said, "Listen. I'm sorry I was rude before today, you know . . . in my studio and at the museum. I swear it was nothing personal. I was just trying to protect Vincent and you . . . and all of us. Now that it's too late for that, well, please accept my apology."

"I totally understand," I told him. "What else could you do?"

"Whew—she forgave me," he said, hand on heart, his playfulness obviously returning. "So. You sure you'll be okay?" he asked me, stepping closer with a look that struck me as more than just friendly concern for my well-being. He saw me read his face and smiled flirtatiously, lifting an eyebrow as if asking a question.

"I'll be fine, really. Thank you," I responded, blushing, and stepped over the threshold onto the cobblestones.

"Vince'll come see you as soon as he can," he said, thrusting his hands into his jean pockets and nodding good-bye.

I waved back at him and walked slowly out of the courtyard into the street beyond, feeling as if I were in a dream.

FIFTEEN

THE WEEKEND WENT BY IN A BLUR, WITH MY body doing one thing and my mind back in the house on rue de Grenelle.

I didn't know when to expect word from Vincent. On Monday morning, as Georgia and I left for school, I spotted an envelope taped to our building's front door with my name printed on it in a beautiful, old-fashioned cursive. I opened it, and from inside pulled a piece of thick white card, on which was written in sweeping script, "Soon. V."

"Who's V?" asked Georgia, with eyebrows raised.

"Oh, just this guy."

"What guy?" she asked, stopping dead in her tracks and grabbing my arm. "The criminal?"

"Yes," I laughed, breaking away from her grasp and pulling her along toward the Métro. "Except that he's not a criminal. He's . . ." *He's a revenant, a kind of undead-guardian-angel type of monster that runs around saving human lives.* "He just hangs out with some iffy people."

"Hmm . . . I think I should meet him."

"No way, Georgia. I don't even know if I'm going to keep seeing him. All I need is for you to interfere and complicate things before I actually decide I like him."

"Oh, you like him all right."

"Okay, I like him. I mean whether I'm going to keep seeing him."

She looked at me skeptically.

"I can't explain it, Georgia. Just let's not talk about it. I promise to let you know if anything happens."

We walked in silence for about two seconds before she said, "Don't worry. I won't try to steal him from you."

I hit her with my book bag as we ran down the stairs to the Métro.

Vincent had said he wanted to see me "in a few days," but we were on day four, and I had begun wondering when, if ever, I would see him again. Maybe he had changed his mind about me once he had gotten stronger. Or maybe Jean-Baptiste had changed it for him. I just thought about his note and hoped he would show.

After the last bell rang on Tuesday, I walked through the school's front gates and headed toward the bus stop. My pace slowed as I spotted a familiar figure standing across the street. It was Vincent.

His black hair shone in the late-September sun, and he radiated energy and life. He looked like some kind of perfect mythological creature. *He* is *some kind of perfect mythological creature,* I reminded myself. I felt breathless. Though his eyes were hidden behind mirrored sunglasses, I saw his lips curve up into a smile when he saw me coming through the gates.

A vintage red Vespa was parked where he stood, and as I crossed the street toward him he held up a matching helmet. After the four-day wait, I felt like throwing my arms around him in relief. But when I got a step away I hesitated, remembering what he had looked like the last time I had seen him.

He had been near death. Lying there almost lifeless on his bed like a scene from an old black-and-white horror film. And now here he was, four days later, every pore of his body oozing health. What was wrong with me? I should be running *away* from him as fast as I could, not into his arms. *Monster, not human,* I reminded myself.

He saw me pause, and although he had been leaning in to greet me, he took a step back and waited for me to make the first move.

"Hey. You look a lot more . . . alive," I said, flashing him a tense smile, while inside me the battle between impulse and caution continued.

He grinned and rubbed the back of his neck with one hand, his expression a cross between sheepish and apologetic. "Yeah. Walking, talking . . ." His voice faded as he watched my expression carefully.

Make up your mind, I thought, prodding myself into action. Reaching out, I took the spare helmet from his hand. "So, the back-from-the-dead thing . . . good party trick," I said, pulling the helmet on.

Vincent's expression was one of immediate relief. "Yeah, I'll have to show you how it works sometime," he laughed and, swinging one leg over the scooter, held out a hand to me.

I took it hesitantly. It was warm. Soft. Mortal. I settled myself behind him and pushed all lingering doubts back to a far corner of my mind. "Where are we going?" I asked, finally letting myself feel the excitement that had been struggling to break free.

"Just a little ride around town," he said, as he kick-started the Vespa and zoomed out into the street.

Holding Vincent felt like heaven, and driving through Paris on a vintage Vespa felt like the best adventure I had had in years. We crossed a bridge over the Seine into Paris, and cut across town to drive along the riverbank. The water glimmered in the autumn light.

After a twenty-minute ride, we came to the Île Saint-Louis, one of two natural islands in the middle of the Seine that are connected to the mainland by bridges, and linked to each other by a footbridge.

Vincent locked the scooter to a gate and then, taking me by the hand, led me down a long flight of stone steps to the water's edge.

"Listen, I'm sorry I couldn't come to you sooner," he said, walking along the quay with me hand in hand. "I had a job to do for Jean-Baptiste. I came as soon as I could."

"That's okay," I responded, refraining from asking him questions. I preferred to forget about all the weird fantasy-novel events from the previous weekend. I wanted to pretend that we were just a boy and a girl spending an afternoon by the riverside. But I had a nagging feeling that the reverie wouldn't last for long.

As we approached the tip of the island, the narrow sidewalk opened out into a large cobblestone terrace. "This place is always crowded during the summer, but no one ever thinks to come here the rest of the year. Which leaves it empty for us," Vincent said as he led me to the north side.

Lowering himself to the edge of the terrace, he spread his coat on the stone and reached his hand up for me to take it. I felt like we were the last two people on earth. This knight in shining armor had swept me away to his little island of peace in the midst of the busy city and wanted to sit with me for a few fairy-tale moments. *This can't be real.*

We watched the tiny waves sparkle and flash like mirrors in the sun atop the fast-flowing viridian river. Enormous puffy clouds drifted across a wide expanse of sky that you rarely saw when walking among the city's buildings. The waves lapped loudly against the base of the wall, their sound mounting to a crashing crescendo when boats motored by. I closed my eyes and let the tranquillity of the place flow through me.

Vincent touched my hand, breaking the spell. His brow was lined with concern as he appeared to search for words. Finally he spoke. "You know what I am, Kate. Or at least you know the basics."

I nodded, wondering what could possibly come next.

"The thing is . . . I want to get to know you. I have a feeling about you that I haven't had for a long, long time. But being what I am makes things"—he paused—"complicated."

Watching his agonized expression, I felt like touching him, reassuring him, but exercised every last ounce of my self-control to keep still and hold my tongue. He had obviously thought about what he wanted to say, and I didn't want to distract him from it.

"You've just been through a great loss. And the last thing I want is to make things more painful for you than they already are. If I were a normal guy, living an everyday life, I wouldn't even be talking to you about this. We would just hang out, see how it went, and if things worked, great. If not, we would each go our own way.

"But I can't do that in good conscience. Not with you. I can't let someone who I feel I could care deeply for begin this journey without knowing the consequences. Knowing that I'm different. That I have no idea what this could mean if it goes further. . . ." He seemed both dismayed by his own words and determined to spit them out. "I hate even having to talk to you like this. It's too much, too fast."

He paused for a moment and looked down at our hands, separated by mere inches of cobblestone.

"Kate, I can't stop myself from wanting to be with you. So I'm putting all of this forward for you to consider. To decide what you want. I want to try. To see how we could be. But I will walk away right now if you give me the word—only you know what you can handle. What happens next, with us, is up to you. You don't have to decide right now, but it would be nice to know how you feel about what I've said."

Drawing my feet up from where they dangled off the edge of the quay, I wrapped my arms around my legs. I rocked back and forth for a few minutes in silence and did something I rarely allowed myself to do. I thought about my parents. About my mother.

She teased me for being impetuous, but had always told me to follow my heart. "You have an old soul," she said once. "I wouldn't say this to Georgia, and for God's sake, don't tell her I told you this. But she doesn't have the same intuition you do. The same ability to see things for what they are. I don't want you to be afraid to go after the things you really want in life. Because I think you will want the *right* things."

If she could only see what I wanted now, she would eat her words.

Shifting my eyes from the passing boats to Vincent, sitting motionless by my side, I studied his profile as he looked out at the water, lost in his own thoughts. It wasn't even a choice. Who was I trying to fool? I had made my decision the first time I saw him, whatever my rational mind had tried to convince me of since then.

I leaned toward him. Reaching up with one hand, I swept my fingers down his arm, running their tips along his warm skin. He turned his head and looked at me with a longing that made my heart skip a beat. I brushed my lips against the bronzed surface of his cheek and braced myself to have the strength to say the words I knew I must. "I can't, Vincent. I can't say yes."

His eyes showed pain, despair even, but not surprise. My answer was the one he had expected.

"I'm not saying no, either," I continued, and he visibly relaxed. "I'm going to need some things if we're going to see each other."

He let out a low, sexy laugh. "So you're making demands, are you? Well, let's hear them."

"I want unlimited access."

"Now that sounds interesting. To what, exactly?"

"To information. I can't do this if I don't understand what I'm getting into."

"Do you need to know everything right away?"

"No, but I don't want to feel like you're hiding anything either."

"Fair enough. As long as it goes both ways."

A slight smile lifted the corners of his perfectly sculpted lips. I looked away, before I lost my courage.

"I need to know when I'm not going to see you for a while. When you do the death-sleep thing. So that I won't worry that I've driven you off with my mortality. Or my incessant questions."

"Agreed. That's easy enough to schedule, when things are normal. But if something were to happen to . . . throw things off . . ."

"Something like what?"

"Do you remember being told about how we stay young?"

"Oh. Right." The awful image of Jules jumping in front of the train returned to my mind's eye. "You mean if you were to 'save someone.'"

"Then I would be sure to get word to you from one of my kindred."

I remembered hearing him use that word before. "Why do you say 'kindred'?"

"It's what we call one another."

"Kind of medieval-sounding, but okay," I said skeptically.

"Anything else?" he asked, looking every bit like a naughty schoolboy waiting to be given his punishment.

"Yes. It doesn't have to be right away, but . . . you have to meet my family."

Vincent laughed outright, a rich sound that startled me with its amusement and relief. Leaning toward me, he took me in his arms and said, "Kate. I knew you were an old-fashioned girl. A girl after my own heart."

I let myself melt into his embrace for a few seconds, and then pulled back and assumed the most serious expression I could muster. "I'm not committing to anything, Vincent. Just to the next date."

All of a sudden I felt that the old me—the pre-car-wreck Brooklyn me—was outside looking in at the new me, the me that not even a year ago had been forced to instantly grow up. The me who had been battle-scarred by tragedy. I was amazed to witness myself sitting next to this breathtaking guy and speaking those cautious words to him. How on earth had I morphed so quickly into this levelheaded person? How could I be sitting there, stoically laying down conditions for something that I wanted more than anything I'd ever had?

Self-preservation. Those two words came to my mind, and I

knew what I was doing was right. My whole being had been torn to shreds when I lost my parents. I didn't want to open myself up to falling for Vincent and risk losing him, too. Deep down I knew I had barely survived my parents' "disappearance." I might not survive another.

SIXTEEN

"LET'S WALK," VINCENT SAID AND, HELPING ME to my feet, held his arm out for me to hold. We strolled as we watched boats plow past us through the dark green water, leaving frothy wakes behind them and sending large, rolling waves clapping against the stones under our feet.

"So how did you . . . die? I mean the first time," I asked.

Vincent cleared his throat. "Can I wait until later to tell you my story?" he asked, sounding uncomfortable. "I don't want to completely weird you out by talking about who I used to be before having the chance to show you who I am now." He shot me an awkward smile.

"Does that mean I don't have to tell you about my past either?" I lobbed back.

"No," he groaned. "Especially since I've barely started to figure you out." He paused. "Just please, don't ask me yet. Any other question, just not that."

"Okay, how about . . . why do you have a photo of me next to your bed?" I prodded.

"Did that creep you out?" he said, laughing.

"Yeah, kind of," I admitted. "Although I saw it about a second after I found you dead on your bed, so the creep factor was already pretty high."

"Well, Charlotte and I had to fight over that one," he said. "Did you notice the photos on my walls?"

"Yes. On Charlotte's, too. She said they were people she had saved."

He nodded. "They're our 'rescues.' And after we saved you, we both laid claim to your picture."

"How's that?" I asked, confused.

"Well, you know that day at the café when you almost became a bit of Paris history?"

I nodded.

"Charlotte waved you over, which is why you moved in time to avoid the falling stone. But I'm the one who told her it was about to happen."

"You were there?" I asked, stopping in my tracks and staring up at him.

"Yes . . . in spirit. Not in body," Vincent said as he pulled me along with him.

"In spirit? I thought you said you aren't ghosts."

Vincent put his hand on mine, and I began to feel like I had been hit with a mini dose of tranquilizers.

"Stop it with the 'calming touch' thing. Just explain. I can handle it." Vincent left his hand on mine, but the warm fuzzy feeling went away. He smiled guiltily, like he had been caught cheating on an exam.

Without patting myself too much on the back, I felt I was handling things pretty well. Besides learning that the guy I liked was immortal, I thought I was taking the supernatural how-things-work lessons in stride. I hadn't freaked out. Much. Okay, except when I saw Jules get killed. And found the obituary photos. And came across Vincent "dead" in his bed. *All of which were totally understandable freak-out occasions,* I reassured myself.

Vincent was talking, so I tried to focus. "I'll come back to the spirit thing. But what I was saying about me being with Charlotte and Charles—that's kind of our modus operandi as revenants. We usually travel in threes when we're 'walking.' That's what we call it when we're . . . um . . . on patrol. That way if something happens . . ."

"Like it did to Jules in the Métro?"

"Exactly. Then the others will alert Jean-Baptiste, who will make sure we get the body."

"And how does he do that? Does he have connections at the city morgue?"

I said it jokingly, but Vincent smiled and nodded. "And the police, among other organizations."

"Handy," I said, trying not to look surprised.

"Very," he agreed. "They probably think Jean-Baptiste is some kind of gangster or necrophiliac, but the amount of money he pays for the services he needs seems to make people forget their questions."

I was quiet, thinking about how complicated the whole undead-lifesaving business must be. And here I had unwittingly crashed their carefully planned party. No wonder I wasn't on Jean-Baptiste's invite A-list.

"Charlotte explained about how when we're dormant our bodies are dead but our minds are still active."

I nodded.

"She was oversimplifying a bit. Actually, for the first of our three dormant days we're 'body-and-mind' dead. Everything is turned off, as if we were any other corpse.

"But on day two we switch into another mode—we're only 'body' dead. If we've been injured since our last dormancy, our body starts healing itself. And our mind wakes up. For two days our consciousness can kind of . . . detach from our bodies. We can travel. We can talk to one another."

I couldn't believe it. There were more "revenant rules." *This can't get any weirder,* I thought. "Floating around outside your bodies? Now I get why Charles said you were ghosts."

Vincent smiled. "When our minds leave our bodies, we call it being *volant.*"

"*Volant* like 'flying'?"

"Exactly. And while we're volant we've got this kind of refined sixth sense. It's not exactly fortune-telling, but we can sense when something is going to happen that the others can use to save someone. It's like seeing into the future, but only for what's happening close to our immediate location, and only a minute or two past where we are."

Strike that . . . it does get weirder.

Vincent must have felt the hesitation in my step and correctly guessed that I was getting overwhelmed. He pulled me over to a stone bench by the side of the quay and sat with me, giving me time to process the whole impossible story. Before us, the reflections of the buildings along the river swelled over the surface of the water.

"I know it sounds strange, Kate. But it's one of the gifts we possess as revenants. One of our only 'superpowers,' as you put it. Like when you saw Jules and me in the Métro: There were actually three of us there. Ambrose was volant, and let us know just before that man jumped. Jules said that he would take it, while I shielded you from seeing him."

Vincent smiled a slightly abashed smile. "Ambrose is also the reason we bumped into you in the Picasso Museum. He saw you from outside and suggested to Jules that we pop inside for 'a lesson in Cubism.'"

"But how did Ambrose even know who I was?" I asked, incredulous.

"Making me bump into you was Ambrose's idea of a joke. I had been talking about you to the others, even before we saved you at the café." He picked up a dead leaf and began crumbling it between his fingers.

"You had?" I gasped, astonished. "What had you been talking about?"

"Ah . . . now don't you wish you knew?" He smiled slyly. "I can't give away all my secrets in one sitting. Let me keep at least a shred of my dignity!"

I rolled my eyes and waited for what would come next. But I was secretly thrilled by this revelation.

"In any case, the day you almost got crushed by the falling masonry, I was volant with Charlotte and Charles and saw the building falling apart a minute before it happened. I told Charlotte you had to be moved, and she gestured at you to come over. That's why we both laid claim to your photo for our 'Wall of Fame.'" He smiled and shifted his gaze from the now tattered leaf to my eyes, gauging my reaction.

"But why the photos? Are they"—I shuddered—"trophies?"

"No. It's not like we're gloating. Or competing. It's deeper than that," Vincent said, his smile replaced by a look of unease. "It's hard not to get kind of . . . obsessed . . . with our rescues, especially the ones we die for. Dying repeatedly isn't easy. And it's hard not to want to know what happened to the person you died for afterward. If the near-death experience changed their life. If the sacrifice you made had a butterfly effect for them, their family, the people who know them, and on and on."

He laughed uncomfortably. "If we weren't careful, we could end up stalking them. It does happen. It's an easy trap for those who aren't warned. Luckily, Jean-Baptiste has a couple hundred years of being undead under his belt. He keeps us to the 'Triple-Recon Plan.'" Vincent smirked. "We can go back and photograph our rescue after saving them. Then we can go in volant form twice to check up on them, but no other communication is recommended. After that, we have to satisfy ourselves with Googling them to our heart's content."

"So Ambrose pretty much threw that rule out the window when he forced us into the same room at the museum."

He smiled. "The rules were already a bit screwed up. Like I said, my fascination with you began well before the crumbling building incident."

Vincent avoided my eyes. Throwing the remains of the mangled leaf into the water, he reached over and covered my hand with his. I heard a warning bell going off in the back of my mind as I sifted through the information he had given me. And then something clicked.

"Vincent, are you saying that even though you didn't die for me, you became 'obsessed' with me after saving my life?"

"*More* obsessed," Vincent admitted, continuing to look away.

"So if the obsession is unavoidable, then what makes me different than any of your other rescues? Maybe the reason you like me is that I just happen to live down the street from you and cross your path more often than most. You saved me, but instead of disappearing from your life like all of the others, I kept popping up and fueled the obsession. How do you know that's not all there is to it?"

He was silent. "That's it, isn't it?" I shook my head in dismay. My stomach seized into a knot of despair.

"I was wondering how someone like you could fall for someone like me. How you went from acting like I was just a stupid admirer the first couple of times I saw you to looking at me like I was your dream girl. And that's the answer. It has nothing to do with me. It's just some sort of unnatural addiction to lifesaving that goes along with being a revenant."

I knew it couldn't be true, I thought to myself.

Vincent lowered his head into his hands and sat like that for a minute, massaging his temples before speaking. "Kate, I've saved hundreds of women and have never felt this for any of them. I was interested in you before I saved your life. I admit, the saving part did make you more unforgettable. It kind of sealed my resolution to know you. Maybe I came off as a jerk the first time we talked, but it's been a long time since I've let myself feel anything about anyone. I'm just out of practice at being human. You have to believe me."

I searched for any hint of deception in his face. He seemed completely sincere. "You have to be honest with me, then, Vincent," I said. "If you suddenly realize that's all that I am—a rescue who you've managed to get closer to—then I want to know immediately."

"I will be honest, Kate. I won't ever lie to you."

"Or keep things from me that I should know."

"You have my word."

I nodded. The sun was already setting, and lights began to appear in the buildings above us, their reflections bouncing off the water like flickering flames.

"Kate, what are you feeling?"

"Honestly?"

"Honestly."

"Afraid."

"Let me take you home," Vincent said, regret filling his voice. He rose to his feet and pulled me up beside him.

No! I thought. And aloud I stammered, "No . . . not yet. Let's not end today like this. Let's do something else. Something normal."

"You mean something besides talking about death, flying spirits, and obsessed immortals?"

"That would be nice," I said.

"How about dinner?" Vincent said.

"Okay." I nodded. "Let me just tell Georgia that I won't be eating at home, though." I took my cell phone out of my bag and texted: Going out for dinner. Please tell M & P I won't be too late.

Vincent took my hand and laced his fingers through mine, sending little shock waves through my heart. My phone rang as we got to the top of the steps. It was Georgia.

"Yes?"

"So, who are you going to dinner with?"

"*So*, why do you want to know?" I smiled, glancing sideways at Vincent.

"Let's just say that I'm taking my role as your legal guardian seriously," she purred.

"You are *so* not my legal guardian."

Georgia laughed. "Who are you with?"

"A friend."

134

"V?"

"Actually, yes."

"Oh my God, where are you going? I'll come by and just pre-tend I was in the area so I can get a look at him."

"No way, and besides, I don't even know where we're going yet."

Vincent gave me a sly smile. "Georgia?" he asked. I nodded, and he reached for the phone.

"Hello, is this Georgia? Vincent here. Should I have cleared this date with you before taking your sister out?" He laughed, and I could tell Georgia was working her irresistible charm on him already.

Finally he said, "No, I don't think that a meet-the-folks ses-sion was in the plans for tonight, but I'm sure we'll run into each other soon. Why not, you ask?" He winked at me, and I shivered. It was incredible how he affected me. In a dangerous way.

"You'll have to ask your sister. She's the one calling the shots."

SEVENTEEN

WE SAT FACING EACH OTHER ACROSS A TINY table in a cavelike restaurant in the Marais. Dozens of flickering candles illuminated the space around us. Our legs were criss-crossed under the table, mine resting between his, and the feeling of his body touching mine kept my blood on a constant low boil from the moment we sat down until we left.

I kept trying to fight the feeling that Vincent and I were already a couple. It was our first real date, after all, and, besides the barely believable information Vincent had given me about his monster-hood, I didn't know anything about him. This was no time to let my guard down. I resolved to keep things light.

"You've been speaking English to me all afternoon, and you haven't made one mistake yet," I complimented him as we waited for our food to come.

"When you sleep as little as we do, you have a lot of time for things like books and films. I'd rather read in the original language and watch movies without having to read the subtitles. So I've managed to learn my favorites: English, Italian, and some of the Scandinavian languages."

"Okay, I'm starting to feel intimidated."

"I'm sure if you had enough decades to work on it, you'd totally show me up," he responded, his eyes vivid in the flickering candlelight.

The waiter set our plates in front of us. *"Bon appétit,"* said Vincent, waiting for me to pick up my fork and knife before touching his own.

"So you eat normal food," I commented, watching Vincent cut a piece off his *magret de canard*.

"What? Were you expecting me to order raw brains? I thought we were going to stay away from unearthly topics of conversation tonight," he said with a grin.

"It's not every night I have dinner with an immortal," I joked. "Give me a little leeway."

"We eat normal stuff. We drink normal stuff. We don't sleep, except when we're dormant, which doesn't really count as sleeping. Anyway, everything else works the same. . . ." His eyes narrowed brazenly, and his lips formed a sexy smile. "Or so I've heard."

I blushed and concentrated intently on my silverware.

"Kate?"

"Mmm?"

"What's the rest of your name?"

I met his eyes. "Kate Beaumont Mercier. Beaumont's my mom's maiden name."

"It's French."

"Yes. I've got French roots on both sides of the family. Anyway, naming your kids after your maiden name is a Southern thing. And the South is where Mom grew up. In Georgia, actually."

"It's all falling into place now." Vincent smiled.

"How about you?"

"Vincent Pierre Henri Delacroix. We get two middle names in France. Pierre's my dad's name, and my grandfather was Henri."

"Sounds very aristocratic."

"Maybe way, way back." Vincent laughed. "But my family was nothing like Jean-Baptiste's. It's easy to tell what kind of background he's from."

"Jean-Baptiste," I murmured. "He doesn't seem very fond of me."

Vincent's face darkened. "I want you to know that, though Jean-Baptiste is like my own family, his opinion of you doesn't matter to me. If you want him to like you, then I will reassure you: It will come. You have to earn his trust . . . he doesn't give it easily. But until then, you are with me. He will respect my choice and be civil from now on."

Vincent saw the doubt on my face and said quickly, "That is, of course, if we keep seeing each other. Which I hope we will."

I nodded to show I understood, and Vincent, seemingly relieved to see I hadn't made a run for it after his overearnest diatribe, changed the subject. "So are you and your sister very close?"

"Yeah, she's not even two years older than me, so we've always joked about being twins. But we're totally different."

"How so?"

I took a bite and thought about how to describe my sister, the social butterfly, without making her sound shallow.

"Georgia is a total extrovert. Not like I'm exactly a shrinking violet, but I don't mind spending time by myself. My sister has to be with people twenty-four/seven. In New York everyone knew her. She always managed to find the best parties and was continually surrounded by her entourage: band members, DJs, performance artists."

"And let me guess . . . you were too busy reading and going to museums to join her." I laughed when I saw Vincent's wry grin.

"No, I went with her sometimes. But I wasn't in the spotlight like Georgia. I was just Georgia's little sister, along for the ride. She took care of me. She always nominated someone in her group to make sure I had a good time."

I didn't explain how she would always choose a "date" for me: gorgeous hipster guys who, to my amazement, enthusiastically took on the challenge of entertaining Georgia's sister. A few of these setups had turned into something more. Not much more, really, but if one of these guys happened to be at a party Georgia and I went to, I knew I had someone to dance with, sit next to, and maybe kiss in some dark corner of the room later in the night. Georgia called them my "party boys."

Now, with Vincent sitting across the table from me, larger than life, they seemed like ghosts. Shadows, in comparison to him.

"I worried how she would handle having to step down from

her queen-of-nightlife throne when we moved," I continued, "but I underestimated her. She's well on her way to reaching the same level here."

"Different city, same scene?"

"She's basically out every night that Papy and Mamie don't force her to stay home. But unlike in New York, I don't go with her."

"I know," he said, spearing a potato with his fork, and then stopped and looked quickly up to see if I had noticed his slip.

"What?" I asked, surprised, and then Ambrose's words suddenly came back to me. *We've been checking her out, and she's not a spy.* "You've been following us!" Feeling simultaneously flattered and appalled, I pulled my legs back from his and kept to my side of the table.

"No one was following Georgia, just following you. And it wasn't me. At least after the day we talked at the Picasso Museum. After that, I felt I owed you some privacy. It was Ambrose and Jules; once they knew that I was . . . interested in you, they insisted on making sure you weren't a danger to us. I never doubted you, though. Honestly."

"A 'danger'?" I asked, dismayed.

Vincent sighed. "We have enemies."

"What do you mean?"

"Let's change the subject," Vincent said. "The last thing I want to do is get you involved in something that could put you at risk."

"Are *you* at risk?" I asked.

"We don't come into contact with them that often. But when we do, it ends in each side trying to destroy the other. So since you asked me to be honest, I have to say yes. But I've had decades of experience protecting myself. I don't want you to worry."

I suddenly remembered my early morning walk with Georgia along the quay. "The night I saw you dive into the Seine after that girl. People were fighting under the bridge. With swords."

"Well, then, you've already seen them. Those were the numa."

Even the word sounded evil. I shuddered. "What are they?"

"They're the same as us, but in reverse. They're revenants, but their fate isn't to save lives. It's to destroy them."

"I don't understand."

"We become immortal when we die while saving someone's life. They win their immortality by taking lives. The universe seems to like equilibrium." His smile was bitter.

"You mean they're resurrected murderers?" I felt a cold blade of panic scrape a path from my stomach to my heart.

"Not *just* murderers. They all betrayed someone to their death."

I inhaled sharply. "What? Wait a minute. Do you mean that anyone who dies after betraying someone to their death turns into an immortal bad guy?"

"No, not all. Just some. It's like us. Not everyone who dies saving someone else is resurrected. I'll explain some other time—it gets a bit complicated. All you need to know is that the numa are bad. They're dangerous. And they never die because they keep on killing. Which is facilitated by their line of work: They're basically glorified mafiosi, running prostitution and drug rings, and in order to have a legal face for their business dealings, they own

141

bars and clubs. Not surprisingly, in their world the opportunity for death and betrayal comes along frequently enough."

"And those are the . . . things, who were fighting under the bridge that night?"

Vincent nodded. "The girl who jumped. She had gotten involved with them. They drove her to decide to kill herself, and then went along to make sure she followed through."

"But she looked so young. How old was she?"

"Fourteen."

I flinched. "So why were you there?" I asked.

"Charles and Charlotte were walking, with Jules volant. Jules saw it before it happened and rushed home to get me and Ambrose. When we got to the scene, the twins held some of the numa off beneath the bridge while the girl . . . well, you saw what happened. I reached her just before she jumped."

"Did you get the . . . bad guys?" I didn't want to say the word, it had such an unsettling effect on me.

"Two of them, yes. A couple others got away."

"So you don't just save people. You kill people too."

"Numa aren't people. If we have a chance to destroy an evil revenant, we do. Humans can always change; that's why we avoid killing them if we can. There is always a possibility of redemption in their future. But not the numa. They started on their path while they were human. Once they're revenants, they're past any hope for salvation."

So Vincent was a killer, I thought. A bad-guy killer, but a killer nonetheless. I wasn't sure how I felt about that.

"And the girl who threw herself off the bridge?"

"She's fine."

"Are you obsessed with her?"

Vincent laughed. "Now that I know she's fine, no." Under the table, he pulled my legs back between his, and some of the warmth returned. "I'm just lucky revenants can't read one another's minds, because Jean-Baptiste would kill me if he knew I had told you about the numa."

"Security breach?" I laughed.

Vincent smiled. "Yes, but I trust you, Kate."

"No problem there," I said. "You probably already know this from your spy network, but I don't have anyone to tell even if I wanted to. It's not like I have crowds of friends waiting around to hear my undead gossip."

Vincent laughed. "No. But you have me."

"I'll be extra careful not to blab about monsters around you, then."

"How is it that we just talked for two hours and I still don't know anything about you?" I complained as we left the restaurant.

"What do you mean?" Vincent responded, starting up the scooter. "I told you a ton about us."

"About you as a group, lots, but you as a person, nothing," I shouted over the noise of the engine. "You didn't let me ask you any questions. Puts me at a disadvantage."

"Get on," he said, laughing. I climbed up behind him and wrapped my arms around him, feeling close to bliss.

We crossed the river and began driving toward our part of town. With the wind whipping my hair wildly about below the edge of the helmet, and the warm body of my . . . potential boyfriend pressed up against me, I wished he would keep driving till we hit the Atlantic Ocean, more than four hours away. But when the Louvre Museum edged into view on the other side of the Seine, Vincent slowed down and pulled over to the riverside. He turned off the bike and locked it to a post before taking my hand and leading me toward the river.

"Okay, ask me something," he said.

"Where are you taking me?"

Vincent laughed. "You get one question, and you're going to use it on that? Okay, Kate. Because you've been so patient, I will answer." We stepped up onto the Pont des Arts—a wooden footbridge leading across the river—and began walking across.

The city was lit up like a Christmas tree, and its bridges illuminated with spotlights that made them appear majestic and otherworldly. The Eiffel Tower twinkled in the distance, and the reflection of the moon shone on the surface of the water swirling below us.

We reached the center of the bridge. Vincent led me gently to the side rail and, standing behind me, wrapped me in his arms and pulled me close to him. I closed my eyes and inhaled, filling my lungs with the river's distinct marine smell, which I had, over the years, come to equate with a state of tranquillity. My heart slowed, and then as Vincent's muscles flexed around my shoulders, accelerated.

We stood there, looking out at the City of Light together for a few euphoric moments before he leaned his head down and whispered, "The answer to your question of where I was taking you would be . . . to the most beautiful place in Paris. With the most beautiful girl I have been lucky enough to set eyes on, and who I desperately hope will agree to meet me again. As soon as possible."

I looked up over my shoulder and registered his sincere expression. He turned me slowly to face him. He gazed at me for a full minute with his big dark eyes, as if trying to memorize every inch of my face.

Then he raised his hand to brush a lock of hair back from my face, tucking it gently behind my ear as he lifted my lips to his.

Our skin barely touched. He was hesitant, as if he knew what he wanted but was afraid of scaring me away. Our lips brushed, and I felt like a chord had been struck inside me, and my body was humming with a pure musical note. I slowly lifted my arms to drape them around his neck, afraid that a sudden move might break the spell. But as his lips met mine once more, the magic escalated and the note grew into a sweeping crescendo that blocked out every other sound.

Paris disappeared. The rippling of waves beneath us, the hum of the cars passing on either side of the river, the whisperings of the couples passing us hand in hand . . . they all disappeared, and Vincent and I were the only people left on earth.

EIGHTEEN

SOMETHING RUSTLED AT THE FOOT OF MY BED. I forced one eye open, and through the haze of an interrupted dream, I saw my sister perched on the edge of my mattress. She looked way too overexcited for this time of the morning. Or was it still night? Raising one eyebrow, she commanded, "Tell me all!" and then, ripping back the covers that I threw over my head, attempted to sound severe. "If you don't, I won't allow you to see him again."

Moaning, I wiped my eyes blearily and propped myself up on my elbows. "What time is it?" I yawned, noticing that Georgia was fully dressed.

"You've got exactly fifteen minutes to get ready for school. I let you sleep in."

I looked over at my clock and saw that she was right. Panicking, I threw off my blankets and began leaping around the room, grabbing a bra and panties out of a drawer and digging through a stack of clean clothes sitting folded on a chair. "I thought that after getting in so late, you might need the extra sleep," she cooed.

"Thanks a lot, Georgia," I groaned, slipping a clean red T-shirt over my head and rummaging through my closet for a pair of jeans. And then, having a sudden flashback to the previous night, I sank into a sitting position on the bed. "Oh my God," I said as I felt my lips forming a reveal-all dreamy smile.

"What happened? Did he kiss you?"

My glowing face must have said it all, because my sister jumped up and said, "That's it, I have to meet him!"

"Stop, Georgia, you're embarrassing me. Give me some time to figure out if I even like the guy," I said as I stuck my feet through the pant legs and stood to shimmy them up my hips.

"We've gone over this before," my sister said, grabbing me by the shoulder and scanning my face for one searching second. "And I'm sorry to inform you, Katie-Bean, but from the look of things, it's way too late for that." And she pranced out of the room, laughing and clapping her hands.

"Glad to provide the morning's entertainment," I grumbled, and leaned over to speed-tie my shoelaces.

The day passed quickly—I fell into a dreamlike state as soon as I sat down in each class, and spent the hours musing about the previous evening. It seemed too good to be true: Vincent confessing his feelings for me by the river, the candlelit dinner, and then . . . my heart lurched every time I thought of the kiss on the Pont des Arts. And of how after that Vincent drove me home and gave me another kiss, short but stunningly tender, in front of my building.

The look of total devotion that I had seen in his eyes as he took me in his arms had shaken me. I hadn't known whether to be afraid of it or respond in kind. But I couldn't let myself reciprocate. I wasn't ready to let my guard down.

At lunch I turned my phone on to check my messages. Georgia always sent me a few inane texts during the day, and sure enough there were two messages from her: one complaining about her physics teacher and a second, also obviously sent from her phone: I love you, baby. V.

I wrote her back:

I thought I told you to buzz off last night, you creep-o French stalker guy.

Her response came back immediately:

As if! Your beet-red cheeks this morning suggest otherwise . . . liar! You're so into him.

I groaned and was about to turn my phone off when I saw that there was a third text from UNKNOWN. Clicking on it, I read: Can I pick you up from school? Same place, same time?

I texted back: How'd you get my number?

Called myself from your phone while you were in the restaurant's bathroom last night. Warned you we were stalkers!

I laughed, and thanked my lucky stars that revenants couldn't read minds, although I'd have to remember to watch what I did on the days he was floating around town as an all-seeing spirit.

Yes x 3. See you then, I wrote, and for the rest of the day gave up all pretense of paying attention in class.

He was waiting for me when I walked out the gates. My heart rate accelerated as I saw him casually leaning against a tree near the bus stop. I couldn't prevent a huge smile from spreading across my face.

"Hey, gorgeous," he said, handing me a helmet as I approached the Vespa. He pulled his glasses off and leaned forward to kiss me on either cheek. And that insignificant gesture that is repeated dozens of times a day in France—every time you say hello or good-bye, every time you are introduced to someone, or run into a friend—those two little pecks that make up the *bises* all of a sudden assumed an entirely different meaning for me.

In what felt like slow motion, Vincent's cheek touched my own, at which point my lungs forgot how to work. He pulled back slightly, and our eyes met as he leaned toward my other cheek and brushed his lips gently against my skin. I opened my mouth to inhale, attempting to send some oxygen to my brain.

"Hmm," he said with a gleam in his eye. "That was interesting." His smile was infectious, and I found myself laughing as I took the helmet from his hands and put it over my head, grateful for the chance to hide my face while I composed myself.

"Since it is unseasonably cold today, I was wondering if you'd be up for some of the best hot chocolate in Paris," he said as he swung his leg over the bike.

"So now you're seducing schoolgirls with promises of chocolate? You're a bad man, Vincent Delacroix," I laughed as he started the motor.

"So what does that make you for accepting my offer?" he yelled over the noise of the Vespa as we pulled away.

"Intentionally gullible," I said, wrapping my arms around his warm body and closing my eyes in delight.

NINETEEN

THAT NIGHT GEORGIA CORNERED ME IN MY ROOM after dinner. "So where'd you disappear to after school? I was waiting for you."

"Vincent picked me up after school and took me to Les Deux Magots."

Georgia's eyes widened. "You've seen him two days in a row?"

"Well, today doesn't really count, being all of fifteen minutes. I had to rush since I have a test tomorrow to study for."

"Doesn't matter! Holy cow, this is getting serious!" She made herself comfortable on the end of my bed. "So. Tell me about this ex-criminal mystery man."

"Well," I said, grasping for things I could actually say. "He's a student."

"Where?"

"Um, I actually don't know."

Georgia looked at me doubtfully. "What's he studying?"

"Ah . . . literature? I think," I ventured.

"You don't know what he's studying, either? Well, what do you guys talk about?"

"Oh, just other stuff. You know. Art. Music." *The undead. Immortality. Evil zombies.* There was no way I could tell Georgia anything about him.

Georgia stared me down for a moment and then snapped, "Fine. If you don't want to tell me about him, that's okay. You don't know much about *my* life either, but it's not for my lack of trying to include you. I've stopped asking you out because I know you'll say no."

"Okay, Georgia. Who are you seeing?"

My sister shook her head. "I don't give you information if you don't give me any either."

I reached out for her hand and pled, "Georgia, I'm not intentionally trying to exclude you from my life. You know I've a hard time with . . . well, everything. But I'm finally getting back on my feet, and I promise to make more of an effort."

"Then you'll come out with me this weekend?"

I paused. "Okay."

"With Vincent?"

"Um . . ."

Georgia shot me a look that said, *See?*

"Okay, okay. We'll go out with Vincent. But not clubbing, Georgia, please."

Georgia's black mood transformed instantly, and she bounced gleefully on my bed. "No club. Fine. How about a restaurant?"

"Sure. I'll check to see if he's around." *More like, if he's alive.*

"Call him now."

"Some privacy, please?"

"Okay," Georgia conceded, leaning over and giving me a kiss on my forehead. She walked to the door, and then turned. "Thanks, sis. Really. It'll be good to have you back."

The streetlights were just coming on as we walked up to the subway station. Vincent and Ambrose, who had been leaning back against the magazine kiosk and chatting, straightened up when they saw us. My heart melted into a soppy mess as Vincent walked up and kissed my cheeks, and then, turning to Georgia, gave her his most dashing smile. "And you must be Kate's legal guardian . . . I mean, sister. Georgia, right?"

Georgia laughed and exclaimed flirtatiously, "Well, just look at you! Katie sure knows how to choose 'em!" She looked like she wanted to stay right there all night, staring into his eyes.

"Georgia!" I exclaimed, shaking my head.

Ignoring me, Georgia looked over Vincent's shoulder at Ambrose and gave him a flirty wink. "Don't worry, Katie-Bean. Looks like Vincent has brought someone along to keep me busy. And you would be . . ."

"Ambrose. Enchanted to meet Kate's lovely sister," he said in French, giving me a sideways glance. I understood. If she knew he was American, she'd start asking questions. Maybe too many questions, although I was sure he was used to making up cover stories. "So where are you taking us, ladies?"

"I thought we'd go to a little restaurant I know in the fourteenth arrondissement," she said.

Vincent and Ambrose gave each other a fleeting look, just as Georgia's phone rang. "Excuse me," she said, and turned to answer the call.

"Not our favorite neighborhood," said Ambrose in a low voice.

"Why?" I asked.

"It's kind of 'their' turf. You know, those people I was telling you about. The 'other team,'" Vincent said, glancing up to make sure Georgia hadn't heard.

"What can they do to us outside, in a busy neighborhood, with two humans along?" asked Ambrose. He stared off into space for a second and then nodded his head and turned to me. "Jules said to tell you, 'Hi, beautiful.'"

"Hey, watch it!" Vincent said.

"He says, 'Whatcha going to do about it?'" Ambrose said, poking Vincent.

"Jules is volant . . . here? Right now?" I said in amazement.

"Yeah," Vincent said. "We're not on official business tonight, of course, but he insisted on coming along. Said he didn't want to miss out on all the fun."

"Can I talk to him?" I asked.

"When we're volant we can be heard only by other revenants—not humans. So Jules can hear what you say out loud, but he can only respond through me or Ambrose," Vincent said. "But you'll want to be careful." He gestured toward Georgia, who was getting off the phone.

"Too bad," she said. "I had a couple of friends who were going to join us, but they're not able to come."

"Shall we?" asked Ambrose, holding his arm out formally for Georgia to take. She laughed delightedly, draping her arm through his, and they headed down the stairs.

Once they were out of earshot I said, "Hi, Jules!"

Vincent laughed and said, "Looks like someone's got a bit of a crush."

"What do you mean?" I asked.

"Jules wants me to tell you that it's a shame you have to fall for someone as boring as myself. He wishes he could take my place and show you how well an older man can treat a lady." He talked back to the air. "Yeah, right, buddy. What are you, like twenty-seven years older than me? Well, at the moment we're both nineteen, so back off."

I did a quick mental calculation. Jules had told me he was born at the end of the nineteenth century. So Vincent must have been born in the 1920s. I smiled as I pocketed that information for later. If Vincent wouldn't tell me anything, maybe I could figure some of it out for myself.

We got out of the subway near the sprawling Montparnasse Cemetery and walked up a pedestrian-only street that was packed with bars and cafés. We stopped in front of a restaurant that had a crowd of about twenty people standing around outside. "This is it!" Georgia said enthusiastically.

"Georgia, look how many people are waiting. It'll take forever before we can get a table."

"Have some faith in your big sis," she said. "A friend of mine works here. I bet I can get us a table right away."

"Go ahead. We'll wait for you out here," I said, leading Vincent and Ambrose across the street and out of the crowd. We leaned up against a closed shop front and watched as Georgia worked her way through the swarm of people.

"Your description of her was right on the nose." Vincent smiled as he put his arm around me and squeezed my shoulder affectionately.

"My sister, the phenomenon," I said, enjoying the hug.

Ambrose stood on the other side of me, watching the crowd and nodding to some rhythm in his head, when suddenly he stopped and looked hard at Vincent. "Vin, Jules said he sees the Man in the neighborhood. Just a few blocks away."

"Does he know we're here?" Vincent asked.

Ambrose shook his head. "Don't think so."

Vincent pulled his arm away and said, "Kate, we've got to get out of here. Now."

"But Georgia!" I said, looking toward the glass door. I could see my sister inside, chatting with the hostess.

"I'll get her," said Vincent, and began pushing his way through the crowd.

Just then, two men who had been walking past bumped hard into Ambrose, pushing him violently against the wall. He groaned and tried to grab for them, but the men dodged him and walked quickly away as he slumped to the ground.

"Hey! Stop!" I shouted at them, as they turned a corner.

"Someone stop them!" I yelled at the crowd of people across the street. People turned and looked in the direction I was pointing, but the men had disappeared from view. The whole thing had happened so quickly that no one had even noticed.

"Vincent!" I called over the crowd. Vincent turned and, seeing my alarm, began to work his way back to me.

"Ambrose, are you okay?" I said, squatting down next to him. "Did that guy . . . ," I began, but stopped, seeing that his shirt was ripped from his neck to his chest and drenched in blood. He wasn't moving.

Oh, please help him not be dead, I thought.

I had seen more violence in the last year than I had in my entire life. I asked, not for the first time, *Why me?* Teenage girls aren't supposed to be on such familiar terms with mortality, I reasoned bitterly, while a feeling of panic rose from the pit of my stomach. I knelt next to his motionless form. "Ambrose, can you hear me?"

Someone began walking over to us from the crowd. "Hey, is he okay?"

Just then Ambrose shuddered and, leaning forward on both hands, began lifting himself off the ground. As he rose, he closed his jacket, effectively hiding the blood on his shirt, although there was already a pretty big puddle on the ground. "Oh my God, Ambrose, what happened?" I asked. I put out an arm to support him, and he leaned heavily on me.

"Not Ambrose. It's Jules." The words came from Ambrose's lips, but his eyes stared blindly ahead.

"What?" I asked, confused.

Vincent finally reached us. "It's Ambrose," I said. "He got stabbed or shot or something. And he's delirious. He just told me he was Jules."

"We have to get him out of here before they come back with reinforcements for his body," Vincent said to me in a low voice, and then said more loudly, "He's fine, he's fine . . . thanks!" to the small group of people who were now coming to our aid. He grasped one of Ambrose's arms and draped it around his shoulder.

"But what about Georgia?" I gasped.

"Whoever did this saw you standing with Ambrose. It's too dangerous for you here."

"I can't leave my sister," I said, turning to make my way through the crowd to get her.

Vincent grabbed my arm and pulled me back to him. "She was inside the restaurant when they attacked. She's safe. Come with me!" he commanded, and I took Ambrose's other arm and pulled it across my back. He was walking, but seemed very weak. We got to the end of the block, and Vincent hailed a taxi and maneuvered us inside before slamming the door. I peered down the street as we pulled away. No sign of Georgia.

"Is he okay?" asked the driver, looking in his rearview mirror and checking out the massive man slumped over in his backseat.

"Drunk," Vincent responded simply, pulling off his sweater as he spoke.

"Well, make sure he doesn't throw up in my cab," the man said, shaking his head in disgust.

"What happened?" Vincent asked me quietly in English, glancing up to see if the driver could understand. He handed his sweater to Ambrose, who unzipped his jacket and stuck it under his shirt. He leaned his head against the seat in front of him.

"We were just standing there when two guys shoved him up against the wall. They ran off before I even knew what was happening."

"Did you see who did it?" he asked.

I shook my head.

Ambrose said, "It was two of *them*. I didn't see it happening ahead of time or I would have warned you."

"It's okay, Jules," Vincent said, placing his hand reassuringly on Ambrose's back.

"Why did you just call him Jules?"

"Ambrose isn't in there. It's Jules," Vincent said.

"What? How?" I asked, gripped by horror as I jerked away from the slumping form next to me.

"Ambrose is either unconscious or . . . dead."

"Dead," responded Ambrose.

"Is he going to . . . come back to life?" I asked, horrified.

"The cycle resets when we're killed. Day one of our dormancy starts the second we die. Don't worry—Ambrose will reanimate in three days."

"So what is Jules doing? Possessing him?"

"Yes. He wanted to get Ambrose out of there before our enemies could come back and take the body."

"You can do that, I mean, possess someone?"

"Other revenants, yeah, under certain circumstances."

"Like?"

"Like if their body's still in good enough shape to move." Seeing my bewilderment, he clarified. "If they're in one piece. And rigor mortis hasn't set in."

"Eww." I grimaced.

"You asked!" He glanced up at the driver who, judging by his lack of interest, was oblivious to the gist of our conversation.

"How about humans?" I asked.

"If they're alive, yes, but only with their permission. And taking into consideration that it's very dangerous for a human's mental state to have two minds active in there at once," he said, tapping his forehead. "They'd go insane if it went on for long."

I shuddered.

"Don't think about it, Kate. It rarely ever happens. It's just something we do in the most extreme situations. Like this one."

"What . . . am I creeping you out, my darling Kates?" the words came from Ambrose's lips.

"Yes, Jules," I responded, wrinkling my nose. "I can honestly say that I am completely creeped out right now."

"Cool," he said, a smile forming on Ambrose's lips.

"Jules, bad time to joke around," Vincent said.

"Sorry, man. It's not often I get to do magic tricks for a human, though."

"Can you just concentrate on slowing down the bleeding if at all possible? This driver's going to freak if we mess up his backseat," Vincent whispered.

"So, if they already killed him, why would those guys want to come back for his body? Why would they even kill him in the first place, if they know he's just going to come back to life three days later?" I asked Vincent, ignoring their surreal conversation.

Vincent seemed to weigh whether or not he should tell me. And then, looking at Ambrose's body half slumped over on mine, he whispered, "It's the only way we can be destroyed. If they kill us, and then burn our body, we're gone forever."

Georgia was furious. And I didn't blame her.

By the time we got to Vincent's house, we had fought it out by text.

Georgia: Where are you guys?
Me: Ambrose sick. Had to take him home.
Georgia: Why didn't you come in and get me?
Me: Tried to. Couldn't get through the crowd.
Georgia: I seriously hate you right now, Kate Beaumont Mercier.
Me: I am SO SORRY.
Georgia: Saw some friends here who rescued me from complete humiliation. But I still hate you.
Me: Sorry.
Georgia: You are NOT forgiven.

Vincent and I tried to help Ambrose, but he righted himself after getting out of the taxi and brushed our hands away. "I've got it now. Damn, this guy is heavy. How can he even move with all these lumpy muscles all over the place?"

When we got to the door Vincent turned to me, looking conflicted.

"I think I'll go home," I said, beating him to the punch.

He looked relieved. "I can walk with you if you can just wait a few minutes for us to get him settled."

"No, I'll be okay. Really," I said. And curiously enough, I meant it. Through all the horror and weirdness of the evening, I felt strangely okay. *I can handle this,* I thought to myself, as I walked out of the gates toward my grandparents' house.

TWENTY

GEORGIA SULKING IS NOT A PRETTY SIGHT. Although I had apologized a million times, she wasn't speaking to me.

Things were pretty uncomfortable around the house. Mamie and Papy tried to ignore the fact that anything was wrong, but on the fifth day after my unforgivable crime, Papy pulled me over and said, "Why don't you come see me at work today?" He glanced over at Georgia's brooding silhouette and gave me a significant look, as if to say, *Can't talk here.* "It's been months since you've stopped by, and I have a lot of new inventory you haven't seen."

After school I headed directly to Papy's gallery. Walking into his shop was like entering a museum. In its muted light, ancient statues were lined up facing one another from either side of the room, and glass cases displayed artifacts shaped in pottery or cast in precious metals.

"Ma princesse," Papy crowed when he saw me, shattering the

room's opulent silence. I flinched. That was my dad's pet name for me, and no one had called me that since his death. "You came. So, what looks new to you?"

"Him, for starters," I said, pointing to a life-size statue of an athletic-looking youth stepping forward with one foot and holding a clenched fist tightly down by his side. The other arm and his nose were missing.

"Ah, my kouros," Papy said, walking over to the marble statue. "Fifth century BCE. A true prize. The Greek government wouldn't have even let it out of the country nowadays, but I bought it from a Swiss collector whose family acquired it in the nineteenth century." He led me past a jeweled reliquary in a glass case. "You never know what you're getting these days, with all these iffy provenances."

"What's this one?" I asked, stopping in front of a large black vase. Its surface was decorated with a dozen or so reddish-colored human figures in dramatic poses. Two armored groups faced each other, and in the middle a fierce-looking naked man stood at the head of each army. They held spears toward each other in a face-off. "Naked soldiers. Interesting."

"Ah, the amphora. It's about a hundred years younger than the kouros. Shows two cities at battle, led by their numina."

"Their what?"

"Numina. Singular, numen. A type of Roman god. They were part-man, part-deity. Could be wounded, but not killed."

"So since they're gods, they fight naked?" I asked. "No armor necessary? Sound like show-offs to me."

Papy chuckled.

Numina, I thought, and muttered under my breath, "Sounds like numa."

"What did you say?" Papy exclaimed, his head jerking upright from the vase to stare at me. He looked like someone had slapped him.

"I said numina sounds kind of like numa."

"Where did you hear that word?" he asked.

"I don't know . . . TV?"

"I very seriously doubt that."

"I don't know, Papy," I said, breaking his laser gaze and searching for something else in the gallery that could bail me out of the situation. "I probably read it in an old book."

"Hmm." He nodded, hesitantly accepting my explanation but keeping his worried look.

Trust Papy to have heard of every archaic god and monster that ever existed. I'd have to tell Vincent that revenants, or at least the evil branch of revenants, weren't as "under the radar" as they thought. "So thanks for the invitation, Papy," I said, relieved to change the subject. "Was there something you wanted to talk about? Besides statues and vases, that is."

Papy smiled wanly. "I asked you to come here to check on you and Georgia. Is this just a skirmish," he said, glancing at the vase, "or a full-out war? Not that it's any of my business. I'm just wondering when you're planning on calling a truce and restoring peace to the household. If it goes on much longer, I might have to leave on an urgent unforeseen business trip."

"I'm sorry, Papy," I said. "It's totally my fault."

"I know. Georgia said that you and some young men left her stranded at a restaurant."

"Yeah. There was kind of an emergency, and we had to leave."

"And you didn't have enough time to bring Georgia with you?" he asked skeptically.

"No."

Papy took my arm and gently led me back toward the front of the store. "Doesn't sound like the kind of thing you'd do, *princesse*. And it doesn't sound very gentlemanly on the part of your escorts."

I shook my head, agreeing, but there wasn't anything I could say to defend myself.

We arrived at the front door. "Be careful who you choose to spend time with, *chérie*. Not everyone has a heart as good as yours."

"Sorry, Papy. I'll sort it out with Georgia right away." I gave him a hug and walked out of the darkened room, blinking in the sunlight. And after picking up a bouquet of Gerbera daisies from a neighborhood florist, I went home for a last-ditch effort at making peace with my sister. I don't know if it was the flowers that did the trick, or if she was just ready to forgive and forget. But this time, my apology worked.

Instead of discouraging me from seeing Vincent, Papy's speech made me even more eager to see him. It had been a long five days, and though we planned to see each other over the weekend and talked by text and by phone every day, it seemed like an eternity. After my peacemaking mission with Georgia, I picked up the phone to call him. But before I finished dialing, I saw his name pop up on my screen and my phone began to ring.

"I was just calling you," I said, laughing.

"Yeah, right," his velvety voice came from the other end of the line.

"Is Ambrose up and about?" I asked. At my request, he had been giving me updates on his kinsman's recovery. The day after he was stabbed the wound had begun closing up, and Vincent assured me that, as usual, Ambrose would be as good as new once he "woke up."

"Yes, Kate. I told you he was fine."

"Yeah, I know. It's still hard for me to believe, that's all."

"Well, you can see him yourself if you want to come over. But do you want to go out first? Since we managed to handle Les Deux Magots without anyone being killed or maimed, I thought I might take you there again."

"Sure. I've got a few hours until dinner."

"Pick you up in five?"

"Perfect."

Vincent was waiting outside on his Vespa by the time I got downstairs.

"You're fast!" I said, taking the helmet from him.

"I'll take that as a compliment," he replied.

***

It was the first cold day of October. We sat outside the café on the boulevard Saint-Germain, under one of the tall, lamplike space heaters that sprout up on all the café terraces once it begins to get chilly out. Its radiating heat toasted my shoulders, while the hot chocolate warmed my insides.

"Now *this* is chocolate," Vincent said as he poured the thick lava of melted chocolate into his cup and added steamed milk from a second pitcher. We sat and watched as people walked by, sporting coats, hats, and gloves for the first time that year.

Vincent leaned back in his seat. "So, Kate, my darling," he began. I lifted my eyebrows, and he laughed. "Okay, just plain old Kate. In our agreed spirit of disclosure, I thought I would offer to answer a question for you."

"What question?"

"Any question, as long as it pertains to the twenty-first and not the twentieth century."

I thought for a moment. What I really wanted to know was who he was before he died. The first time. But he obviously wasn't ready to tell me.

"Okay. When did you die the last time?"

"A year ago."

"How?"

"A fire rescue."

I paused, wondering how far he would let me go. "Does it hurt?"

"Does what hurt?"

168

"Dying. I mean, I suppose the first time it's the same as any other death. But after that, when you die to save someone . . . does it hurt?"

Vincent studied my expression carefully before answering. "Just as much as if you, as a human, were hit by a subway train. Or asphyxiated under a pile of burning timbers."

My skin crawled as I tried to wrap my mind around the fact that some people . . . or revenants . . . whatever . . . experienced the pain of death not just once but repeatedly. By choice. Vincent saw my unease and reached for my hand. His touch calmed me, but not in the supernatural way.

"Then why do you do it? Is this just about having an over-blown sense of community service? Or repaying your debt to the universe for making you immortal? I mean, I respect the fact that you're saving people's lives, but after a few rescues, why don't you just let yourself get older, like Jean-Baptiste, until you finally die of old age?" I paused. "*Do* you die of old age?"

Ignoring my last question, Vincent leaned in toward me and spoke earnestly, as if making a confession. "Because, Kate. It's like a compulsion. It's like pressure building up inside until you have to do something to get relief. The 'philanthropic' or 'immortal' motives wouldn't make the pain and trauma worth it on their own. It's going against our nature *not* to do it."

"Then how has Jean-Baptiste resisted it for . . . what? Thirty years straight?"

"The longer you're a revenant, the easier it gets to resist. But even with a couple of centuries under his belt, it takes him a mammoth amount of self-control. He has a really good reason, though. He not only shelters our little clan but supports other groups of revenants around the country. He can't be dying left and right and still manage that much responsibility."

"Okay," I conceded. "I get it that you have a compulsion to die. But that doesn't explain why, in between all the dying, you do things like dive into the Seine after a suicide attempt. You obviously weren't going to die from that."

"You're right," Vincent said. "The occasions where we actually die saving someone are rare. Once . . . twice a year at most. Usually we're just doing things like preventing pretty girls from getting crushed by crumbling buildings."

"Very suave," I said, nudging him. "But that's exactly what I mean. Where's the reward in that? Is that a compulsion too?"

Vincent looked uncomfortable.

"What? That is a valid question. We're still talking twenty-first century here," I said defensively.

"Yeah, but we're going a bit beyond the original question." As he studied my stubborn expression, his cell phone rang.

"Whew, saved by the bell," he said, winking at me as he answered. I heard a high-pitched, panicky voice coming from across the line. "Is Jean-Baptiste with you? Good. Just try to calm down, Charlotte," he soothed. "I'll be right there."

Vincent pulled out his wallet and laid some change on the table. "It's a family emergency. I have to go help out."

"Can't I come with you?"

He shook his head as we stood to leave. "No. There's been an accident. It might be a bit"—he paused, weighing his words—"messy."

"Who?"

"Charles."

"And Charlotte's there with him?"

Vincent nodded.

"Then I want to go. She sounded upset. I can help her while you take care of . . . whatever it is that you need to do."

He looked up at the sky, as if waiting for some divine inspiration on how to explain things to me. "This isn't how it usually goes. Like I was saying—we normally die for someone only once or maybe twice a year. It's a fluke that Jules and Ambrose both died just as you and I started hanging out."

We reached the scooter. Vincent unlocked it and put his helmet on.

"This is your life, right? And you promised not to hide things from me. So maybe this is something I should see if I want to know what hanging out with revenants really means." A little voice inside me was telling me to give it up, to go home, and to stay out of Vincent's "family's" business. I ignored it.

He touched my stubbornly clenched jaw with one finger. "Kate, I really don't want you to come. But if you insist, I'm not going to stop you. I hoped it would be longer before you had to see the worst of it, but you're right—I shouldn't shelter you from our reality."

Pulling my helmet on, I tucked myself in behind him on the scooter. Vincent started the engine and headed toward the river.

We drove past the Eiffel Tower and pulled over into a little park in front of Grenelle Bridge. I knew the spot because it's the end of the line for sightseeing boats before they head back to the center of Paris.

One of those tour boats was pulled over to the riverbank, and in front of it an anxious crowd watched from outside a protective fence of police barriers. Two ambulances and a fire truck were parked on the lawn next to the river, their lights flashing.

Vincent propped the scooter against a tree without bothering to lock it up and, holding my hand, jogged up to the fence to speak with a policeman standing behind it. "I'm family," he said to the man, who didn't budge, but glanced inquiringly back at his superior.

"Let him through. He's my nephew," came a familiar voice, and Jean-Baptiste strode through a horde of paramedics and pushed the barrier aside to let us pass. Vincent kept his arm wrapped tightly around my waist, making it obvious that I was coming with him.

Now that we had an unobstructed view, I saw three bodies on the riverbank. One was a good distance away from the others. It was a little boy, probably five or six years old, and he was lying on a stretcher, wrapped in a blanket. A woman sat by his head, weeping silently as she rubbed his wet hair with a towel. After a moment, two paramedics flanking his small, shivering form helped him up to a seated position, facing away from the other two bodies, as they asked him and the woman questions. He was obviously okay.

Unlike the body laid out a few yards away. It was a little girl, probably the same age as the boy. Her head lay in a pool of blood. A distraught woman sat next to her, screaming unintelligibly.

Oh no, I thought. *I don't know if I'm going to be able to handle this.* It took all my strength to stay calm and not burst into tears myself. I knew I wouldn't be any help if I started losing it.

And finally, another ten feet away, was a third body—this one adult. I couldn't tell if it was a man or a woman because the face was covered in blood. An emergency blanket was draped over the body, which was long past needing it for warmth. *They must be hiding something gory,* I thought, and then my eyes fixed on the girl kneeling next to him.

Unlike the other survivors, Charlotte wasn't hysterical. She was crying bitterly, but her body language communicated defeat rather than shock. Her hands were on the top of the blanket, pressing down on her brother's corpse as if she was trying to keep him from flying up into the air. She looked around when Vincent called her name and, seeing us, stood.

"It's going to be okay, Charlotte," Vincent whispered once his arms were around her. "You know it is."

"I know," she sobbed. "But that doesn't make it any easier. . . ."

"Shh," Vincent cut her off, holding her against himself in a powerful embrace, before letting her go and handing her gently to me. "Kate came to be with you. She can take you home in a taxi now if you want."

"No." Charlotte shook her head, simultaneously reaching out

to grasp my hand as if it were a safety net. "I'll wait until you guys get him in the ambulance."

Vincent turned to me. *Will you be okay?* he mouthed. I nodded, and he left us to walk toward Jean-Baptiste. The two men approached a third ambulance that had just arrived. Ambrose stepped down out of the passenger side of the cab looking as strong and healthy as a model on a gym brochure.

Charlotte had slumped back down to the ground and was running her hand over Charles's blanket as if trying to warm him up with the friction. "So," I said gently, "if you don't want to talk about it, just say. But what happened?"

She exhaled deeply, her drawn face giving me a hint of what she would look like if she were her true age. She raised a trembling hand and pointed toward the deserted tourist boat. "The boat. It was rented for a children's birthday party. Charles and I were walking nearby, with Gaspard volant, and he let us know before the two children fell in. Charles jumped in and reached the boy just after he went under. He swam him over to me on the shore, where I gave the child mouth-to-mouth. Then he went back for the little girl as the motor was pulling her under. He tried to get her, but the propeller hit her first. And then it got him."

Her voice was numb as she recounted the story, but as soon as she finished, she began crying softly again, her shoulders shaking against my arm. I felt tears well up in my eyes and pinched myself hard. *Get ahold of yourself,* I thought. *Charlotte doesn't need you crying right along with her.*

I looked down the bank toward the water as two police divers emerged. The paramedic standing next to Ambrose noticed them too and walked briskly in their direction. It wasn't until he got a few feet away and they held an object toward him that I began to guess what was going on.

Charlotte felt my body tense and looked up toward the divers. "Oh, good. They found it," she said in a monotone as the paramedic reached for the plastic bag, half full of bloody water.

I couldn't stop the tears this time, and through the blur I saw what it held. My body went numb and the breath left my lungs as violently as if I had been kicked in the stomach. In the bag was a human arm.

TWENTY-ONE

IT WAS WHEN THE PARAMEDICS ZIPPED CHARLES into a body bag that I lost it. As I watched, the body bag replicated and then there were two. And now it was my own parents I was looking at in the bags, my body having flown across the Atlantic and backward in time to the New York City morgue not even a year ago.

They wouldn't even show me my dad. But I had insisted on seeing my mom, who, with "only" a broken neck, was judged more presentable than my mutilated father. And now I was back in that room, staring at the coral-hued toenail polish on my mother's naked toes. Georgia stood next to me weeping as I tore out strands of my hair and braided them in with my mother's. I knew she would be cremated, and I wanted part of me to accompany her. At that thought, my memories came to an end, but I stayed in the scene, unwilling to leave my mother in the blindingly white room.

"Kate. Kate?" Strong hands turned me until Vincent's face was inches from my own. "Are you okay?"

I nodded, in a daze.

"Why don't you ride in the ambulance and I'll bring the scooter home and meet you there?"

I nodded again and attempted to hold myself together as I wedged myself between Charlotte and the driver in the vehicle's cab.

When we arrived at Jean-Baptiste's house, Jeanne met us at the front door. She took Charlotte away from me, leading her upstairs toward her room in a familiar way that made it clear they had been through this before. Through the hall window, I saw Jean-Baptiste hand a wad of bills to the ambulance driver as Jules carried the unwieldy body bag through the front door and gently placed it on the floor. I succeeded in wobbling my way down the back hallway into Vincent's room, where I threw myself facedown on his bed and let myself sob.

I knew I wasn't crying about Charles's death. That had just set me off. Or boomeranged me backward, more like. And now I felt myself perched at the rim of the same black abyss I had finally managed to crawl out of a few months earlier. I felt the overwhelming temptation to lean forward, just an inch, and let myself fall headlong into its comforting darkness. The thought of letting my mind leave my body behind was tempting. I wouldn't even need to be around to clean up the mess.

Someone sat down on the bed, but I kept my face buried in the pillow. Vincent's warm voice came from above me. "It's okay,

Kate. I know it's really hard to see something like that, and I wish you hadn't. You just have to remember that it's not a real—mortal—death. And that it's for a reason. Charles saved a little boy's life by giving up his own. Temporarily."

His words went in through my ears but stopped at my brain. I couldn't process what he was saying. It just didn't make sense according to everything I'd ever learned or experienced in life. I couldn't just cut off my feelings, knowing that someone was mangled by a boat propeller—even if they were only "temporarily" dead. "Is Charles . . . ," I started.

"Everyone's fine. Charles's body is back in his room. He'll be in perfect shape in a few days. Charlotte is fine now that she has him back here at home and can watch him heal." He paused. "You're the only one I'm concerned about."

I tried to sift through what I had seen and what he had said and to think of it rationally, but everything inside me rejected it. I scooted away from Vincent and pulled my hand from his. I couldn't look at him.

"How can you live like this?" I asked finally, my voice shaking.

"Well, I've had a long time to get used to it," he said, biting his lower lip.

"Exactly how long?" My voice sounded empty. I knew Vincent had been keeping things from me for a reason, but I resented the fact that I still knew so little about him.

"Do you want to hear this now?" he asked, and sighed.

"I *have* to hear this now," I responded quietly.

"I was born in 1924."

I did the math. "You're eighty-seven."

"No, I'm nineteen. I died in 1942, when I was eighteen. It's been a year since I died rescuing someone, so I'm nineteen now. And the oldest I've ever been is twenty-three. I've never been married. I've never had children. I've never experienced anything that would make me feel much older than I am right now."

"But you've seen eighty-seven years go by. You've had eighty-seven years of life."

"If this is what you call *life*," he said, shaking his head. "But it's a trade-off. I get to act like a guardian angel with a death wish, and in exchange I get a certain version of immortality." His voice was tinged with something just short of bitterness. Regret, maybe.

He tried to smile, and then looked at me pleadingly. "Please, Kate. Can that be enough truth telling for now? This has been a hard enough day for you without my upsetting you with more science fiction."

I nodded. He ran his fingers through my hair and pulled an errant lock back, tucking it behind my ear. I flinched at his touch. "What is it, Kate? Please talk to me."

My thoughts flew in a dozen different directions. Finally I looked at him straight on, steeling myself to say the difficult words.

"I have to be honest. I've never felt like this before. I've never . . ." My eyes searched the ceiling for something that would give me courage to continue, and finding nothing, I sighed deeply before meeting his gaze. "I've never felt this strongly about someone. And if I let myself keep feeling this way about you . . ."

Vincent's face was composed, but his eyes were full of torment as he waited for the verdict that he knew was coming.

I pushed myself to continue. "I can't imagine having to live through what happened today on a regular basis. And when it's your turn, it will be even worse. I can't stand the thought of seeing you die again and again. It reminds me too much of my parents' deaths."

I choked on my words and began to cry, and Vincent moved toward me, but I held a hand out to stop him. "If I were to end up loving you, I couldn't live like that. In constant agony. Knowing that you were going to be resurrected, or whatever it is that you do afterward, wouldn't be enough to make up for having to live through your death time and time again. You can't ask me to do it. I *can't* do it."

I rose abruptly to my feet, wiping my tears away, and stumbled toward the door. He followed me silently down the passageway to the foyer and stood motionless as I picked my coat up off the bench and began struggling with the door handle. Vincent opened it for me and, placing a hand on my shoulder, gently turned me toward him.

"Kate, please look at me." I couldn't lift my eyes to his face. "I understand," he said.

I finally looked up and held his gaze. His eyes were hollow. Empty. "I'm so sorry for the pain I've caused you," he whispered, and dropped his hand from my shoulder.

I turned to go while I still had the strength to leave him, and as the gate swung shut behind me, I began to run.

TWENTY-TWO

I MADE IT TO MY ROOM WITHOUT SEEING MY grandparents or Georgia, and shut myself in. As I curled up into a corner of my bed, time seemed to stop and stand still. I felt torn between the certainty that I had done the right thing and the nagging doubt that in the space of ten minutes I had ruined any chance I might have had for a bright, hopeful future. For love.

Though I hadn't known him for long, I felt that if things continued the way they had been I would fall in love with Vincent. There was no doubt about that. And if this were just the starting point, I knew that it wouldn't be just some lighthearted romance. My heart would be swept away. I was sure of it.

And feeling like that about him, I couldn't risk the pain of seeing him repeatedly injured, killed, or even destroyed. He had said it was possible: His immortality had its limits. After losing Mom and Dad, I refused to lose someone else I loved.

The old dictum was backward. It should be "Better not to

have loved at all, than to love and have lost." I had done the right thing, I reassured myself. So why did it feel like I had made the biggest mistake of my life?

I wrapped myself in a blanket cocoon and inched deeper into misery. I let the pain consume me. I deserved it. I never should have opened myself up.

Hours later, Mamie knocked to tell me it was time for dinner. I took a second to compose my voice, and then yelled, "Not hungry, Mamie. Thanks!" A few minutes later I heard a gentle tapping on the door.

"Can we come in?" Georgia's voice came from the other side, and without waiting for a response, my sister and grandmother tiptoed cautiously into the room. Sitting down on either side of me, they put their arms around me and waited.

"Is it Mom and Dad?" Georgia asked finally.

"No, for once it isn't about Mom and Dad," I sputtered, half laughing, "at least, not just about Mom and Dad."

"Is it Vincent?" she asked.

I nodded tearfully.

"Did this . . . Vincent"—I felt Mamie and Georgia look at each other over my head—"do something to hurt you?" Mamie said, running her fingers up and down my back.

"No, it was me. I just can't . . ." How could I possibly explain this to them? "I can't let myself get close to him. It feels like too much of a risk."

"I know what you mean," Georgia said. "You're afraid to love someone again. In case they disappear too."

I put my head on Mamie's shoulder and breathed, "It's too complicated."

Smoothing my hair back with her hand, and planting a kiss on the top of my head, she responded quietly, "It always is."

I bought a bagful of novels at an English bookstore, and then retreated into the dark cave of my bedroom, telling Mamie I was "hibernating" for the weekend. She understood, and after leaving a platter set with water, tea, fruit, and an assortment of cheese and crackers on my dresser, she left me alone.

I spent the rest of my day in someone else's story. The rare moments that I put the book down, my own pain returned in burning stabs. I felt like a circus knife thrower's target. If I held my mind immobile, I might avoid being hit by the blades whizzing by my head. From time to time I fell asleep, but was immediately awakened by dark, tortured dreams that, once I awoke, dissolved without a trace.

I couldn't help looking over my shoulder at times, wondering if I might see Vincent lurking in the shadows. *Does he come to see me when he's volant?* I wondered. He could be floating around my bedroom for all I knew. Or maybe not. Maybe it was a case of "out of sight, out of mind" for him, and my outburst had been effective enough to stop him from trying to see me again. *That was what I wanted,* I told myself. Wasn't it?

If I let myself think, that would be the end. So I disconnected my brain and let my body carry on without a mind to steer it. All in all, it seemed like I was pulling it off. I could live without him.

I was self-contained. Self-sufficient. Maybe I wasn't happy, but I wasn't sad. I was just . . . there.

School was a welcome relief. It helped the days pass by in numb monotony. Finally, returning home one day, I realized in a rare jolt of clarity that it had barely been two weeks since I had left Vincent standing in his doorway. It had felt like months. I had been congratulating myself for completing a marathon when I was hardly past the starting line.

As I climbed the Métro steps onto my street, I was surprised to see a familiar figure leaning against a nearby phone booth. It was Charlotte. When she spotted me, her pretty face lit up. "Kate!" she cried, skipping up and leaning forward to kiss me on both cheeks.

"Charlotte. What a surprise!" I smiled, glancing around curiously to see if she was with someone else.

"Waiting for Charles. And here he is," she said, her eyes fixing on the subway stairs behind me.

Charles walked up, all his limbs intact, looking healthier than ever but in a much fouler humor. He scowled when he saw me. "What's the human doing here?" he asked.

"Um, I have a name. And to answer your question, I live here," I responded defensively. "You're not the only person in Paris who uses the rue du Bac Métro."

"No, I mean, what are you doing here with Charlotte?"

"I just ran into her. Accidentally." *Why am I making excuses to this obnoxious adolescent?* I wondered, annoyed with myself.

"I thought that since you ditched Vincent, we'd never see you again."

"Well," I said, pasting a fake smile across my face, "here I am. So, Charlotte, it was nice to see you. Gotta go."

I turned to walk away, but Charles shouted after me. "You just can't get enough of us dead guys, huh? What do you want now? You want us to save your life again? Or are you going to lead us into a death trap like you did Ambrose?"

"What are you talking about?" I yelled, spinning to face him.

"Nothing. I'm talking about nothing. Just forget I ever said a word," he spat. Thrusting his hands into his jeans pockets, he turned and stalked off.

Charlotte looked at me apologetically.

"What was that about? What did I do?" I gasped.

"Nothing, Kate. You didn't do anything. Don't worry, it's all Charles's problem."

"Well then, why did he attack me like that?" I was still motionless with shock.

"Hey, do you want to walk down to the river?" she asked, ignoring my question. "I was kind of hoping I'd run across you at some point, seeing we're neighbors and all. Not that I haven't seen you around, of course. I just didn't feel like it was appropriate to run down the street after you."

"Don't tell me you were following me," I said, half joking.

Charlotte didn't answer, but grinned at me like a cat.

"What? *Have* you been following me?"

"Don't worry, Vincent didn't ask me to. It's just that following people is what we do, and when we're doing it nonstop, it's hard not to follow people who interest us."

"*I* interest *you*?"

"Yes."

"Why?"

"Let's see. Well, you're the first girl Vincent has fallen for since becoming a revenant. Which already qualifies you as fascinating to the rest of us."

"I can't talk about . . . him," I began to protest.

"Okay. We will avoid the topic of Vincent completely. Promise."

"Thanks."

"You also interest me because . . ." For once she looked much younger than her fifteen-year-old body. "I had kind of been hoping you would be a friend. Before you left, that is. It's a bit lonely hanging out with guys all the time. Thankfully Jeanne is there, or I'd probably have already lost it."

My expression must have been quizzical, because she hurriedly went on to explain. "It's not like I can go out and make friends with just any human. They wouldn't understand. But since you already know what we are . . ."

I gently cut her off. "Charlotte, I am incredibly flattered that you want to be friends with me. I really like you, too. But I'm still so upset about Vincent that if I hung out with you and we ran into him, it would be too hard on me."

She looked away and nodded her head nonchalantly, as if already distancing herself from me.

"I thought you hung out with Charles most of the time," I said.

"Oh, he's off on his own a lot lately," she said, trying to sound flippant but not managing very well. Her voice trembled as she continued, "So recently I've found myself a bit more on my own than I'm used to." Her attempt to look brave was ruined by the tear I noticed coursing down her cheek as she turned away.

"Wait!" I said, grabbing her hand, and pulled her back to face me.

Staring at the ground, she brushed away another tear. "I'm sorry. Things have just been kind of . . . hard lately."

I guess I'm not the only one with problems, I told myself, my resolve crumbling as I saw the sadness on her face. "Okay, yeah. Let's walk to the river." Her empty eyes met my own, and she managed a glimmer of a smile as she took my arm and we walked down the street together.

As we neared the water, I pointed out an antique taxidermy shop. "My mom and I used to always go in there," I said. "It's like a zoo, except all the animals are dead. Now I can't even pass by without thinking about Mom. I haven't dared go in, in case I had a meltdown right there in the middle of all the stuffed squirrels."

Charlotte laughed—the response I had been hoping for. "That's how I felt too after my parents died. Everything reminded me of them. Paris felt like a ghost town to me for years after," she said as we walked down the steps to the quay.

"Your parents died? I mean, before you did?" I asked, the hole in my heart beginning to ache again. We began strolling past a long line of houseboats that were moored to the riverbank.

Charlotte nodded. "It was World War Two. During the Occupation. My parents ran a clandestine press out of our apartment near the Sorbonne, where my father taught. The Germans found it and shot them. Charles and I were at my aunt's house that night, or they probably would have killed us, too.

"We were proud of our parents and wanted to continue in their footsteps. So when we began hearing about the roundups . . ." She paused, then explained, "When the police rounded the Jews up to send them to the concentration camps." I nodded to show her I understood, and she continued, "We hid some friends from school and their parents in our apartment, in a room with a false wall, where the printing press had been concealed. We secured enough ration cards to feed and clothe the six of us for over a year before a neighbor caught on and reported us."

I stopped in place. "Who would ever do such a thing?" I said, aghast.

She shrugged and continued, taking my arm and forcing me to move again. "We were able to get the family safely to another hiding place, but Charles and I were caught the next day and shot."

"I can barely believe that was happening right here in Paris."

Charlotte nodded. "They say that thirty thousand of us 'resisters' were shot during the course of the Occupation. At least, that's the official number. Some were actually lawbreakers. But others were innocent bystanders who were taken hostage and killed to revenge their countrymen's acts of resistance."

"That was so brave of you and Charles to help that family."

"Well, wouldn't you have done the same? How could we have acted differently?"

We neared a stone bench and sat down.

"I don't know," I responded finally. "I would hope I would have acted like you did. But there must be very few people who are actually that brave. Maybe that's why you became one of them. I mean, a revenant," I said.

"That's what Jean-Baptiste thinks. That saving lives was pre-programmed into us. That it came naturally. Who knows?" She paused thoughtfully. "What I *do* know is, now that I can spare others the pain I went through when my parents were killed—by saving lives—it makes the continual trauma of our existence easier to bear."

I nodded, and watched as she pensively picked at her finger-nails. "So what's up with Charles?" I asked finally.

"It's all part of the same story," she said. "He's had a hard time dealing with his failure to save that little girl's life in the boat accident. For the last couple of weeks he's been . . ." She looked like she was weighing how much to tell me and settled for, ". . . obsessing about it."

"Will he get over it with time?" I asked.

She shrugged. "I finally told Jean-Baptiste about it this morn-ing. He's going to have a talk with Charles."

"Maybe that will help," I offered.

She shook her head, as if unconvinced. "Let's change the subject."

"Okay," I said, grasping for a new topic of conversation. "So what's so bad about living with a houseful of hot men? Excluding Gaspard and Jean-Baptiste, that is, who I guess could be called 'hot' in their own way . . . ," I trailed off.

She burst out laughing. "Definitely not hot," she agreed.

"There's so much testosterone packed into that air, I'm surprised I haven't grown a mustache just from breathing it!"

Now it was my turn to laugh. It felt foreign to me, as if I were suddenly speaking Chinese. It didn't feel natural, but it didn't feel bad.

Charlotte shot me a wry grin, proud that she had cracked through my armor. "Honestly," she conceded, "they're all like family to me. We've lived together for decades."

"The revenants out in the countryside have to constantly relocate so that the locals don't recognize them once they've died saving someone. They're always on the move from one of Jean-Baptiste's country homes to another. It suits most of them just fine, but I couldn't do it. These men are all the family I've got, and I could never leave them."

"Have you ever . . ." I paused, unsure of how probing my questions could be.

"What?" Charlotte asked, intrigued.

"Do you have a boyfriend?"

Charlotte sighed. "It would be just as hard for me to have a boyfriend as it is to have girl friends. I guess that in the beginning I could make excuses for vanishing three days every month, but that wouldn't work for long. And then disappearing for a few days every time I died. No, it just couldn't work. And I can't do the casual relationships like Jules and Ambrose do. When I fall in love, it sticks."

"So you've been in love before?"

She blushed and looked down at her hands. "Yes. But he

doesn't . . . he didn't feel the same way." Her words were almost inaudible.

"Then why not date a revenant?"

She leaned forward, a sad smile forming on her lips as she wrapped her arms around herself and looked out over the water. "There aren't many of us around, so the choices are rather slim."

I didn't know how to respond, so I took her hand in mine and gave it an encouraging squeeze. She smiled, and then said, "I better be getting back home. For Charles. Thanks for the chat. I can't even tell you how nice it is to hang out with a girl."

I felt the same way. I hadn't made any friends here in Paris. And even though it meant spending time with someone who was practically a member of Vincent's family, I had to admit I really enjoyed being with Charlotte. "We'll do it again," I promised.

If you are friends with Charlotte, you're bound to run into Vincent at one point or another, a little voice in my mind nudged me. *Oh, shut up,* I told it, wondering if the pain in my heart would ever subside. It had to, I decided. The longer I spent away from Vincent, the better I would feel. I was sure of it.

TWENTY-THREE

INSTEAD OF IMPROVING, THE NEXT WEEK I FELT worse, and by Friday a creeping despair began to engulf me as I realized the entire weekend stretched ahead with not a single activity planned as a distraction.

At lunch, I turned my phone on to see my daily texts from Georgia:

> Have you seen you-know-who's ho outfit?
> Calculus sucks.
> Going out tonight, wanna come?

I hesitated, and then forced myself to respond to the last text: Where?

She wrote me back immediately:

> Meet you after school.

At four o'clock, Georgia was waiting for me at the gate wearing an expression of sheer amazement. "No way, Katie-Bean . . . you're really coming out with me tonight?"

"Depends," I said blithely, trying not to sound as desperate as I felt. "Where are you going?"

"There's a dance party at this underground club. The owner's a *very* good friend of mine." She flashed me a sly smile. My sister, the incorrigible flirt. "Seriously, it's a really cool place, in this labyrinth of old wine cellars that runs under a couple of buildings near Oberkampf. It's always packed with musicians and artists; you'll love it."

Although my heart wasn't into clubbing, this was my only offer for the weekend. Actually, for the month, if I was being realistic. "I'm in," I said. "What time are you going?"

"Around nine."

We took the bus into town, and then changed to the Métro. Once on our street I told Georgia, "I don't feel like going home yet. I think I'll wander. Don't leave without me."

"I'll pick your outfit," she said, smiling, and headed up our street. I turned in the other direction and made my way past the busy boulevard Saint-Germain to drift through the small winding streets crisscrossing the area next to the river.

On a busy corner stood a café with a large terrace where my grandmother took me as a child for the delicious tarte tatin, a baked apple tart served upside down with a caramelized glaze. The café was called La Palette, as in an artist's palette, its name dating back to when it was a hangout for local painters and sculptors. It was too far from home to have chosen as my local café, but totally worth the occasional visit.

A frigid wind gusted through the streets, and the normally teeming terrace was almost deserted. I pushed my way through the front door into the warm, delicious-smelling café. A waiter caught my eye and gestured toward an empty table tucked into an almost hidden niche behind the front door. Perfect. Anonymity was exactly what I wanted today.

I sat down, stowed my book bag under the table, and began to check out the café's clientele as I waited for the waiter to return. A group of students rowdily chatting in one corner. Several tables of businesspeople with drinks set atop their documents. A striking-looking woman in her late twenties sitting by herself.

I focused on the last of these. Thick blond, almost white, hair flowed down her shoulders, and her high cheekbones and light blue eyes made her look vaguely Scandinavian.

A man with his back to me approached her from the café's bar. He sat down in front of her, picked up the coffee cup sitting across from hers, and drained the dregs with one quick motion. Then he reached across to hold her hand, which was lying delicately on the tabletop.

He said something to her, and her gaze dropped from him to the table. I saw a tear run down her lovely cheek, and the man's hand rose automatically to brush it away. He smoothed a loose lock of her platinum hair back behind her ear in a motion that I recognized.

And with a sudden realization, my heart stopped. As an icy chill overtook me, I grabbed for my bag and knocked the glass salt shaker to the floor, where it shattered loudly. The woman's eyes flew to me as she said something to her companion.

He turned in my direction, and then froze with a look of devastation marring his handsome face. My instincts had not been wrong. It was Vincent.

Just then the waiter materialized in front of me, holding a broom and a dustpan. "Sorry," I managed to blurt as I grabbed my coat from the chair and pushed by him to stumble out of the café.

I ran all the way home, my face so numb it felt like it had been shot full of Novocain. *I left him,* I reminded myself, *not the other way around. Why shouldn't he have found someone else?*

The thought came to me that he might have lied about not being in love with anyone since his childhood romance. He might have been with the gorgeous blonde the whole time. My shattered heart told me that was wrong, though. Vincent wouldn't lie to me. And neither would Charlotte, when she said I was the first girl Vincent had fallen for since becoming a revenant.

Unfortunately, conceding that he was free of blame, and that I was the one who had walked away, didn't make the pain in my chest hurt any less.

When I got home, I went straight to Georgia's room and threw the door open without knocking. "Let's go," I said breathlessly. She smiled and held up a short, lacy dress.

TWENTY-FOUR

AROUND NINE WE LEFT THE HOUSE AND CLIMBED into a car waiting outside. I squeezed into the backseat with two girls I recognized from school, while Georgia leaped into the passenger seat and gave a handsome guy I'd never seen a peck on the lips.

I knew that this was Georgia's way of saying hello to boys she liked, so decided to ask for details later. She made introductions. "Lawrence—British; Mags—Irish; Ida—Swedish; this is my sister, Kate, who is in desperate need of a good night out. If she goes home bored, I will hold you all personally responsible." She cranked up the radio, Lawrence steered the car toward the river, and we were off.

The bar was in a slightly rough neighborhood on the east side of Paris, an area popular with artists, models, and musicians who hadn't yet made it to the big time. Several trendy bars had popped up there in the last few years, and the sidewalks were crowded with small clusters of ultra-hip people, shivering in the cold as they smoked outside.

We stopped in front of a building in an alley that seemed to quake from the pounding beat of the music inside. A huge bouncer stood at the door, wearing only jeans and a white tank top stretched tightly across his impressive chest muscles. Lawrence yelled something over the blaring music, and the man cracked the door open to let us in.

The space was as big as a ballroom, but only about eight feet high. A DJ booth stood to one side, with a long fluorescently lit bar running the length of the opposite wall. The room was carved out of rough stone, with scattered concrete columns supporting the ceiling. White spotlights set up in the corners made the uneven cave walls eerily theatrical.

"Drinks!" shouted Georgia, and we headed toward the bar. In a buttery British accent, Lawrence asked me what I wanted, and got both of us a Coke. "Designated driver," he said, winking at me and smiling. We clinked our glasses together in a toast, and then turned to lean back on the bar.

"So are you and Georgia . . . ?" I asked Lawrence, letting him fill in the blank.

"Nope," he responded, his smile creasing his cheeks with dimples. "I like guys."

"Got it," I said, sipping on my straw, and we turned back to scoping out the room.

I never failed to marvel at Georgia's impeccable talent for finding the newest, hottest places to hang out. Beautiful people danced in the middle of the floor, while others mingled at the edges, shoulders slumped in skinny, brooding hipness. I noticed a famous young actress sitting in one corner, with a gaggle of admirers pretending not to fawn on her, and sprawled across a pile of cushions in an alcove carved out of the wall, I spotted a singer from a trendy British band.

My sister stood a few feet away from me, kissing a model-looking guy on the cheeks, when I saw a rugged figure walking slowly but steadily across the room in our direction. People clapped him on the back as he made his way through the crowd.

When he was a few feet away, Georgia set her glass on the bar and threw her hands in the air as he picked her up by the waist.

"Georgia, my sexy Southern belle," he said, lowering her to the floor. I smiled. The fact that we had never actually lived in the South was a moot point. Georgia had used the dozen or so holidays we spent in my mom's home state to cultivate a molasses-thick accent that Scarlett O'Hara would have traded her petticoat for. When she was in the mood, she used her drawl, along with her name, to imply that we came from somewhere more "exotic" than Brooklyn. Foreigners, at least those who spoke English well enough to notice accents, ate it up.

The man leaned in to give her a kiss on the lips. The fact that this one lasted a whole second longer than the others she had been bestowing left and right made me suspect that this must be someone special.

Taking him by the hand, she dragged him in front of me. Finally getting a view unhampered by the crowds, I saw that he was everything that Georgia always went for, combined into one man. At least six-five, he looked like a mix between a surfer and a football player: windswept blond hair and suntanned skin but massive enough in build to single-handedly plow through an entire defensive line. His brown eyes were so light and crystalline that they looked like frozen butterscotch. And the way he held Georgia in a proprietary way confirmed they were an item.

"Finally we meet! Georgia's little sister, Kate. I've heard about you. You didn't tell me she was so pretty, Georgia."

My sister drawled, "Now why would I go and do a thing like that?" Turning to me, she said, "Kate, this is Lucien. He owns the bar."

"Nice to meet you," I said.

He squeezed Georgia's shoulders and leaned down to whisper something in her ear. Then, stretching back to his full height, he made a signal to the bartender indicating our group.

"Sweet Georgia Brown," whistled Lawrence from my side. "Free drinks all night. Your sister has the magic touch."

"I know," I admitted as I watched Lucien kiss my sister's hand before letting himself be pulled away by a frantic-looking manager. As he disappeared into the crowd, he grinned and gave me a wink.

A group of scruffy-looking guys walked into the room and headed our way. Lawrence leaned over and said, "Band alert. These guys are the hottest new group in town."

"Then they've got to be friends of Georgia," I sighed.

He smiled and nodded as they approached. One walked right

up to Georgia and wordlessly pulled her out onto the dance floor. She leaned over and shouted something in his ear, and then smiled at me as one of his friends came over and took my hand. "Alex," the guy yelled, brushing the long hair out of his eyes.

We danced next to Georgia and her friend for the next couple of songs. Alex's flashing blue eyes and flirty grin definitely got my heart beating again. The way he smiled appreciatively at me showed me he didn't mind being assigned as my "party boy." He was handsome. He was human. So why wasn't I able to relax and enjoy myself?

I finally leaned over to tell Alex I was going to get a drink. He gazed at me regretfully and mimed a sexy kiss as I walked away. I mentally kicked myself for my stupidity, but knew I couldn't do anything else. Not tonight. Not for a while. Not until Vincent's face left my aching brain in peace.

Lawrence had left by the time I got back to the bar, but seeing me, the bartender automatically poured another glass of Coke. I took it and went to sit on a giant leather cushion against the wall.

Leaning back against the cold stone, I squinted as I watched the wavelike movements of the teeming masses for a few minutes before closing my eyes. I let the music work its trancelike beat on my brain. A few seconds later, I heard a low, smooth voice say, "Tired?"

Opening my eyes, I saw that Lucien had grabbed a cushion and was sitting next to me. I smiled at him. He didn't look quite as tough now that he wasn't fighting off crowds of hangers-on, but there was a slight aura of permafrost hovering about him.

Owning one of the trendiest bars in town had to have an effect on one's ego, I told myself.

"Not really tired, just not in a dancing mood."

"So. Does Georgia's sister have a boyfriend?"

Okay, this guy is really direct. "Ah, no," I said. "Not at the moment."

"Well," he said, rubbing his hands together for effect. "That's good news for my friends!"

"Um. I'm . . . not really in the market."

"But you wouldn't be opposed to meeting people." He raised a bushy blond eyebrow.

"Actually . . ."

Unwilling to hear my response, he stood and took my empty glass back to the bar, returning with a full one. "You'll have to come with Georgia to a party I'm having in a couple of weeks. Everyone who's anyone will be there." He squatted down and handed me the glass. "And so will you!"

His playful pat on my shoulder gave me an unexpected visceral reaction: I recoiled. From the way his body tensed as he stood, I could tell that he had noticed. *What is wrong with you?* I chided myself, surprised by my reaction. He was just trying to be friendly—but I must be sorely out of practice at social interaction. Before I could say something to make up for my unintentional cold shoulder, he turned to talk to someone who had been impatiently waiting for his attention. I sipped my Coke and checked my phone: It wasn't even midnight.

Rising to my feet, I threaded my way between the dancers until

I reached Georgia. She gave me a concerned smile, and I shook my head. "Sorry, Georgia. Just can't get into it. Going home," I yelled over the music, gesturing toward the doorway in case she couldn't hear me.

She nodded. "Are you going to be okay getting back alone?"

"I'll take a taxi."

Georgia gave me a hug and then said something to the guy she was dancing with. Smiling, he took my hand and led me across the floor to the entrance. While I got my coat, he pulled out a cell phone and ordered a taxi for me, walking me out to the street and waiting with me until it pulled up to the curb. "Thanks," I called after him. He waved, already walking back toward the club.

As I opened the cab door, I glanced back down the alley and saw Lucien standing outside, talking on his cell phone. As he looked up he caught my gaze, and I raised my hand to wave good-bye. He shot me a confident smile and saluted.

A slender redheaded boy standing with him turned his head to see who Lucien was waving to but quickly looked away.

I breathed in sharply and continued to stare as the car drove away. One second had been enough for me to recognize the boy with the bitter look on his face. It was Charles.

TWENTY-FIVE

I DIDN'T HEAR GEORGIA GET HOME THAT NIGHT, and slept late into the morning. When I awoke, it was to a feeling of expectation.

Half dreaming, Vincent's face from the day before floated through my mind. As he scanned the café with a brooding expression, I was overwhelmed with a mix of longing and pride. The dark, handsome boy was mine. At this thought a delicious feeling enveloped me, and I slowly opened my eyes.

And then my conscious mind kicked in and my heart plunged. Vincent wasn't mine. He was someone else's. And I was right back into the black hole of sadness and regret that had been my prison for the past three weeks.

Resolving to get out of the house, I decided to have my breakfast at the Café Sainte-Lucie, which I noticed had reopened the previous day.

On my way past the living room, I spotted Papy in his armchair, reading a newspaper and looking every bit like an older version of my father. He still sported a full head of hair at seventy-one. His noble looks, which had been inherited by Georgia, had unfortunately skipped right over me.

He peered over his paper. "How's my princess?" he asked, pushing his reading glasses up to his forehead.

"Fine, Papy. I'm just going out to have breakfast with J.D." I held up my copy of *The Catcher in the Rye* before stuffing it into my bag. He caught my hand in his and placed it on the chair arm next to him, using grandpa sign language for, *Stay for a minute.*

Papy spoke softly. "Mamie says she's worried about you. Do you want to talk?"

I shook my head and gave him a grateful smile.

"You know I'm here whenever you need me," he said, pulling his glasses back down to his nose.

"Thanks, Papy," I whispered, squeezing his hand before turning to leave.

I could never tell him about my problems. Even if I had just broken up with a regular human boyfriend, Papy couldn't really understand. He and Mamie lived in a perfectly functioning dreamworld. They were still madly in love and spent their time doing things they both enjoyed. They had a normal life. A stable life. They had everything I wanted.

The café owner welcomed me back personally, seating me in the front corner of the room, where I would have some privacy. I sipped my *café crème* and ate a croissant as I lost myself in my book. It must have been a half hour later when I realized that the chair across from me was occupied. Jules sat in front of me with a wicked grin on his face, his chestnut eyes sparkling with humor.

"So, Miss America, you thought you could pull a disappearing act and just abandon all of us. No such luck."

I almost laughed with happiness at seeing him again, but played it cool, asking, "What's the deal with you dead guys? Are you following me, or what? Last night Charles, and now you!"

"You saw Charles?"

"Yeah, he was at this club I went to over near Oberkampf." My voice slowed as I saw Jules's amazement.

"Which club?"

"Honestly, I don't even know what it was called. There wasn't a sign or anything."

"Did he say anything to you?"

"No, I was just leaving when I saw him standing outside. Why?"

Jules considered what I had told him, then shifted the conversation in a different direction. "So . . . when're you coming back?"

My smile faded. "I can't, Jules."

"You can't what?"

"I can't come back. I can't let myself be with Vincent."

"How about being with me, then?" Seeing him wink flirtatiously, I laughed. "Can't blame me for trying," he said, grabbing my hand across the table and lacing his fingers through mine.

I shot him an embarrassed smile and said, "You're incorrigible."

"And you're blushing."

I rolled my eyes toward the ceiling and said, "Being the young, dashing artist, Jules, I'm sure you have lots of girls just beating down your door."

"Yeah, we dead guys really score with the chicks." He let go of my hand and sat back in his chair, wearing a cocky expression. "Actually, since you have so adamantly refused my attentions, I feel free to tell you that I have several girlfriends that I see on rotation, just to make sure nothing gets too serious."

"Is one of them the barely dressed model I saw in your studio that day?"

"*That* is purely a professional relationship. Unlike what ours would be if you would just give me a chance." He puckered his lips in a sexy kiss.

"Oh, Jules. Stop!" I groaned and mock-punched him in the arm.

"Ow!" he said, rubbing the spot with his hand. "Damn, you're not just pretty, you pack a mean punch, too!"

"If you're going to sit here and torture me, then you can just get up and go back to that fancified mortuary you all live in," I said.

"Ooooh! She dares send the poor zombie boy away in shame! What if I bring news?"

I looked up at him. "News of what?"

"News that Vince is pining away for you. That he's inconsolable." Jules's tone was serious now. "That he's not only *technically* a 'dead man walking' . . . now he's emotionally one too."

My stomach clenched, and I fought to keep my voice steady. "Look, Jules, I'm really sorry. I wanted to give it a chance, but after seeing Charles carried home in a body bag . . ." I paused. Jules was staring at me with challenge in his eyes. It gave me strength.

"I can't let myself fall for Vincent if it means having a constant reminder of death. I've had enough of that to deal with in the last year."

He nodded. "I know about that. I'm sorry about your parents."

I took a deep breath, and my aching heart hardened as I spoke. "Besides, I don't think you're being honest with me. I saw Vincent yesterday sharing a very tender moment with a gorgeous blonde."

Jules acted like he hadn't heard me. Turning over his paper place mat, he took an artist's charcoal pencil out of his shirt pocket and began doodling on it. He talked as he drew.

"Vince wanted me to check on you. He doesn't dare approach you himself. He says he doesn't want to cause you any more agony. After seeing you sprint out of La Palette yesterday, he was afraid that you might have drawn the wrong conclusion. Which you obviously did."

I felt my temper flare. "Jules, I saw what I saw. How much more obvious could it have been?"

Jules seized my gaze. "Kate, you're obviously not stupid, so I'm assuming you must be incredibly blind. Geneviève is one of us. She's an old friend who's like a sister to us. Vincent's in love, but not with her."

My breath caught in my throat.

Satisfied that he had gotten my attention, he looked calmly

back down at his paper, concentrating intently on his scribbling as he continued. "He's trying to figure things out. To find a way around the situation. He asked me to tell you that."

Jules's gaze flickered up at me and then back down at his place mat. "Not bad," he said. He tore off a square and then, standing up, handed it to me.

It was a sketch of me, sitting there in the café. I looked like a Botticelli Venus, radiating serenity and natural loveliness. "I look beautiful," I said in awe, looking up from the drawing to his serious face.

"You *are* beautiful," he said, leaning over and kissing me softly on the forehead, before turning and striding out of the café.

TWENTY-SIX

WHEN I GOT HOME THE NEXT AFTERNOON FROM another book-reading session at the Café Sainte-Lucie, Mamie was coming out of the apartment with a visitor. Most of her clientele—paintings dealers and museum curators—stopped by on weekdays during working hours. So if someone came on the weekend, you could be sure it was a private collector.

The well-dressed man stood in the hallway with his back to me, holding a large, slender, brown-paper-wrapped package, watching Mamie lock our front door behind them. "You can take the elevator, and I'll carry the painting up the stairs," she was saying, when the man turned around. It was Jean-Baptiste.

"Oh!" I exclaimed. My body froze as my mind struggled over this head-on collision between my two worlds: the undead clan I had almost gotten mixed up with, and my own comforting mortal family.

"My dear girl, I've frightened you. My apologies!" His voice came out smooth and monotone, as if he were reading a script. He was dressed as he was the first time I saw him, wearing an expensive suit with a patterned silk ascot at the neck, and gray hair carefully oiled and combed back from his aristocratic face.

"Katya, dear, this is a new client of mine: Monsieur Grimod de La Reynière. Monsieur Grimod, my granddaughter, Kate. You got home at just the right time, dear. Could you carry this painting up the stairs to my studio? I'm afraid it's too big to put on the elevator."

Jean-Baptiste continued staring at me in amusement while Mamie opened the door to the tiny elevator. I could feel my anger mounting as he lifted a smug eyebrow. His trespassing into my world felt like a violation.

As in many Parisian apartment buildings, our elevator was tiny. It barely held two people standing side by side, but a third, or a large painting in this case, was impossible.

I lifted the paper-wrapped painting carefully by the edges and began inching my way up the remaining three flights of stairs. The painting was about half my size in height, but the frame had been removed, so it wasn't heavy.

I got to the top of the stairs just as Mamie unlocked her studio door, chatting animatedly with Jean-Baptiste as they entered. I stared at the back of his stiffly held form and wondered just what Vincent's "uncle" was doing here in my house. *First Jules, now Jean-Baptiste!* I thought. How could I move on if Vincent's "family" kept popping up in my life? My emotions had been in roller-coaster mode since talking with Jules, but I was determined to stick with my original decision—I was putting my heart at risk if I continued to see Vincent.

As I stepped through the doorway, I breathed the comforting odor of oil paints and varnish deeply into my lungs. Mamie's studio had always been one of my favorite places to hang out.

Six maids' rooms that took up the entire top floor of our building had been combined to make one large workspace, and most of the ceiling and roof had been knocked through to install frosted-glass skylights, which flooded the room with diffused sunlight.

Mamie's current restoration projects were scattered around the room on easels. A time-darkened old master painting of a herd of cows in a meadow sat across from a brightly colored Postimpressionist painting of cancan girls high-kicking their petticoats in a dance hall line, seemingly shocking a Spanish woman dressed in black, who prudishly held a fan in front of her lips on a nearby canvas.

"Let's have a look at this," Mamie said, taking the package from me and laying it down on a large worktable standing in the center of the room. She carefully removed the paper, and then turned the painting over and held it up to inspect it. It was a life-size portrait of a young man from the waist up, wearing a dark blue Napoleonic-looking soldier's uniform and a tall black plumed hat. The sitter was obviously Jean-Baptiste himself.

"My, you can certainly see the family resemblance," Mamie said in awe, looking from the painting to her client and back again.

Leaning forward, he touched a small rip in the canvas, at the level of the man's forehead. "The tear is here," he said.

"Well, it's a clean slice, so it will be easy to repair. Just a patch to the back, and we may not even need to touch it up. What did you say made the incision?"

"I didn't say, but it was a knife."

"Oh," exclaimed Mamie in surprise.

"Nothing to worry about. Grandkids roughhousing, you know. They've been banned from playing in the study from now on," he said, looking calmly at me as he spoke.

"Well, if you could just wait here, I've left my receipt book down in the apartment. Kate, could you please make Monsieur Grimod a coffee?" She nodded toward a coffeepot set up on a corner table and bustled out the door, leaving it open behind her.

The elderly revenant and I stood motionless until we heard the sound of the antique elevator lurching into motion. Then he took a step toward me.

"What are you doing here?"

"We must talk," he said, his authoritative voice grating on my nerves. "Jules tells me you saw Charles. Please tell me where."

I decided that the sooner I told Jean-Baptiste what he wanted to hear, the sooner he would leave. "He was standing outside a club I went to near Oberkampf. It was Friday, around midnight."

"Who was he there with?" Although he seemed nothing but composed on the surface, I could tell from a twitch at the corner of his mouth that things were not well.

"It looked like he had come there alone. Why?"

He glanced toward the door as if calculating the time he had to speak.

"I came here for two reasons." He spoke softly and quickly. "The first was to ask you about Charles. He disappeared a few days ago after"—he glanced at his portrait with distaste—"boning up on his knife-throwing skills.

"And the second was to pay an inconspicuous visit to your family. I needed to see where you were from."

My anger returned in a second. "What, you're spying on me? What do you mean 'where I'm from'? If my grandparents have money?" I shook my head in disgust. "Well, they do, but not as much as you. I don't see why it matters anyway." I began walking away from him, toward the door.

"Stop!" he commanded, and I did. "Money doesn't matter to me. Character does. Your grandparents are honorable. And safe."

"What, honorable enough to fix your painting?"

"No. Honorable enough to take into my confidence. If the need were ever to present itself."

As the meaning of his words began to dawn on me, my back stiffened. He was spying on my family to see if I was good enough for Vincent. He must not have gotten the memo that it was definitely and definitively *over*. "There will never be a need. Don't worry, Monsieur Grimod, I will not be intruding upon your precious home life again." Appallingly, I felt a tear run down my cheek, and I wiped it angrily away.

The sharp lines of his face softened. Touching my arm lightly with his fingers, he said, "But dear girl, you must come back. Vincent needs you. He is inconsolable."

I looked down at the ground and shook my head.

Jean-Baptiste placed his perfectly manicured fingers under my chin and lifted it until my eyes met his. "He is willing to make extreme sacrifices to be with you. You don't owe us—him—anything, but I would beg you to please come hear him out."

My resolve began to crumble. "I'll think about it," I whispered finally.

He nodded, satisfied.

"Thank you." His voice cracked as his lips uttered words they must rarely speak. He walked rapidly toward the door and began making his way down the stairs, as I heard the elevator ascend.

Mamie stepped out, looking down at her notebook, and then up at me as she came through the door. Glancing around the empty studio in confusion, she asked, "Well, where did he go?"

TWENTY-SEVEN

IT WAS RAINING. HARD. I WATCHED THE RAIN-drops hit my floor-to-ceiling windows with a force that made them ricochet into the pond that was forming on my balcony.

I had been thinking about Vincent ever since Jean-Baptiste had talked to me a few hours before, comparing what he had said to what Jules had told me in the café. Vincent was trying to work things out. To find a solution. Should I give him a chance to talk, or would that just be opening myself up to the risk of more pain?

What's better, I thought, *to be safe and suffer alone, or to risk pain and actually live?* Although my head and heart were leading me in two different directions, I was certain that I didn't want my life to resemble what it had for the last three weeks: a drab existence void of color, warmth, and life.

I walked to the windows and peered out into the darkening sky, wishing the answer to my question could be printed there in plain letters across the rain clouds. My gaze lowered to the park below, and I saw the form of a man leaning back against the park gate. He was standing in the pouring rain, no umbrella, looking up at my window. I stepped out onto the balcony.

A gust of cold air caught me, and I was immediately drenched by the beating rain, but I was able to see the upturned face, three stories below. It was Vincent. Our eyes met.

I hesitated for a second. *Should I?* I asked myself before realizing I had already made up my mind. Ducking back into my room, I grabbed a towel from a chair and dabbed my face and hair as I searched for my rain boots. Pulling them from under my bed, I raced out into the hallway, bumping into Mamie outside the kitchen.

"Katya, where are you going?" she asked.

"Have to go out. I'll call you if I'm going to be late," I said as I threw my coat on and grabbed an umbrella.

"Okay, darling. Just take care. It's pouring outside."

"I know, Mamie," I said, grabbing her and hugging her violently before I ran out the door.

"What has gotten into you?" I heard her call as the door slammed behind me and I sprinted down the stairs.

Once out the front door, I turned the corner of the building toward the park, and then came to an abrupt halt. There he was. Standing in the lashing rain, looking at me with an expression that made me stop in my tracks. It was an expression of dizzying relief. As if he had come across a pond of crystal clear water in the middle of a desert. I recognized it because I felt exactly the same.

I dropped my umbrella and threw myself on him. His strong

arms wrapped around me, lifting me up off the ground in a desperate embrace. "Oh, Kate," he breathed, nuzzling his head against mine.

"What are you doing out here?" I asked.

"Trying to be as near to you as possible," he said, kissing the raindrops off my cheek.

"How long . . . ," I began to ask.

"It's become a bit of a habit. I was just watching until I saw your light turn out. I never thought you'd see me," he responded, setting me down. "But let's get you out of the rain. Will you come back with me? Home? So we can talk?"

I nodded. He picked up my umbrella and, holding it over our heads, wrapped an arm around my shoulders and held me close the whole way.

As we stepped into the dappled light of the foyer, I faced Vincent and gasped. He was gaunt. He had lost weight, and his hollow eyes had dark circles beneath them. I hadn't noticed that in La Palette, having other things (like a gorgeous blond revenant) on my mind. But standing here, a couple of feet away from him, his deteriorated state was unmistakable. "Oh, Vincent!" I said, reaching toward his face.

"I haven't been well," he explained, catching my hand before I touched him and folding it into his. As soon as his skin touched mine, my insides turned into a warm gooey mess. "Let's go to my room," he said, and led me down the servants' hallway and through his open door.

The curtains had been flung open. Scattered embers glowed in the hearth, and the room smelled like a campfire. I stood and watched Vincent add some kindling to start the fire back up. He piled some logs on before returning to me.

"Are you cold?" he asked.

"I don't know if it's cold or nerves," I admitted, and held out my hand to show him how I was trembling. He immediately reached out to take me in his arms. "Oh, Kate," he breathed, kissing the top of my head. I felt him shiver when his lips brushed my hair.

He took my head in his hands, and his words rushed out in a torrent. "I can't tell you how I've struggled during the last few weeks. I tried to disappear out of your life. To let you go. I wanted you to be able to live a normal life, a safe life. And I was almost convinced I had done the right thing until I came to see you."

"You came to see me? When?" I asked.

"Starting a week ago. I had to see if you were okay. I watched you come and go for days. You didn't look like you were doing better. You actually seemed worse. And then when Charlotte overheard your sister and grandmother talking at the café, I knew I had been wrong to let you go."

"What did she hear?" I asked, a bad feeling forming in the pit of my stomach.

"They were worried about you. They talked about depression. About what they should do for you. About whether Georgia should take you back to New York."

Seeing my shock, Vincent settled me on the couch and sat down next to me. His fingers kneaded mine absentmindedly as

218

he spoke, and the motion and the pressure made me feel more grounded.

"I've been talking to Gaspard about this. He knows as much, or maybe more, than Jean-Baptiste about us. About our situation as revenants. I feel I've arrived at a solution that we could live with. That wouldn't demand as much from you. An *almost* normal existence. Can you listen?"

I nodded and tried to contain my feeling of hope. I had no idea what he was about to say.

"I apologize for not telling you more about myself from the start. I just didn't want to scare you off. I think that placed a barrier between the two of us. So I want to start from scratch.

"First: my story. I was born in 1924, as I told you, in a little town in Brittany. Our town was occupied soon after the Germans invaded in 1940. We didn't even try to fight them off. We didn't have the weapons, and it all happened too quickly to prepare a defense.

"I was in love with a girl named Hélène. We had grown up together, and our parents were best friends. A year after the Occupation began, I asked her to marry me. We were just seventeen, but age didn't seem to matter in the unpredictable atmosphere of war we lived in. My mother urged us to wait until we were eighteen, so we did.

"Our town was at the mercy of the German garrison stationed nearby, and we were expected to provide them with food, drink, and supplies. As well as . . . other, unofficial services." I could hear the fury rising in Vincent's voice as he continued, but

I remained silent, knowing that revisiting these memories must be hard for him.

"My parents and I were eating dinner at Hélène's house the night that two drunk German officers showed up at her family's door, demanding wine. Hélène's father explained that they had already turned over the entire contents of their wine cellar to the army, and had nothing left to offer them.

"'We'll see about that!' one of them said, and taking out their guns, they ordered Hélène and her younger sister to strip. Their mother rushed toward the officers, screaming her protest. They shot her, and then turned and shot my mother, who had jumped up to defend her friend. My father was the next to be killed.

"Hélène's father had lunged behind the door for the hunting rifle he kept hidden there, but before he could take aim, one of the Germans grabbed it from him and shot him in the leg, while the other pistol-whipped me as I tried to jump him. They kept us alive, but only so we could watch, bleeding and handcuffed to the doors. They . . . attacked . . . Hélène and her sister. Hélène put up a fight. They shot her, too." Vincent's voice cracked, but his eyes had become as hard as flint.

"The three of us were left to bury our dead. I offered to stay and care for Hélène's father and sister, but they asked me to go fight our attackers instead. I left that same night to join the Maquis."

"The Resistance," I said.

He nodded. "The rural arm of the Resistance. We hid out in the forest during the day and descended on German camps at night, stealing weapons and food and killing when we could.

"One day two of us were arrested in daylight, on suspicion of raiding a weapons shed the night before. Although I hadn't taken part in the raid, the friend I was with had organized the whole thing. They didn't have anything on us. But they were determined to make someone pay for the scandal.

"My friend had a wife and a child back in his hometown. I had no one. I told them that it had been me, and they shot me in the town square, as an example for the rest of the inhabitants."

"Oh, Vincent," I said, horrified, and my hands rose to my mouth.

"It's okay," he said softly, pulling my arms down and looking firmly into my eyes. "I'm here now, aren't I?"

He continued, "The story was in the next day's papers, and Jean-Baptiste, who was staying in a family home in the area, came to the country 'hospital' where they had laid me out. Claiming I was family, he took my body back with him and cared for me until I woke up two days later."

"How did he know that you were . . . like him?"

"Jean-Baptiste has 'the sight'—it's kind of like a radar for the 'transforming undead.' He sees auras."

"Like the New Agey kind of auras?" I asked doubtfully.

Vincent laughed. "Yeah, kind of like those. He tried to explain it to me once. Revenants' auras have their own color and vibrancy. After their first death, Jean-Baptiste can view revenants from miles away. He said it's like a spotlight pointed up into the sky.

"That's how he found Ambrose a couple of years later, after his American battalion was slaughtered on a Lorraine battlefield.

Jules died in World War One; the twins in World War Two; and Gaspard in a mid-nineteenth-century French-Austrian war."

"Gaspard was a soldier?"

Vincent laughed. "Does that surprise you?"

"Wouldn't he be a bit too nervous for battle?"

"He was a poet forced to be a soldier. Too sensitive a soul to have seen what he did on the battlefields."

I nodded pensively. "So almost all of you died during wartime?"

"Wartime is just the easiest time to find people who are dying in others' stead. It must happen all the time, but usually goes unnoticed."

"So what you're saying is that there are people dying all over France who could come back to life . . . under the right circumstances." My head hurt. It was all a bit overwhelming, even after having had more than a month to get used to the idea that the world I lived in was no longer the one I had always known.

Vincent laughed. "Kate, it's not just a French thing. I'll bet you walked past a good number of revenants in New York City without knowing that you were crossing paths with a zombie."

"So why you? I mean, in particular. I would guess that most lifesaving firefighters or policemen or soldiers don't wake up three days later."

Vincent said, "We still don't understand why some people are predisposed to be revenants. Jean-Baptiste thinks it's something genetic. Gaspard believes it's merely fate—that some humans have just been chosen. No one's found proof that it's anything other than that."

I wondered if it was magic or nature that had created Vincent and the others. It was getting harder for me to tell the two apart, now that the rules I had been taught were being turned upside down.

Vincent pulled over the table and poured me a glass of water. I took it gratefully and sipped as I watched him pile a few more logs onto the now dwindling fire.

He settled himself onto the floor in front of me. The couch was so low, and Vincent so tall, that his eyes were just underneath mine as he spoke cautiously now, carefully weighing each word.

"Kate, I've been trying to figure out how to work with this. I told you that I once lived to twenty-three. That was five years of avoiding the compulsion to die. Jean-Baptiste had asked me to hold out so that I could get a law degree in order to handle the family's papers. It was hard, but I was able to do it. He gave me that task because he knew I was stronger than the others. And I've seen him resisting his own urges for up to thirty-five years at a time. So I know it's possible.

"The woman you saw me with the other day. In La Palette..." Vincent wore a pained look.

"Yes, Geneviève. Jules told me she was just a friend."

"I hoped you would believe him. I know it must have looked... compromising. But I asked Geneviève to meet with me that day so that I could ask about her situation. She's married. To a human."

My jaw dropped. "But . . . how?"

"Her original death was around the same time as mine. She had just gotten married. And her husband lived. So when she animated, she went back to him, and has lived with him ever since."

"But he must be . . ."

"He's in his eighties." Vincent finished my thought.

My mind tried to wrap itself around the thought of the beautiful blond woman married to a man old enough to be her great-grandfather. I couldn't imagine what her life must be like.

"They're still madly in love, but it's been a hard life," Vincent continued. "She wasn't able to control her urges to die, and her husband encouraged her to follow the fate she was dealt as a revenant. He's proud of her, and she dotes on him. But soon enough it'll be his turn to die, and she'll be alone. It is one option, but not one that I would ever ask someone else to endure."

Vincent leaned forward and took my hands in his. They were warm and strong, and his touch sent a rush of excitement coursing through my body that lodged in my heart. "Kate," he said, "I can stay away from you. It would be a miserable existence, but I could do it if I knew you were happy.

"But if you want to be with me, too, I can offer you this solution: I will resist dying for as long as I am with you. I've talked to Jean-Baptiste, and we'll figure out a way for me to handle it. I won't put you through the repeated trauma of living through my deaths. I can't do anything about the fact that you will be without my physical presence for three days a month. But I can control the rest. And I will. If you decide to give me the chance."

TWENTY-EIGHT

WELL? WHAT *COULD* I SAY?
    I said, "Yes."

TWENTY-NINE

WE SAT ON THE FLOOR CUDDLED UP NEXT TO each other, facing the fire. "Are you hungry?" Vincent asked.

"Actually, I am," I confessed, surprising myself. I hadn't had much of an appetite for about . . . three weeks.

While he went to the kitchen, I phoned my grandmother. "Mamie, would you mind if I skipped dinner? I'm going to eat out."

"From the tone of your voice, would I be correct in guessing that this is about a certain boy?"

"Yes, I'm at Vincent's house."

"Well, good for you. I hope you can clear this all up and join us again in the land of the living." I flinched. If only she knew.

"We have a lot to talk about," I said. "I might be out late."

"Don't worry, darling Katya. But remember you have school tomorrow."

"No problem, Mamie."

My grandmother paused for so long that I wondered if she had hung up. "Mamie?" I asked after a few seconds.

"Katya," she said slowly, as if pondering something. Then, in a decisive voice, she continued, "Darling, forget what I just said. I think it's better to get things sorted out than to try to be sensible about getting a good night's sleep. Does Vincent live with his parents?"

"With his family."

"That's good. Well, if you decide to spend the night, give me a call so I won't worry."

"What?" I exclaimed.

"If it means having to take a sick day, then that's fine. You have my permission to stay at his family's house . . . in your own bed, of course."

"Nothing's going to happen between us!" I began to protest.

"I know." I could hear her smile through the headset. "You're almost seventeen, but you are older than that in your head. I trust you, Kate. Just take care of things and don't worry about coming home for me."

"That's very . . . progressive of you, Mamie," I said, paralyzed with amazement.

"I like to think I'm up with the times," she joked, and then said ardently, "Live, Katya. Be happy. Take risks. Have fun." And she hung up the phone.

My grandmother just gave me permission to have a sleepover with my boyfriend. That takes the cake for weirdness-of-the-day, I decided. *Even more than Vincent's pledge not to die for me.*

He returned with a huge tray of food. "Jeanne comes through for us once again," Vincent said, laying the tray down on the table. It was piled with thinly sliced charcuterie, *saucissons*, cheeses, baguettes, and five or six different kinds of olives. There was bottled water, juice, and a pot of tea. Exotic fruits were piled in a bowl, and tiny macaroons in different colors were stacked in a pyramid on a high-stemmed cake plate.

I popped a tiny ball of fresh goat cheese into my mouth and chased it with a sliver of oil-drenched sun-dried tomato. "I feel spoiled," I said dreamily, leaning my head on Vincent's shoulder. It felt so good to touch him after three weeks with only my pillow to hug.

"Good. That's exactly what I want you to feel. The only way I can compensate for this extraordinary situation is to make it up to you in an extraordinary way."

"Vincent, it's amazing just being here with you. I don't need anything else."

He smiled and said, "We'll see about that."

As we ate, something Jean-Baptiste had said earlier in the day popped into my mind.

"Vincent, what happened to Charles?"

He was silent for a moment. "What did Jean-Baptiste tell you?"

"That Charles threw a knife at his portrait and ran away."

"Yeah. Well, that was the end of the story. It started with the boat wreck and just got messier."

"What happened?"

"Well, the day after the rescue, when his mind woke back up,

Charles had Charlotte help him track down the mother of the girl who had died. He started following her around in volant form, wallowing in the guilt of not having saved her child. After he reanimated a couple of days later, he began stalking the woman. Leaving presents at her door. Taking flowers to the funeral home. He even attended the little girl's funeral."

"Very creepy."

Vincent nodded. "Charlotte was worried and told Jean-Baptiste the whole story. He sat Charles down and forbade him to see the woman. He even mentioned sending the twins to one of his houses in the south, to distance Charles from the situation until he got his head back together.

"And that's when Charles flipped. He was out of control, ranting about how unfair the whole thing was. How he didn't want to be a revenant for eternity, forced to sacrifice himself for people he didn't even know, and exiled if he tried to get involved in their lives. He blamed Jean-Baptiste for feeding and caring for him after he woke up, and not letting him die 'as nature intended' after he was shot. And that's when he threw the knife."

"At least he didn't throw it at Jean-Baptiste!"

"He might as well have, the way it hurt JB. Then he stalked out of the house, and Charlotte just about had a nervous breakdown." Vincent paused. "We're sure he'll come back once he gets it out of his system."

"He seems to have had a chip on his shoulder even before the boat accident," I said.

"Yeah. He's always been the most existentially minded of all of us. Not that I haven't thought long and hard about our purpose here. He's just had the hardest time accepting it."

That would explain a lot, I thought, feeling a little bit sorry for Charles.

"When did he leave?"

"Two days ago."

"That's when I saw him," I said. "Friday night, a bit after midnight."

"That's what Jean-Baptiste said. So . . . you were out clubbing without me?" He gave me a teasing smile. I could tell he was trying to lighten the atmosphere by changing the subject.

"I was attempting to dance my sorrows away."

"Did it work?"

"No."

"Maybe it would work if I were there," he said smugly. "Should we go out dancing some night?"

"I don't know. I've never seen a dead guy dance. Think you can keep up with me?" I joked, and in response Vincent grabbed my shoulders and leaned forward to press his lips firmly against mine.

My senses were instantly concentrated into those few tiny millimeters of our skin that were touching. And then he broke the connection, leaving my heart pounding in my throat, as if the kiss had yanked it up out of my chest.

"I take that as a yes?" I panted.

"I missed you," he said, and leaned in for more.

* * *

"It's late. You should be getting back," Vincent said after a couple of hours of lying on the couch and cuddling and catching up on all my nonevents.

"Actually, I have special permission from Mamie to stay at your family's house tonight, if I need the time to patch things up with you." I felt a wicked grin spread across my face.

"What?" From his look of surprise, it seemed I had finally told him something shocking instead of the usual vice versa. "I've got your grandma on my side? Will wonders never cease?"

"I'm not sure it's exactly on *your* side; it's more on my side. Or maybe even hers. She doesn't want me to waste away from misery under her own roof."

Vincent laughed. "Well, we wouldn't want to misuse Mamie's trust. You can take my bed. I don't need it anyway." He winked. "Anything to spend more time with *ma belle* Kate."

I melted inside.

While he concentrated on getting the fire restarted, I got up and wandered around his room, looking at his things for more clues as to who this mystery boy really was. When I reached his bedside table, I froze. Where my photo had stood was a small pot of flowers.

"I gave your photo to Charlotte," Vincent said, walking up behind me. "It was too hard for me to see your picture every day when I knew I couldn't see you in the flesh."

I touched his arm to show I wasn't upset. "I'll give you another one. That wasn't the most flattering of portraits, I have to say."

"Good idea," Vincent said and, digging a camera out of the table next to his bed, held it up like a trophy.

"Right now?" I grimaced, wondering if I looked as tired as I felt.

"Why not?" he asked, and standing next to me, he put his arm around my shoulder and held the camera out in front of us. "Hold still. It's better with no flash," he said, and pressed the shutter release. He turned the camera around so we could see the shot.

My heart was in my mouth as I looked at the image of myself standing next to this godlike boy. His eyes were half-shut, and in the dim light of the room the circles under them actually made him appear more handsome than ever—but with a hint of darkness.

And me . . . well, I was glowing. Next to him, I looked like I was where I was supposed to be. And I felt it too.

We sat up on Vincent's bed and talked until late in the night. Finally my eyes began to close on their own, and he asked if I wanted to sleep. "Want, no. Need, maybe. Too bad your revenant insomnia can't rub off on me." I smiled, stifling a yawn.

He pulled a light blue-green T-shirt out of a cupboard and tossed it to me across the room. "To match your eyes," he said.

I rolled my eyes at the cheesy remark but was secretly pleased that he happened to know my exact eye color. The shirt was big enough to come halfway down my thighs. "Perfect," I said, and looked up to notice that Vincent had turned around to face the wall.

"Go ahead," he said in a playful voice.

"What are you doing?" I asked him, laughing.

"If I am forced to watch Kate Mercier strip down to her undies in my very own bedroom, I'm afraid I won't be able to answer to Mamie for what might happen." The huskiness in his voice made me wish, for just a second, that he would follow through with his threat.

Pulling the shirt over my head, I said, "Okay, I'm decent."

He turned around and looked at me, whistling under his breath. "You're more than decent! You look practically edible."

"I thought revenants weren't into eating human flesh," I teased, blushing in spite of myself.

"I didn't claim we never lapsed when pushed beyond our limits," Vincent countered.

Wondering if all our conversations were going to be this bizarre, I shook my head with a smile and fished my phone out of my bag. Texting Georgia, I asked her to tell the school I was staying home "for personal reasons" and that I would bring a note from my grandmother on Tuesday.

And soon afterward, sitting on the bed with my back against the wall and my head on Vincent's shoulder, I fell asleep.

When I awoke in the morning, I was covered in blankets and resting on a whisper-soft feather pillow. Vincent was gone, but there was a note on the table.

Has anyone ever told you how cute you are when you sleep?

The urge to wake you up and tell you was too tempting,

so I left instead of risking your sleep-deprived wrath. Jeanne's got breakfast for you in the kitchen.

Throwing the previous day's clothes on, I walked groggily down the hallway to the kitchen. When Jeanne saw me walk in, she gave a cry and, running over to me, grabbed my head between her plump hands and planted a huge kiss on each of my cheeks.

"Oh, my little Kate. It's good to have you back. I was so happy when Vincent told me you were stopping by last night. And he actually ate this morning, for a change! I thought he was on a hunger strike, but he was just so sick over losing you. . . ." She stopped herself, putting a hand over her mouth.

"Listen to me run on, and you having just woken up. Sit, sit. I'll get you some breakfast. Coffee or tea?"

"Coffee," I said, flattered by all the attention.

Jeanne and I chatted while I was eating. She wanted to know everything about my family, where I was from, and what it was like to live in New York. I stayed for a little while after I finished eating, but couldn't wait to see Vincent.

Jeanne could tell. Picking up my empty cup and plate, she shooed me out of the kitchen. "I'm sure you don't want to spend your day in here with me. Go find Vincent. He's working out in the gym."

"Where's the gym?" I asked, curious about a side of Vincent's life I didn't yet know.

"Silly me, I keep thinking you know your way around, when you've only been here a couple of times. It's in the basement. The door to the left as you leave the kitchen."

I heard them before I saw them. The clang of steel against steel. The heavy breathing, groans, and exclamations. It sounded like the special effects sound track for a martial arts film was being played full blast in an echo chamber. I got to the bottom of the stairs and gasped as I looked around.

The room extended the entire length of the house. The stone ceiling was curved in a barrel arch. Tiny windows were hewn into the top of the wall along its length, at what must be ground level outside. Rays of sunlight angled into the room, transforming swirling dust motes into spooky-looking columns of smoke.

The walls were lined with arms and armor, everything from medieval crossbows, shields, and swords to battle-axes and pikes. Mixed in were more contemporary swords and an assortment of hunting rifles and old army guns.

In the middle of the room, Vincent was swinging a massive, two-handed sword at another man, whose black hair was pulled back into a short ponytail. He parried, holding up his own dangerous-looking blade to deflect the blow. Their speed and force was astonishing.

Vincent was wearing baggy black karate pants but was barefoot and shirtless. When he spun with the sword, his rock-hard abdominal muscles and broad chest rippled as he raised and lowered his weapon. He was chiseled, but not pumped up like Ambrose. His body was perfect.

After a few minutes of blatant spying, I stepped down into the room, and the other man glanced toward me and nodded.

"Kate!" Vincent called, jogging over to me. He took my face in his hands and gave me a sweaty peck on the lips. "Good morning, *mon ange*," he said. "Gaspard and I were just working out. We'll be done in a few minutes."

"Gaspard!" I exclaimed. "I didn't even recognize you!" With his wild hair pulled back from his face, he looked almost . . . normal. And in the intensity of the fight, he had lost all his awkwardness and hesitation.

"Don't let Gaspard's usual mad-poet appearance fool you," stated Vincent, reading my mind. "He's used the last hundred and fifty-odd years to study weaponry, and deigns to serve as martial arts instructor for us youngsters."

Gaspard forced the sword into its sheath. He approached and, making a half bow, said, "Mademoiselle Kate. I must say it is a pleasure to see you here again." Without his sword in hand, he quickly lost his smooth manner and transformed into the jittery man I had met once before. "I mean . . . under the circumstances . . . that is, with Vincent being so inconsolable . . ."

"If you stop there," I laughed, "I'll still be able to take it as a compliment."

"Yes, yes. Of course." He smiled nervously and nodded toward Vincent's sword lying on the floor. "Would you like to give it a try, Kate?"

"Do you have life insurance?" I laughed. "Because I could quite possibly kill the three of us if you let me hold a deadly blade."

"You might want to take off that sweater," Vincent said. I self-consciously pulled it off to reveal only a tank top underneath. He whistled appreciatively.

"Stop it!" I whispered, blushing.

Gaspard lifted his sword, and his face became calm. He smoothly urged me forward with his chin. Vincent positioned himself behind me, holding the grip in my hands between his own.

The sword looked like it had been stolen from the set of *Excalibur*—the kind you saw knights in suits of armor staggering around with under its massive weight. The hilt was in the shape of a cross, with a grip long enough to fit one hand over the other and still leave lots of space. Together, Vincent and I raised the sword off the ground. Then Vincent let go, and it dropped to the floor.

"Holy cow, how heavy is that thing?" I asked.

Vincent laughed. "We work out with the heaviest swords so that when we go to something smaller and more wieldy, it's like holding a feather. Try this instead," he said, and grabbed a smaller rapier off the wall.

"Okay, I can deal with this one," I laughed, testing its weight in my hand. Gaspard stood at the ready, and I advanced with Vincent standing behind me, arms around my own. Feeling his bare torso pressed tightly against my back and warm skin brushing my naked arms, I forgot what I was doing for a second, and the sword drooped toward the floor. Forcing myself to focus, I pulled it upright. *Concentrate,* I thought. I wanted to have at least a passing chance at avoiding complete humiliation.

They showed me a few traditional fencing moves in slow motion, and then changed to more dynamic, martial-arts-style swoop-and-spin movements. After five minutes I was already winded. Sheepishly I thanked Gaspard, saying I'd better sit the rest of the session out and start from scratch another time.

Taking the sword from my hand, Vincent gave my waist a playful squeeze and let me go. I watched from the sidelines for the next half hour as they changed from weapon to weapon, both of them displaying an awe-inspiring mastery of each one.

Finally I heard steps on the stairway, and Ambrose walked into the room. "So, Gaspard, are you done playing with the weakling and ready for a real man?" he jibed, and then, catching sight of me, flashed me a big smile.

"Katie-Lou, well I'll be. So we didn't manage to scare you off for good?"

I smiled and shook my head. "No such luck. Looks like you just might be stuck with me."

He gave me a hug, and then leaned back to look at me affectionately. "Fine with me. We could use some eye candy around here."

Hanging out with a houseful of men was going to be good for my self-esteem, I thought, whether or not those men were technically alive.

"Okay, back off, Ambrose. You might be bigger than me, but I've got a sword," Vincent said.

"Oh really?" laughed Ambrose and, reaching up with one hand, grabbed a battle-ax as tall as him from off the wall. "Let's see what you've got, Romeo!" And at that, the men began a three-way fight that topped anything I'd ever seen in the movies—and without any Hollywood special effects.

Finally Vincent called for a time-out. "Not that I couldn't

fight you all day, Ambrose, but I have a date, and it's bad manners to keep a lady waiting."

"Convenient, that, just as you were starting to get tired," chuckled Ambrose. Turning back to his teacher, he slowed to a more sustainable pace.

Vincent picked up a towel from a chair and mopped the sweat off his face. "Shower," he said. "I'll just be a minute." He walked to one corner of the room and stepped up into a pine box the size of a sauna, with a large showerhead sticking out of the open top.

Ambrose and Gaspard continued their workout, the older man looking like he could go for hours without a break. I watched, amazed, as they stopped and changed weapons, and began working on some fencing-style footwork while Gaspard called out instructions.

Until I had picked up that two-handed sword, I never imagined how difficult martial arts could be. The movies make it look so easy, with all the flying up walls and acrobatic swordplay. But here, with the sweating and grunting and force expended with every single movement, I realized that I was witnessing truly breathtaking skill. These men were lethal.

The hissing of the shower stopped, and Vincent stepped out with only a towel around his waist. He looked like a god straight out of a Renaissance painting, his brown skin stretched tightly over his muscular torso and black hair falling back from his face in waves. I felt like I was in a dream. And then that dream walked right up and took me by the hand. "Let's go up?" he asked.

I nodded, speechless.

THIRTY

ONCE WE WERE BACK IN HIS ROOM, VINCENT pulled some clean clothes out of a paneled cupboard set into the wall. He grinned at me. "Were you planning on watching?" I blushed and turned around.

"So, Vincent," I said, pretending to inspect his photo collection as I heard him dress behind me. "Can you come to dinner this weekend to meet my grandparents?"

"Finally, she asks. And unfortunately, I must decline."

"Why?" I asked, surprised. I turned to see him walking up to me with an amused expression.

"Because I will not be in any condition to meet your family this weekend, much less make conversation or even sit, propped up, at a dinner table."

"Oh," I said, "when are you dormant?" My voice faded as the strange word tripped off my tongue.

He picked his cell phone up from a table and checked the calendar. "Thursday, the twenty-seventh."

"That's Thanksgiving," I said. "We've got Thursday and Friday off school. It's a shame you won't be around."

"The clock stops for no man, especially my type. Sorry."

"Well, how about before then?" I asked. "Today's Monday. How about tomorrow night?"

He nodded. "That would work. It's a date. So . . . I'm meeting the grandparents? What should I wear?" he teased me.

"As long as you're not wearing a body bag, I should think you'll do just fine," I laughed, turning back to his collection of portraits.

Among the head shots of angelic children, battle-worn soldiers, and tough teenage hoodlums was an old black-and-white photo of a teenage girl. Her dark hair was crimped into a 1940s hairstyle, and she wore a flowery dress with squared shoulders. Both hands were raised to one side of her face, where she was securing a daisy behind her ear. Her dark lips were open in a playful smile. She was stunning.

"Who is this?" I asked, knowing the answer before the words had finished leaving my mouth.

Vincent walked up behind me and placed his hands on my arms. He smelled freshly washed, like lavender soap and some kind of musky shampoo. I sank back into him, and he wrapped his arms around me. "That's Hélène," he said softly.

"She was beautiful," I murmured.

He dropped his head to lean his chin on my shoulder, kissing it softly before he did. "Until I saw you, I didn't let myself think of any woman besides her. My life since her death has been spent avenging it."

Hearing the pain in his voice, I asked, "Did you ever find the soldiers who did it?"

"Yes."

"Did you . . ."

"Yes," he replied before I could say the words. "But it wasn't enough. I had to go after every other murderous villain I could find, and even when the worst of the occupiers and collaborators were gone, it wasn't enough."

It was hard to think about Vincent destroying people, either human or revenant. Although now that I had seen how well he fought, I knew that he and his kindred were probably capable of taking out an army. But what kind of person could spend more than half a century thinking only of vengeance?

The cool, dangerous edge that had both attracted and alarmed me when we met—it had a basis. Now I knew what it was. I envisioned his face contorted with fury, and shuddered at the thought.

"What is it, Kate?" Vincent said. "Would you prefer that I took her photo down?" I realized that I was still staring at the picture of Hélène.

"No!" I said, turning around to face him. "No, Vincent. She's a part of your past. I don't feel intimidated by the fact that you still think of her."

As the words left my lips, I realized that I was lying. I did feel intimidated by this beautiful woman. Vincent's only love. Even though the hairstyle and clothes placed her securely seventy years in the past, he had guarded her memory so closely that it had influenced everything he had done—and not done—since she died.

"It's been a long time, Kate. Sometimes it feels like yesterday, but usually it feels like a lifetime ago. It *was* a lifetime ago. Hélène is gone, and I hope you'll believe me when I tell you that you have no competition, from her or anyone else."

He looked like he had more to say but couldn't decide how to say it. I didn't push him. Getting off the topic of ex-loves was fine with me. I took him by the hand and led him away. And though we left the photos behind, my sense of unease remained.

"Get comfortable. I'll be right back," he said, and left the room. I turned my attention to the bookshelves, which were lined with books in several languages, all mixed together. Most of the English ones I recognized. *We have a similar taste in reading material,* I thought, smiling.

Spotting a row of fat photo albums on a lower shelf, I pulled one out and opened it. *1974–78* was handwritten on the inside cover, and I giggled as I began flipping through, seeing photos of Vincent wearing distinctly hippyish clothes and long hair with sideburns. Even though there was something ridiculous about the styles, he was just as handsome then as he was today. Nothing had changed but his accessories.

I turned a page and saw Ambrose and Jules standing together with competing enormous Afros. On another page, Charlotte was wearing Twiggy-style makeup and a micro-minidress, posed next to a Charles who looked like a teenage Jim Morrison: scraggly hair, shirtless, with rows of beaded necklaces. I couldn't stop myself from laughing out loud at that one.

"What's so funny?" Vincent asked, closing the door behind him. He set a bottle of water and a couple of glasses on the table and turned to me. "Aha, you've found my secret stash of blackmail photos."

"Show me some more, these are priceless," I said, bending over to slot the album back into its space.

I stood back up to find him standing inches away from me. "I don't know, Kate. Swallowing my pride enough to show you photos of me looking like a clown through most of the twentieth century might just cost you something."

"How much?" I breathed, transfixed by his sudden nearness. I unconsciously moistened my lips.

"Hmm. Let's see," he whispered, as he raised his hands to my waist and held me firmly. His fingers kneaded the small of my back, making my knees dissolve.

"It might cost you just a few kisses here...."

He leaned his head down to the side of my neck and held his mouth an inch away from my ear, exhaling warm breath onto my skin. I felt goose bumps rise all over my body as he slowly leaned forward and pressed his lips to the side of my neck.

I shuddered, and sighed instinctively as he began working his way with soft kisses downward, then moved slowly forward to my throat. When he got to the place between my collarbones, he paused and said, "Or maybe here...," and I felt him carefully touch the tip of his tongue to the soft skin in its hollow.

I moaned and reached my arms around his neck. He pulled me closer and, maintaining his torturously slow pace, began kissing up the front of my neck in little steps, until he reached my chin. My head fell back, and he cupped it with one hand, supporting me as his lips worked the short way from my chin to my mouth.

"Or here," he said, pausing before he brushed his lips against my own so lightly that my body tingled in anticipation. I waited, but nothing else came. Forcing my eyes open, I saw that his were closed, a look of concentration and willpower creasing his brow. He began to draw back, and his grip on me loosened.

I let a second pass. And then in desperation I grabbed his face and pulled him back to me. As our lips met, I crushed myself against him and threw my arms around his neck. He stumbled forward slightly and lifted his hand to the wall for support. I felt the bookcase press behind my shoulders and leaned backward against it, pulling him toward me.

"Whoa!" he said finally, managing to extricate himself from my grip. He took a step back, panting and holding me away from him. "Kate, I'm not going anywhere," he said with a mock look of reproof on his face. "I have to warn you that my bedroom isn't the best place to stage an assault on me. It's where I'm at my weakest, with my bed a mere twenty feet away."

I tried to focus on his words, but I couldn't quite pull myself back into the real world. "And you look so tempting," he said, his ragged breath slowing, "that I find it very hard to resist taking you to bed here and now."

He turned and quickly walked away from me, throwing his curtains aside and opening the window to let in the cold November air. I felt its icy fingers clear the fog in my head, and slid down the bookcase into a sitting position.

"You might be more comfortable over here," Vincent said, scooping me up into his strong arms and depositing me onto the couch. He set a glass of water in front of me. "Something to cool your ardor, *mademoiselle*?" he murmured, with an amused smile.

I nodded gratefully and drank deeply from the glass. Then, handing it back to him, I rolled over toward the back of the couch, in an attempt to bury my face. *Oh my God. What have I done?* I thought, cringing at the memory of leaping on him and practically devouring his face, just when he had made it clear that he was done.

"What, Kate?" Vincent chuckled, pulling my hands away from my reddening face.

"Sorry," I said, with a broken voice. I cleared my throat. "Sorry for . . . um . . . jumping on you in your own room. I'm not usually . . ."

"It's okay," Vincent said, hushing me, with a look on his face like he was about to crack up.

"No, it's not. I don't usually throw myself on people. I mean, I've only kissed about three guys in my life, and that's the first time I've ever lost myself like that. I'm just a bit . . . embarrassed. And surprised."

Vincent stopped trying to control himself and burst out laughing. Then, leaning over and kissing me on the forehead, he said,

"Well, it's a good surprise, then, Kate. I can't wait to get another chance. But not here. Somewhere very safe. Like on the Eiffel Tower with a hundred Japanese tourists standing around us."

I nodded, secretly relieved that he wanted to go slowly, but at the same time wondering why.

Vincent read my thoughts. "It's not that I don't want to take things . . . further. Trust me. I do." His eyes were smoldering. My heartbeat accelerated accordingly. "Just not quite yet. I want to enjoy getting to know you without rushing into . . . the main event." He ran his finger along my jawline and down my neck. "The wait will be fun, but it's not going to be easy."

As he leaned in to brush his lips lightly against mine, I felt like I had officially won the Perfect Boyfriend Contest. Hands down. *Although at the moment I can't help wishing he wasn't quite so perfect,* I thought, my temperature rising at his touch as he finished kissing me and pulled back. Trying to distract myself and avoid spontaneous combustion, I straightened my clothes and smoothed down my messed-up hair.

"We better get out of here before I ignore everything I just said. I'll walk you home," he said, picking up our coats and my bag. He opened the door and waited for me.

"I must say, I had my suspicions," he said cryptically.

"Suspicions of what?" I asked.

"That there was a savage beast hiding behind that good old-fashioned demeanor of yours," he laughed.

Biting my lip, I walked past him and into the hallway.

THIRTY-ONE

GOING HOME THAT NIGHT WAS LIKE AWAKING from a long sleep. When I was with Vincent I occasionally forgot about all the weird revenant stuff, but still felt like I was wandering through a Salvador Dalí dreamscape. Mamie and Papy's world felt amazingly comforting after twenty-four hours in a surrealist painting.

"So?" said Georgia as we sat down to dinner. "What is the status of this 'thing' with Vincent? Did your little pajama party give you two enough time to work out your problems?" She grinned wickedly at me and popped a piece of bread into her mouth.

Mamie tapped her on the arm reprovingly and said, "Katya will tell us what she wants us to know when she wants us to know it."

"That's okay, Mamie," I offered. "Georgia can't help herself from living vicariously through me, since she has no life of her own to speak of!"

"Ha!" said Georgia.

Papy rolled his eyes, obviously wondering how his peaceful home had so quickly transformed into a sorority house.

"So?" asked Georgia, wheedling now.

"We seem to have worked things out," I said, and turning to Mamie, asked, "Is it okay if he comes to dinner tomorrow night?"

"Of course," she responded with a broad smile.

"Woo-hoo!" crowed Georgia. "No more Kate pining away in her bedroom. I should go over to his house and thank him myself."

"That's enough now, Georgia," said Papy.

"You can thank him tomorrow night," I said, and quickly changed the subject.

At seven thirty the next night I got a text from Vincent: Good evening, *ma belle*. Could I please have your digicode?

I sent him the four-number and two-letter code, and a minute later our doorbell rang. I pushed the interphone, buzzing open the door to the stairwell. "Third floor, left," I said through the speakerphone.

My pulse sped up as I opened our front door and stood in the hallway waiting for him. He was up the three flights of stairs in no time, carrying a huge bouquet of flowers in one hand and a bag in the other. "These are for your Mamie," he said, leaning over to give me a quick, soft kiss on the lips.

The pounding of my heart went into overdrive. Vincent lifted his eyebrows suggestively. "Are you going to ask me in, or were you testing to see if I could cross your threshold without the invitation?" Then he whispered, "I'm a revenant, not a vampire, *chérie*." His teasing expression made me forget my nerves, and taking a deep breath to compose myself, I reached for his hand and led him through the doorway.

"Mamie's right here," I said as she walked out of the kitchen toward us. She had gone to her salon that morning and was looking stunningly elegant in a black-and-white wool dress and four-inch heels.

"You must be Vincent," she said, leaning over to kiss his cheeks, her gardenia-scented perfume enveloping us like a grandmotherly hug. She backed up a step to get a look at him. She seemed to be grading him, and from her expression he was getting an A.

"For you," he said, handing her the massive flower arrangement.

"Oh, from Christian Tortu," she said, spotting the florist's card. "How lovely."

"I'll take your coat," I said, and Vincent shrugged off his jacket, revealing a robin's-egg blue cotton shirt tucked into dark corduroys.

I could barely believe that this crushingly handsome boy had dressed up and brought flowers expressly to impress my family. He had done it all for me.

"Papy, I would like to introduce you to Vincent Delacroix," I said as my grandfather approached from his study.

"Nice to meet you, sir," Vincent said in a formal manner as they shook hands. He held up the bag and said, "For you."

Taking it, Papy pulled out a bottle and looked startled as he inspected the label. "Château Margaux, 1947? Wherever did you find this?"

"It's a gift from my uncle, who says he has already had the pleasure of making your acquaintance, madame," Vincent said, looking back at Mamie.

"Oh?" she said, her interest piqued.

"He recently brought you a painting to repair. Monsieur Grimod de La Reynière."

Mamie's eyes widened. "Jean-Baptiste Grimod de La Reynière is your uncle?"

Vincent nodded. "I have lived with him since my parents died."

"Oh," Mamie said, her eyes softening. "I am sorry to hear that you have that in common with our Katya."

Fearing more in-depth questions, I took Vincent by the hand and quickly turned toward the sitting room. "Would you like something to drink? Maybe a bit of bubbly?" Papy asked as we sat down next to the fire.

"That would be nice. Thank you," said Vincent.

"Yes, please," I said, nodding at Papy, and he left the room, just as Georgia made her way in.

She looked stunning in a green silk frock that made my own simple black dress look drab in comparison. Vincent stood up politely. "Georgia," he began, "I know that Kate apologized for me after we left you at that restaurant. But I just wanted to tell you myself. I am so sorry. I never would have done it if Ambrose hadn't been in such a bad state. Even so, it was unforgivable."

"I consider myself a very understanding person," she said, with just a tinge of her fake Southern accent coming through. "If you weren't so darn cute, I'm not sure I would let this one go. However, under the circumstances . . . ," she trailed off as she slowly kissed his cheeks.

"For God's sake, Georgia! Could you try to leave a bit of him for me?" I exclaimed, shaking my head in disbelief.

"I'll take that to mean I'm forgiven," Vincent said, laughing.

Meals in France can last for hours. And when guests are invited, they usually do. Luckily, since tonight was a school night, we only spent a half hour over each course. I didn't want my grandparents to have enough time to get too far past the polite conversation stage into the personal information stage with my mysterious guest.

"So, Vincent, I would guess you're a student?" Papy asked about halfway through the hors d'oeuvres. Vincent answered that he was studying law. "At such a young age? Not wanting to pry, but how old . . ." My grandfather let his sentence fade out so he wouldn't have to ask a direct question.

"I'm nineteen. But my uncle had me tutored privately, so I'm a couple of years ahead."

"Lucky boy!" Papy nodded approvingly.

After that, Vincent deflected more personal questions by asking his own. Papy was delighted to tell him in detail about his business and the travels he had made to pick up the special objects he dealt in, which had taken him all over the Middle East and North Africa.

Vincent mentioned his interest in antique and ancient weaponry, and that conversation alone got us through the main dish, a tender-as-butter side of beef. Mamie asked him about his uncle's painting collection and seemed impressed by his broad knowledge of the artists and stylistic periods.

By the time we had gotten to dessert, Vincent and my family were talking and laughing together as if they had known one another for years. He and Georgia teased each other and teased me, and I could see Mamie glancing between Vincent and myself and looking pleased with what she saw.

Finally, after settling into the comfortable sitting room chairs with decaf espressos and a plate of chocolate truffles, Mamie asked Vincent if he would like to join us for dinner in two weeks. "It's Kate's seventeenth birthday on December ninth, and since she refused to let us give her a party, we thought we'd have an informal dinner here at home."

"Now *that* is very interesting information," Vincent said, smiling broadly at me.

I put my head in my hands and shook my head. "I don't like to make a big deal about birthdays," I moaned.

Vincent gestured to the others and said, "Well, too bad that the rest of us do!"

"It's settled, then?" asked Mamie, looking at me for approval.

I grimaced but nodded my head.

"Now that we're handing invitations out left and right, how about coming out with me and Kate on Friday night, Vincent?" asked Georgia.

"I would love to, but I already have plans that night." He winked at me.

"Not with Kate, you don't!" said Georgia defensively. "She's promised my friend Lucien to come to a party at his club. And from what I've heard, you might want to accompany her, since he's promised to supply a crop of handsome friends for all the single ladies showing—" Georgia stopped midsentence, seeing the dark look spreading across Vincent's face.

"Are you talking about Lucien Poitevin?" he asked.

Georgia nodded. "Do you know him?"

Vincent's face turned flame red in seconds flat. He looked like a pressure cooker about to explode. "I know *of* him. And quite honestly, even if I didn't already have plans, I would have to refuse." I could tell he was using great restraint to sound calm.

"Vincent!" I whispered. "What—" He cut me off by taking my hand and unintentionally (I hoped) squeezing it so hard it hurt. *This is officially very bad,* I thought.

"Who is this Lucien Poitevin?" asked Papy sternly, frowning at Georgia.

"He's a very good friend!" she retorted, glaring at Vincent.

The room was quiet. Vincent finally leaned toward her and said in his most diplomatic voice, "I wouldn't say this if I wasn't a hundred percent sure of myself, but Lucien Poitevin doesn't deserve to stand in the same room as you, Georgia, much less be counted among your friends."

There was a collective dropping of jaws. Georgia, for once, seemed lost for words. She looked like she had been slapped. And then had a bucket of ice poured down her back.

Mamie and Papy gave each other a look that made it clear they had been worrying about Georgia's nocturnal activities.

Georgia gave both me and Vincent an evil glare and then stood abruptly and stormed out of the room.

Mamie broke the silence. "Vincent, could you clarify why you think Georgia shouldn't be associating with this man?"

Vincent was staring at the coffee table. "Excuse me for causing this lovely dinner to end on a bad note. It's just that I know of this person, and wouldn't want anyone I cared about to have anything to do with him. But I've said enough. Again, my apologies for upsetting your granddaughter in your own home."

Papy shook his head and held a hand up, as if it was no trouble, and Mamie stood to collect the cups. As I got up to help her, she said, "Now don't worry yourself, Vincent. We try to keep a certain measure of openness and honesty in this household, so your comments are not unwelcome. I'm sure Georgia will apologize for her temper next time she sees you."

"Don't bet on it," I said under my breath.

Hearing me, Vincent nodded grimly. "I should be going," he said. "I'm sure you all have a busy day ahead of you tomorrow."

"I'll walk you out," I said, intending to grill him as soon as we got outside.

Papy stood to get Vincent's coat. After thanking my grandparents for the evening, Vincent stepped out into the hallway. I followed, taking my coat and closing the door behind us.

"What—" I began.

Vincent put a finger to his lips, and we maintained a tense

255

silence until we got outside. As soon as the door shut behind us, he grabbed me by the shoulders and looked intently into my face. "Your sister is in grave danger."

My confusion transformed into alarm. "What are you talking about? What's wrong with Lucien?"

"He's my sworn enemy. The leader of the Paris numa."

I felt like someone had picked me up and thrown me against a brick wall. "Are you sure we're talking about the same person?" I asked, refusing to believe it. "Because when I met him—"

"You met him?" Vincent choked. "Where?"

"At that club where I went dancing with Georgia."

"The same place you saw Charles?"

"Yeah—in fact, Charles was talking to him outside when I left. I don't see—"

"No. This is terrible," Vincent said, shutting his eyes.

"Vincent. Tell me what's going on," I said, a sick feeling rising in my throat. If Lucien was a monster, what did that mean for my sister? I shivered as I thought of the kiss Georgia shared with Lucien that night in his club. She obviously didn't know about his dark side. Georgia couldn't see past her own nose when it came to discernment. As my mom lamented once when a boyfriend of Georgia's was arrested for burglary, "She can't ever see the bad in people. Your sister's not stupid, she just doesn't possess an ounce of intuition." *This time that flaw could be fatal,* I thought.

Vincent pulled his phone out of his pocket. "Jean-Baptiste? Lucien's got Charles. I'm sure. Yeah . . . be there in a minute."

"Please! Talk to me!" I begged him.

"I have to get home. Can you come with me?"

"No." I shook my head. I had to go back and clean up the mess that Hurricane Vincent had left for my family.

"I have to go," he said.

"Then I'll walk you home," I insisted. "You can tell me on the way."

"Good," he said, taking my hand as we began walking down the lamp-lit streets toward his house. "So, Kate. You know how there's a bad guy in every story?"

"I guess."

"Well, Lucien's the bad guy in my story."

"What do you mean *your* story?" I ventured uneasily. "I mean, is it just a case of the two of you being on opposite sides of the good-and-evil divide?"

Vincent shook his head. "No. It's me against him. We have a long history."

"Wait," I said, putting together the puzzle pieces in my mind. "Is he the one you guys are always referring to? 'The Man,' or whatever?" I paused, thinking. "Was it Lucien you saw at the Village Saint-Paul . . . and who Jules spotted nearby when Ambrose got stabbed?"

Vincent nodded.

"Who is he?" I asked.

"As a human, during World War Two, he was part of the French Militia, or *la Milice*, a paramilitary force formed by the German-controlled French government to fight the Resistance."

"The Vichy regime?"

Vincent nodded. "Besides executing and assassinating Resistance members, the Milice helped round up Jews for deportation. They were famous for their torture methods: They could extract information and confessions from anyone they captured.

"To be honest, they were more dangerous than the Gestapo or SS, since they were one of us: They spoke the language, knew the topography of the towns, and were friends and neighbors of the people they betrayed." Vincent looked me in the eyes. "It was a dark time for my country."

I nodded and remained silent. We crossed a tree-lined avenue and continued toward his house.

"Lucien betrayed hundreds, or indirectly, thousands, of his own countrymen to their deaths, torturing and murdering his way up through the organization's ranks. He quickly became a top man in the Vichy regime's information and propaganda ministry.

"In June of 1944, a group of Resistance fighters, dressed as members of the Milice, broke into the Ministry of Information building where Lucien and his wife had been moved for their safety. It was late at night. They found the couple in their bed and killed them."

My jaw dropped. It seemed like he was telling the story from personal experience. "Were you one of them?" I ventured.

Vincent nodded. "Along with a couple of other revenants. The rest were humans who didn't know what we were."

"But Lucien was still human then. You told me revenants try not to kill humans."

"Our order was to capture and imprison Lucien until he could be tried by the authorities for his crimes. But one human in our group had had his family killed by Lucien himself, and he couldn't restrain himself. He shot them both."

I shuddered at the gory scene reenacted in my mind. In stories like this, you always want the bad guys to be taken out. But thinking about the actual act: to be shot with his wife . . . in his bed. It was too horrible to consider.

"Lucien remembered our faces from that night, and when he came back as a revenant, he hunted us down. He succeeded in killing the majority of the humans who had taken part in the assassination, and was eventually able to destroy the other two revenants involved. I'm the only one left. We've come up against each other on several occasions, but he's never managed to kill me. Nor I him."

"Then why in the world would Charles have been talking to him?" I asked.

"This is what you have to understand about Charles. He's not a bad kid. He's just messed up. I told you he's had a hard time accepting our fate. It's a difficult existence, continually living and dying. When you save someone and see them go on to have a good life, it makes it all feel worthwhile. But sometimes things don't turn out like that.

"The person you rescued from a suicide attempt tries again and succeeds. The kid you save in a drug deal gone bad doesn't see it as a reason to mend his ways and returns to the mess he was in before. That's one reason Jean-Baptiste doesn't want us following our rescues' lives too closely.

"But one of the worst feelings is when you try and fail. Charles couldn't save the little girl. He saved the other child, but he can't focus on that success. He is obsessed with his failure. And its consequences on the child's mother.

"He has a good heart," he continued softly. "Maybe too good of a heart. But this was the final straw for him. The only reason I can think of that Charles would go to Lucien is because he can't cope with our lifestyle any longer. He wants to die. If he puts himself in their hands, all he has to do is ask them to kill him and burn his body. And they'd be all too happy to comply."

"He's committing suicide?" I stopped walking, horrified by the thought of Charles delivering himself to his death.

"That's what it looks like." Vincent took my arm and pulled me forward. We were almost there.

"If Lucien is a vicious killer, then . . . what about Georgia?" Charles's story was heartbreaking, but all I could think about at the moment was the danger my sister could be in.

"What's their relationship?" Vincent asked.

"It seems like they're kind of dating."

"Do you think it's serious?"

"Georgia doesn't *do* serious."

Vincent thought about it. "Lucien is always surrounded by women, and he would have no reason to kill someone like Georgia. If she doesn't let herself get sucked into his clan and their activities, then the worst she probably risks is getting used and dumped by him."

Well, that's comforting, I thought, not at all comforted. *She's swapping spit with a homicidal maniac, but if she doesn't get too involved, she should be fine.* Although I was still frightened, Vincent's words *had* made me feel less panicky. It was true: Georgia never got too involved in anyone besides herself.

We arrived at Jean-Baptiste's gate. Vincent took my hand in his. "Listen. I'm sorry if I've messed up things between your sister and your grandparents tonight. But I couldn't just sit there and say nothing after hearing her mention that . . . monster."

"No, you were right. And it didn't matter where you said it, in front of everyone or one-on-one: Georgia would have had the same reaction."

"You've got to talk to her," he urged. "Even if things don't go too far with Lucien, she's hanging out with some dangerous people."

I nodded at him. "I'll do my best."

Danger was constantly lurking in the shadows for Vincent and his kindred. But now that one of my family members was at risk, it seemed much more real. It made me feel closer to him. We now had a common foe. But I hoped that Georgia would listen to me and remove herself from that danger.

"What are you going to do now?" I asked.

"I'm going to get the others and start hunting Lucien down." Vincent's voice shifted an octave lower and his eyes blazed with anger. He looked lethal.

"You're going to be careful, right?" I asked, fear gripping me as

I realized what this could mean.

"I would take him out tonight if I could. But there's a reason I haven't been able to destroy him yet. If he doesn't want to be found, we're not going to find him. The cards are in his hands."

Then, seeing my expression, some of the steeliness went out of his features. "Don't worry, Kate. Try to come over after school tomorrow if you can."

"Are you still going to be alive tomorrow after school?"

"Yes," he said with his lips. But his eyes were telling a different story. He would do anything to destroy this enemy. It was clear that his own safety wasn't his priority.

"I'm sorry I have to leave you like this," Vincent said, drawing me to him and brushing his lips against mine. Every point of contact with his body seemed to trigger a shower of fiery sparks inside me. *Is danger an aphrodisiac?* I wondered. I'd rather him be safe than have a Fourth of July celebration in my nerve endings. But since I didn't have a say, I grabbed him tighter and responded to his kiss.

Too soon, he pulled away. "I have to go."

"I know. Good night, Vincent. Please be safe."

"Good night, *mon ange.*"

I knocked softly on Georgia's bedroom door. It opened violently a second later, and my sister stood there looking like a Fury. "What the hell was that about?" she raged, slamming the door shut behind me.

I perched on the edge of her bed while she threw herself

belly-down onto a fluffy white rug in the middle of her floor and stared at me.

"I'm sorry Vincent embarrassed you in front of Papy and Mamie. But from what he's told me, Lucien does sound like really bad news."

Georgia almost spit her reply. "Oh yeah? What exactly does he say?"

"He said that Lucien's kind of in a . . . Mafia type of organization." I tried to remember how Vincent had described the numa that night in the Marais restaurant. "And that his colleagues are involved in all sorts of illegal dealings."

"Like what?"

"Prostitution, drugs—"

"Oh, give me a break!" Georgia rolled her eyes. "You've seen Lucien. He's an entrepreneur. He's got bars and clubs all over France. Why in the world would he even need to be involved in stuff like that?" She looked at me with distaste.

"I really don't think Vincent would make that up," I replied.

"Yeah?" she asked bitterly. "How's he know him?"

"He doesn't," I lied. The last thing I wanted to do was to make some sort of link between Vincent and Lucien with Georgia and me in the middle. "He just knows his reputation."

I paused, weighing how far I should go. "He said there's even talk of Lucien's associates being involved in murders."

Georgia looked shocked for a moment, and then shook her head. "I'm sure that in the world that Lucien moves in, there have got to be some shady dealings. It must go with the territory. But to suggest that he could work with murderers . . . I'm sorry, I just don't believe it."

"It's okay," I said. "You don't have to believe it. But do you have to see him again?"

"Kate, we're barely even seeing each other. It's not serious. We only see each other out in public. I'm sure he dates other people, and so do I. No big deal!"

"Well, if it's not a big deal, and there's even the slightest chance that he's bad news, then why don't you just . . . you know . . . ditch him? Please, Georgia. I don't want to worry about you."

For a split second after hearing my pleading voice she looked uncertain, and then a stubborn look stole over her pretty face. "I don't *have* to see him again. But I'm *going* to see him again. I don't believe a word you or Vincent has said about him. And why are you and your new boyfriend getting all involved in my private life anyway?"

I knew I couldn't say a thing that would change her mind. And how would I say it, anyway? "The reason my boyfriend hates yours is because Vincent's a good zombie and Lucien's a bad zombie?" I could only hope she would lose interest in Lucien before anything bad happened.

She was really mad now. Her light dusting of freckles was becoming mottled by angry red patches. I knew my sister, and when she got to this point, there was no more reasoning with her. I began to stand, but she sprang up and beat me to the door. Opening it, she pointed to the hallway. "Go."

THIRTY-TWO

THE NEXT DAY GEORGIA LEFT FOR SCHOOL BEFORE I even got to the breakfast table. From behind his newspaper, Papy asked tiredly, "Are you girls on World War Four now, or is it Five?"

I didn't see her between classes, and she disappeared afterward. My sister was avoiding me, and that hurt. But I knew I had done the right thing by warning her about Lucien. Vincent had said that nothing might happen to her. But in these circumstances, "might," for me, was too big a word.

I headed to Jean-Baptiste's on the way home, texting Vincent from the street, and the gates were opening by the time I arrived. He was waiting for me, the same worried look on his face as he had worn when he left me last night.

"Any news?" I asked as we walked to his room.

"No." He leaned forward and opened his door, politely standing aside to let me by before following me in. *There are some advantages to dating a guy from another era,* I thought. Though I am a big believer in gender equality, chivalry scores high in my book.

"We were out all night searching. It's like all the numa in town just up and disappeared. We went to every bar and restaurant that we know they have a finger in, and only saw human employees—no trace of them."

"That could have been really dangerous, couldn't it?" I tried to imagine what would happen in a standoff between the good and evil revenants. The undead leaping around with swords among a frightened bar clientele.

"*If* they had been there, then it could have been dangerous. But with humans around they wouldn't dare attack us."

I thought about Ambrose getting stabbed just a few feet away from a crowd of humans and suspected Vincent was downplaying the danger for my benefit.

"But no one was in sight for us to interrogate. They don't have one fixed residence like us. So it's impossible to know where they're based."

"How's Charlotte taking it?" I asked.

"Not well," Vincent said. "She's out with the others right now, looking."

"Why aren't you with them?"

"Tonight's the 'big night.' And I'm already feeling weak. I wouldn't be much help if we actually found anything."

"So when does it start . . . the dormancy thing?" I asked.

"During the night," he responded. "The evening I begin

266

dormancy, I usually end up watching movies and loading up on some calories, since I'm no good for anything else." He waved his hand toward the coffee table, which was set with tea and an assortment of mini pastries.

I looked at him in amusement. "Jeanne?"

"Who else?" he responded with a chuckle. "Every time you stop by she acts like we're receiving visiting royalty."

"As she should," I said, holding my chin a bit higher before throwing myself onto the couch in order to attack a mini chocolate éclair. "So where's the TV?" I asked.

"Oh, I watch in our screening room. Ambrose is a movie buff, and he convinced Jean-Baptiste to build our own cinema here. It's in the basement, alongside the gym."

"Now that is something I would love to see," I said.

"I may just have one or two of your favorite films waiting downstairs for you. We could even order some pizza and dine in style. Is it a date?"

"A real date! I accept!" I almost squealed, and then, trying to dampen my enthusiasm, continued, "Only since you claim you'll be such boring company, of course. Otherwise I'd be fine just sitting here, staring into your eyes all night."

Vincent paused, looking at me suspiciously for a second, and then, grinning, asked, "Sarcasm?"

"Yes," I laughed. "You're pretty quick for an old guy."

"Damn, and I thought I had finally found a true romantic," he joked, and then hesitated as a serious look stole over his face. "Speaking of boring company, do you mind talking about what we'll do while I'm asleep?"

"Sure," I said, wondering what could possibly come next.

"Tomorrow I'll be body-and-mind dead. I would rather you not see me when I'm unable to communicate. But starting Friday morning, my mind will be awake. So that you won't feel like I'm stalking you, do I have your okay to come and see you . . . in volant form?"

"Hmm. That's got to be the strangest offer I've ever received," I laughed. "I don't know . . . can you do anything to let me know you're there? Like write me a ghostly text message? Or make my pen move?"

He shook his head. "Only if someone comes along who can hear me, like Charlotte or Jules."

Thinking of my messy bedroom, which I hoped he hadn't already secretly seen while floating around, I countered, "Aren't you going to be on 'walking duty' with someone?"

Vincent smiled, tiny lines of fatigue creasing the corners of his eyes. "Well, yes, if anyone's walking I'll be going along. But I'd like to come see you in my downtime."

"Then why don't I come here?" I asked. "That way whoever's home can 'interpret' for me."

"If you don't mind, that would be nice," Vincent said. I noticed he was steadying himself on the couch with one hand.

"Are you okay, Vincent?" I asked.

"Yes. Although I'm starting to feel weak. No biggie." He exhaled deeply and sat down on the couch next to me. "So tomorrow's a no-go, but I'd love to see you Friday."

"Deal. I'll come over in the morning. Since tomorrow's Thanksgiving in the States, school's out tomorrow and Friday. I'll just bring my homework and do it here."

We ordered pizza and curled up on the couch to wait for it to arrive. "How did it go last night with Georgia?" he asked.

I had been scrupulously avoiding the issue, hoping I wouldn't have to tell Vincent that I had failed.

"We're not speaking," I admitted.

"What happened?"

"I didn't tell her that you knew Lucien. I was afraid she might say something to him. I just told her that you knew his reputation, and what kind of criminal dealings he and his associates were known for. She didn't buy it. She wants you and me to stay out of her business."

"You're upset," he said, wrapping his arms around me.

"Yes. I'm upset . . . not that Georgia and I are fighting. That's nothing out of the ordinary. I'm upset because I'm afraid for her. She told me that they're only seeing each other casually. But I can't help but worry."

"You've done everything you can," Vincent said. "You can't control your sister. Just try to put it out of your mind."

Easier said than done.

After our pizzas were delivered, we moved downstairs to the screening room and plopped down onto a massive old worn-leather couch to watch *Breakfast at Tiffany's*, which Vincent had pulled from their vast movie collection. Sitting there in the darkened room and munching on slices of mushroom and Parmesan, for once I actually felt like Vincent and I were doing something a real, normal couple would do . . . that is, if I didn't think about what was going to happen to him after midnight.

I left around nine. He insisted on walking me home, and we strolled along the darkened Paris streets at a snail's pace. He seemed as weak as if he were actually eighty-seven years old. It was hard to believe that this same guy had been wielding a sword the weight of a couch just a few days earlier. When we got to my door, he gave me a slow, tender kiss and turned to go.

"Be careful," I said, not knowing the etiquette of saying good-bye to someone who was going to spend the next three days dead. Vincent winked and blew me a kiss, and turning the corner, he was gone.

THIRTY-THREE

MAMIE HAD ASKED US IF WE WANTED TO HAVE A traditional Thanksgiving dinner, but neither Georgia nor I felt like it. Anything American reminded me of home. And home reminded me of my parents. I asked Mamie if we could treat it like any other day, and she agreed.

So I spent Thanksgiving Day on my bed reading, trying not to think of my boyfriend, dead on his bed a few blocks away.

On Friday morning, I walked the five minutes from my house to Jean-Baptiste's. Standing outside the massive gates, I typed the digicode that Vincent had texted me into the security box and watched the gates swing open.

Once at the front door, I wasn't sure whether I should knock or just walk in. As I raised my hand the door opened, and Gaspard stood in front of me, nervously wringing his hands.

"Mademoiselle Kate," he said, giving me an awkward little

bow. "Vincent told me you were here. Come in, come in." He didn't even attempt to give me the *bises*, and, afraid that my mere presence was giving him a heart attack, I didn't insist.

"Any news?" I asked.

"Sadly, no," Gaspard said. "Come back to the kitchen. Vincent's telling me to ask if you want a coffee."

"No, no, I just had breakfast. I'm fine."

"Ah, okay then. Vincent says if you want to come back to his room, he's ready to help you with your . . . trig?" Gaspard looked confused.

"Trigonometry," I said to him, laughing. And then to the air I said, "Thanks, Vincent, but I left it at home. You get to look over my shoulder for English lit and European history today."

Gaspard laughed a nervous laugh. "Vincent says that I should be the one to help you with that. My, my, it's true, I have been around to see a bit of history. But I wouldn't want to bore you with my tales."

Sensing that helping a teenager with her history homework would be the last way he would want to spend his morning, I politely declined, to his obvious relief.

"Charlotte's out, but I'll let her know you're here when she returns," he said, dropping me off in front of Vincent's door.

"Thank you," I responded.

Vincent's room was as I had seen it the first time. Windows and curtains closed. Fire cold in the hearth. And Vincent cold on the bed. I shivered as I saw his motionless form behind the gauze bed curtains.

Shutting the door behind me, I placed my bag on the couch and approached the bed. He lay there completely immobile. Devoid of life. It struck me how different he looked from somebody who was merely sleeping, with their chest in perpetual motion, breath coming in and out of their mouth. Pulling the drapes back, I gingerly sat down on the bed and gazed at him, magnificent even in death.

"Okay, I feel a bit silly talking to you like this," I said to the empty room. "Like in a minute you're going to jump out of the closet and laugh your head off."

The room was silent.

Hesitating, I ran my fingers lightly down his cold arm, trying not to recoil at the inhuman feel of his skin. Then, even more slowly, I leaned over to touch his mouth with my thumb. The skin was cold, but soft, and I thrilled at the sensation of my fingertips against his curved, perfect lips. Encouraged, I caressed his thick, wavy hair with my hand before touching my lips very lightly to his own. I didn't feel anything. Vincent wasn't there.

"Am I taking advantage of the situation," I whispered, wondering if he was there to hear me, "since you couldn't say no even if you wanted to?"

Though the room remained silent, I was possessed by the strangest feeling—like someone was writing on a tablet in my mind. It felt like a great effort was being expended. Like an enormous weight was being shifted. And then these two words slowly materialized in my head: *I'm yours.*

"Vincent, was that you?" I asked, startled. My body felt like a tree strung with a million Christmas lights that had all been switched on at once.

"Okay, if that was you, it kind of freaked me out. But that's fine. And if it wasn't you, then I must be completely losing it from hanging out with a dead guy. Thanks a lot for compromising my sanity," I said, feigning sarcasm, but badly, since I was shaking.

I could almost feel a sensation of amusement drifting through the room, but it was so feeble that I assumed I was making it up. "Now you're making me paranoid," I said. "Before I start doing a Joan-of-Arc-hearing-voices impersonation, I think I'll work on my history homework."

Silence.

Leaving the bed curtains open so that I could see him, I went to sit on the couch, digging my books out of my bag and spreading them on the coffee table.

It was then that I noticed an envelope sitting on his bedside table. I saw my name written in Vincent's beautiful script, and pulled a sheet of thick paper from inside. It was embossed with the initials VPHD centered at the lower edge, and encircled with a border of vines and leaves. *Kate,* it started.

I'm not always the best at expressing myself to you, so I'm taking advantage of the fact that I will be completely unresponsive when you read this, and therefore incapable of messing things up.

I want to thank you for giving me a chance. When I first saw you, I knew I had found something incredible. And since then all I've wanted was to be with you as much as possible.

When I thought I had lost you, I was torn between wanting you back and wanting the best for you—wanting you to be happy. Seeing you so miserable during the weeks we were apart gave me the courage to fight for us . . . to find a way for things to work. And seeing you happy again in the days we've been back together makes me think I did the right thing.

I can't promise you an ordinary experience, Kate. I wish I could transform myself into a normal man and be there for you, always, without the trauma that defines my life as "the walking dead." Since that isn't possible, I can only reassure you that I will do everything in my power to make it up to you. To give you more than a normal boyfriend could. I have no idea what that will mean, exactly, but I'm looking forward to finding out. With you.

Thank you for being here, my beauty. Mon ange. My Kate.

Yours utterly,

Vincent

What do you do after reading the most romantic love letter—the only love letter, for that matter—you've ever received?

I walked over to the bed and, climbing up onto its high mattress, sat down beside Vincent's body. I cupped his cold face with my warm hand and then, stroking his hair with my fingers, began to cry.

I cried for the loss of my former life. For the days when I would wake up in my old room, walk down the stairs, and see my mother and father sitting at the breakfast table waiting for me. I cried because I wouldn't ever see them again, and my life would never be the same.

I thought of how, after all that loss, I had found someone who loved me. He hadn't said it, but I had seen it in his eyes, and read it in the words he had written. My normal world was gone, in more ways than one. But I had a chance for happiness in a completely new one. A world better suited to science fiction and horror films, perhaps, but also one where I could find tenderness, friendship, and love.

Although I still longed for my old life, I knew I had been given a second chance. It was right here, suspended like a ripe fruit in front of my eyes. All I had to do was reach out my hand and take it. But first I had to let go of what I was grasping in white-knuckled fear: the past.

I was being offered a new life in exchange for the old. It felt like a gift. I felt like I was home. I opened my hand and let go. And then I cried until my swollen eyes drifted shut and I fell asleep.

* * *

When I awoke an hour later, I didn't know where I was for a few seconds. And then I felt Vincent's cold body by my side, and I was suffused with an overwhelming sense of peace that made me feel stronger than I ever had before.

I heard a noise and turned to see Charlotte poking her head through the door. "I stopped by before, but you were asleep. Are you up now?"

"Yes," I said, sitting up and slipping off the bed.

"Oh, good." She slid inside and closed the door. "You've been crying," she said after kissing my cheeks.

I nodded. "I'm fine now. But you don't look so hot yourself."

Charlotte's normally radiant glow had turned sallow, and all the life that seemed to be popping and sparking around her before had disappeared. She looked sad and exhausted. "It's Charles," she said.

"Still no word?" I asked, pulling her down to sit next to me on the couch.

She shook her head, bereft.

"I've tried calling him a million times. I've left dozens of messages. We've put all the numa-controlled locations under surveillance, have paid our tipsters, and even raided an old ware-house where we thought they might be holding him. And we've found nothing."

"I'm sorry." Not knowing what else to say, I rubbed her shoulder comfortingly.

"He's my twin, Kate. We've never been apart except for when

we're dormant. I feel like I've lost a half of myself. And I'm really afraid for him."

I nodded. "Vincent told me what he suspected."

"I just don't understand," she whispered, shaking her head.

She leaned in toward me, and I hugged her slender frame against my own.

"Vincent's been leaving us alone for the last few minutes, but he says he wants to be part of the conversation now."

"Okay," I said.

She nodded, listening to him, and her eyes welled with tears.

"What did he say?" I asked.

"He said, 'We're all lost souls here. It's a good thing we've got each other.'"

Vincent's right, I thought. *Even though I'm not a revenant, I fit right in.* I took a package of Kleenex out of my book bag and handed one to her.

She dabbed her eyes, and then looked at me, surprised. "Vincent says that he talked to you this morning, and that you heard!"

"So I wasn't imagining it!" I said, awestruck. "Ask him what he said."

"He said he told you, 'I'm yours.'"

"That's it!" I said, jumping up off the couch and glancing over at his body before realizing for the millionth time that he wasn't there. "But how is that possible?" I asked her. "He told me once that revenants can only communicate with other revenants when they're volant."

Charlotte listened, then said, "Vincent says that he's been

278

studying up since then. That it's rare but has been reported in cases where a human and a revenant have been together for years and years. Geneviève is the only revenant we know like that. And her husband can get impressions of what she wants, but he can't actually hear words."

"But we've been together for weeks, not years," I said doubtfully. "How can it work for us?"

"He says he has no clue, but wants to try again," Charlotte said excitedly.

"Okay," I said, walking over to the bed.

"No, come over here," Charlotte said. "It will just distract you to look at his body. He says to close your eyes and block everything else out. Like you do at museums." I smiled as I remembered the art-induced trance he had spotted me in at the Musée Picasso. I closed my eyes and breathed slowly, letting the room's tranquillity permeate my body. Slowly I began to feel the same sensation I had before. Of someone trying to write letters in my mind.

"What are you hearing?" she asked me.

"I'm not hearing anything. I'm kind of seeing something . . . like someone is writing words."

"He says you're trying to visualize. Stop using your inner eye and use your inner ear. Like if you were listening to music that you heard coming from far away. Try to sharpen it and tune in."

I concentrated, and began to hear a kind of swishing noise, like the wind through leaves, or a kind of static.

"He says to stop trying so hard and just be," said Charlotte.

I relaxed, and the static turned into a rustling noise like a plastic bag being blown around in a breeze. And then I heard it. *Pont des Arts*.

"Pont des Arts?" I said out loud.

"You mean, the bridge crossing the Seine?" Charlotte asked, confused, and then nodded. "Vincent says it was the site of a very important event."

I laughed. "Um, yeah. That would be the first time we kissed."

Charlotte's sad face brightened. "Oh my God. I always knew Vincent would be terribly romantic once he found the right person." She leaned back onto the couch, lacing her hands over her heart. "You're so lucky, Kate."

We practiced our undead-to-human communication skills for the next half hour, with Charlotte bending over in laughter at my off-the-mark answers and Vincent's silly exercises.

"Fight off the . . . lint in bed?" I asked, confused.

"No, *Night of the Living Dead*!" Charlotte roared with laughter.

Finally I was getting most of the phrases right, although I still couldn't hear a voice that sounded like Vincent's pronouncing them. It was more like words popping out of the blue. And only a few words at a time.

"Go get lunch?" I asked finally.

"Right! That's good! Vincent says it's time for a lunch break, and that Jeanne's waiting for us."

When we got to the kitchen, Jules and Ambrose were tucking into a lunch of roast chicken and fries, and Jeanne was sitting next to them, absorbed in their recap of the morning's scouting mission. She jumped up when she saw Charlotte and me enter the room, and gestured at places already set for us.

"Hey, guys, Vincent can talk to Kate. You know . . . while he's volant," Charlotte said with a smug look on her face.

Everyone froze and stared at me, but after a second Jeanne came unstuck and announced, "I'm not completely surprised. I've always told you that I could feel you all floating around when you're volant. I can even tell which one of you is there. But no one ever believed me."

"That's impossible!" exclaimed Ambrose in amazement, and to the air said, "No way, Vincent!"

"Not exactly impossible," Jules replied. "Vincent told me he had been studying Gaspard's records for examples of revenant-human relationships and had found a few unsubstantiated accounts of communication."

"I know," Ambrose replied. "He told me that too. But those were just rumors—freak stories. Trust Vincent to push the envelope and try it out for himself."

Curious, I asked, "What other kind of 'unsubstantiated rumors' are out there? Anything I should know about?"

Ambrose popped a french fry into his mouth and chewed with a sly smile. "You think of all the scary ghost stories, Katie-Lou, all the weird old wives' tales, all the fairy tales you've ever heard, and then remember . . . they all started with a kernel—or maybe just a grain—of something true. Just be glad you didn't fall for a vampire." He shoved another fry in his mouth and then stood, stretching his impressive pecs and biceps, and said, "Jules . . . wanna take a walk on the wild side?"

Jules wiped his mouth with his napkin and then stood, carrying his plate to the sink. "Thanks, Jeanne. Delicious, as usual." Jeanne beamed. "Vincent, you coming with us?"

Will you be lonely? The words popped into my head. I smiled.

"No, you go on with the boys. It looks like they could use a babysitter," I replied with a smirk.

"No way . . . he just talked to you right then?" Ambrose said, mouth agape.

I nodded and smiled.

"Lucky man," Jules said to me, leaning over to kiss my cheeks. "What I wouldn't give to be in your head." Instead of the usual quick air-kisses, he took his time kissing both of my cheeks tenderly.

"Jules!" I gasped, feeling myself blush.

He stood, looking up in space, and raised both arms as if in surrender. "Okay, okay, man. Hands off, I get it! But it's not often we get a young pretty human in the house. In fact, it's *never*." He turned to go, and then looked back over his shoulder at me. "Bye, Kates, and just remember . . . I'm completely available for the next couple of days while Vincent is otherwise indisposed." He winked. My face burning, I turned away, studiously ignoring him as he left the room.

"What was that about?" asked Charlotte curiously.

"Honestly, I have no idea," I groaned.

THIRTY-FOUR

"ARE YOU STAYING FOR DINNER?" JEANNE ASKED as Charlotte and I left the kitchen.

"Actually, I hadn't thought about it, but it would be nice to see Vincent—I mean, hear Vincent"—I paused, shaking my head at the weirdness of what I had just said—"when the guys get back. Yes, I'll stay, thanks!"

She nodded, satisfied, and got back to her bustling. We left the kitchen and headed down the hallway.

"I'm going to study, Charlotte," I said, opening the door to Vincent's room.

"Okay," she said lightly. "But if hanging around a dead guy proves to be too distracting, feel free to use the library upstairs. Or my room. I'll be downstairs working out."

"Do you do the weapons thing too?" I asked.

She nodded proudly and said, "The guys have more upper-body strength than me, but I'm faster and smaller, so even though I can handle a sword as well as the rest of them, I focus more on karate."

"Wow. Respect!" I said.

"Wanna come?" she asked.

"No, no. I'll study in Vincent's room. It kind of feels comforting having him near," I said. "Even if he's not . . . near. Which reminds me. He can't be in two places at once, can he?"

"Nope, he won't be spying on you while he's out walking with the guys. Unless he leaves them to come home. Which he won't." She squeezed my hand in hers before heading back down the hallway and disappearing down the stairs.

I called Mamie to let her know I wouldn't be home for dinner. "Georgia's busy too," she said, "so maybe Papy and I will take the opportunity to go out. If we're not here when you get home, don't wait up!" I laughed at the girlishness in her voice.

I spent the afternoon studying World War I, which seemed more interesting now that I knew someone who had fought in it. The hours passed quickly, and I switched over to English literature, which, I have to admit, seemed more like pleasure than work.

As for Charlotte's comment, Vincent's body lying a few feet away from me as I read wasn't distracting. It was comforting. It struck me again that I—the orphan stripped of her roots and displaced to live in a foreign land—finally felt home. I felt centered. Whole.

As I finished a chapter on Victorian writers, I heard the ring tone of Vincent's phone coming from the direction of the bed. *How strange,* I thought. Everyone who knew Vincent well enough to phone him would know he was dormant. I followed the sound to his bedside table and, opening its small drawer, pulled the phone out. CHARLES, read the caller ID.

My heart raced as I pressed the button to answer. "Charles? This is Kate. Are you okay? Everyone's looking for you!"

A sobbing sound came from the other end of the line. "Is Vincent there?"

"No. He's dormant. Where are you?"

"He's dormant," Charles repeated aloud, and then his crying became a jagged, gasping weeping. In a lowered voice, he said, "Listen. Tell my kindred I'm so sorry. I didn't mean for it to happen like this. . . ." His voice was cut off by the metallic sound of a blade leaving a sheath. There was a clattering as the phone hit the ground, and then there was silence.

"Oh my God, Charles! Charles!" I screamed into the phone, and then a low voice, smooth as an ice floe, began speaking.

"Tell Jean-Baptiste that if he wants Charles's body, he'll have to come and get it."

"What did you do to him?" I yelled into the phone, my voice staccato stabs of panic.

"We'll be waiting in the Catacombs. At midnight, young Charles goes up in smoke." The line went dead.

The door flew open and a wild-looking Charlotte burst into the room. She looked at the phone in my hand and cried, "What? What happened?"

"Oh, Charlotte." I felt the blood drain from my face as I held the phone out to her. "Call the boys. Tell them to come home right now."

"Was it about Charles?" she asked, beginning to tremble.

I nodded.

She scrolled through Vincent's numbers and placed a call. "Jules, come back now. It's about Charles." She hung up and said, "They're almost home. They'll be right here. Kate . . ." She searched my face for some reason for hope. I couldn't give it to her. "He's dead," she said. It was a statement, not a question.

"Yes."

"And the numa have him?"

"Yes."

Charlotte sank to the ground and hugged her knees against herself. Tears coursed down her ashen cheeks. I kneeled down and put my arms around her, just as the door flew violently open and Jules and Ambrose rushed in.

"What happened?" Jules said, throwing himself down in front of Charlotte.

"Ask Kate," she sobbed. "Oh, Ambrose," she said, holding her arms out to the man crouched beside her. He lowered himself to a sitting position and wrapped his powerful arms around her, hugging her close.

It was the first time I had seen the two of them interact, and even in the midst of this trauma, something clicked in my mind. There was something there between Charlotte and Ambrose. He handled her carefully, as if she were breakable.

And she soaked in his comfort like a sponge.

He was the unrequited love she had mentioned that day by the river. The one who "didn't feel the same way." She hadn't been talking about a human. She had been talking about Ambrose. As soon as the thought crossed my mind, I knew it was true.

"Kate?" Jules asked, snapping me out of my thoughts.

"Charles called Vincent's phone," I said. "He asked for Vincent, and when I told him he was dormant, he asked me to tell you all that he was sorry. He hadn't wanted things to happen this way. And then . . . it sounded like a sword."

Charlotte let out a whimper, and Ambrose tightened his hold.

"Someone else picked up the phone and said that if you want Charles's body, you have until midnight to get it in the Catacombs."

"The Catacombs!" Jules said to Ambrose, incredulous.

"Figures. We've looked everywhere else." Ambrose's voice was tinged with venom. Charlotte began crying harder. "Shhh," whispered Ambrose, dipping his head down so that his face touched her cheek. "It'll be okay."

"Vincent says we have to go tell Jean-Baptiste and Gaspard," Jules said.

The same second I realized Vincent was in the room, I heard the words, *I'm here. It's okay.* I breathed a sigh of relief knowing he was nearby.

As we made our way down the upstairs hallway, I saw Gaspard walk out of a room saying, "Okay, okay, I'm hurrying, Vincent. What's the panic?" And then, seeing Charlotte's twisted face, he whispered, "Oh my. Yes. I see," and opened the door across from his, leading us all inside.

The group filed into a room that looked like it had been beamed over from the castle of Versailles. On one end of the room, velvet draperies cascaded from the ceiling to curtain a bed below. Mirrors and paintings lined the paneled walls, and an enormous tapestry worked with a hunting scene took up most of the wall facing the bed.

Jean-Baptiste was in the middle of the room, sitting at a delicate-looking mahogany desk, writing with a fountain pen. "Yes?" he said calmly, and finished writing his sentence before he looked up at us.

I repeated verbatim what I had told the others a few minutes before.

"And did the second person on the phone identify himself?" asked Jean-Baptiste.

"No," I responded.

I saw the others glance at one another warily.

"Could it have been Lucien?" he asked.

"I only spoke to him once, in a noisy club. I really couldn't tell."

"It's got to be a trap," Gaspard said, wringing his hands.

"Of course it's a trap," Jean-Baptiste said. After a second of silence, I saw him nod and say, "I see." Rising from his desk and walking across the room to face me, he said, "Vincent says that your sister plans on attending an event that Lucien is giving tonight."

I had forgotten all about the party. "Oh my God—that's

right," I gasped, blanching as I thought of the danger she could be in. "It's a big party being held near Place Denfert-Rochereau. A place called Judas."

"Denfert?" Ambrose let out a spiteful laugh. "That's just what they call it now. It used to be d'Enfer, 'Hell's Square.' Right above the Catacombs. The perfect spot for a band of demons to set up shop."

"It makes total sense for Lucien and his clan to camp out among the dead," Jules added. "They probably provided half of those bones themselves."

THIRTY-FIVE

I HAD BEEN TO THE CATACOMBS BEFORE, ON A guided tour for the general public. Made up of a series of medieval mines underneath the city, they are filled with the bones of centuries of Paris's dead.

Paris had been inhabited for millennia, so understandably, by the seventeenth century all the city's tiny churchyard cemeteries were overflowing. Some accounts told of bodies floating around the city whenever the Seine River flooded. Finally the government condemned the city's small graveyards, dug up the bodies from the existing graves, and moved the bones to the underground caverns beneath Paris's streets.

The Catacomb walls were lined with the bones of its ancient residents, arranged in decorative shapes like hearts, crosses, and other patterns. It was the most gruesome spectacle I had ever seen. And to think that someone would actually spend time there . . . I shuddered, unable to imagine the kind of monster that would be drawn to such a place.

"Did he say where in the Catacombs we were to go?" Jean-Baptiste asked. "The tunnels run for miles around the area."

I shook my head.

Gaspard left the room and returned holding a large roll of parchment. "Here's the map of the sewers and Catacombs," he said.

"Okay," said Jules. "If Lucien wants us to meet him in the Catacombs while he's giving this big party, I'm guessing there is an entrance through the club he owns. Almost every basement in the neighborhood has stairs leading down to the Catacombs. One of us should watch that access point."

"I want to go too."

The group fell silent, and everyone gaped at me in astonishment.

"Whatever for?" Jean-Baptiste asked.

"My sister's in danger." My voice cracked with emotion.

Jules put his arm around me tenderly. "Kate, your sister's not in danger. Lucien and his crew have bigger fish to catch tonight. They'll be thinking about how to destroy us. A human will be the last thing on their minds."

Ambrose nodded. "And no offense, Katie-Lou, but with your fighting skills you'd be more liability than asset." He glanced at Jean-Baptiste. "However, we shouldn't leave Vincent's body alone if the numa knows it's here."

Jean-Baptiste looked at Gaspard and nodded. "I'll stay," Gaspard agreed, and then spread the map across a table. The group huddled in to look at it over his shoulder, everyone contributing their personal knowledge to develop the plan.

"Jeanne has dinner ready in the kitchen," Jean-Baptiste finally said. "You should all have something to eat, or at least take something with you. You'll need your strength to fight."

Soberly the group filed out of the room. The entire meeting had taken less than an hour. But it was coming up on nine, and the deadline was quickly approaching.

Jules stayed behind and walked with me out of the room. "Vincent is asking me to talk to you for him, since your communication is still limited."

I nodded.

"He says he has to go with us. We'll need his help to locate Charles. He says he wants you to go back to your grandparents' home to wait."

"No," I said stubbornly, and then said it again to the air. "No, Vincent. I'm worried sick about all of you, and Georgia, and want to be here when you get back."

Jules listened and then said, "He agrees that you're as safe here with Gaspard as you would be at home. But he doesn't want you to worry about Georgia. At least, not tonight. As long as she stays at the party she'll be safe. They would never fight us in front of hundreds of people."

Trust me, the words ran through my mind.

"I do," I said.

The next half hour was controlled mayhem. Jeanne put a spread of food out on the table and then disappeared down the stairs into the basement. I followed her to the gym-slash-armory and watched as she opened and closed cupboard doors. She pulled heavy instrument cases out of closets and spread them open on the floor with the same efficiency she used to take croissants out of the oven.

"What can I do to help?" I asked.

"Nothing. It's done," she said as she pulled out an enormous case for a double bass. It opened to show an empty shell with built-in compartments dividing its velour-lined interior into a dozen different sections. Seeing the shape and size of the weapons hanging on the walls, it wasn't hard to guess what the case was intended for.

Charlotte was first down the stairs and began pulling weapons off the wall. Choosing a couple of swords, a dagger, some weird ninja-looking objects like throwing stars, and other things I couldn't name if I had to, she nestled them into their slots in an electric guitar case.

Stripping down to her bra and panties, she began layering: first a long-sleeved skintight black shirt, then black leather pants tucked into tall leather boots. Jeanne helped her strap on what looked like a Kevlar vest, and then she threw a dark zip-up sweater over the ensemble. A black sleeveless fake-fur vest, with a balaclava stuffed into one pocket, finished her uniform. She looked like Attila the Hun's right-hand woman. She looked deadly.

Her entire packing-and-changing routine took less than five minutes, and by the time she was done, Ambrose and Jules were downstairs, packing their own cases with weapons.

Ambrose had the double-bass case and was filling it with a veritable armory of battle-axes, maces, swords, and other dangerous-looking blades. Jeanne laid out the boys' clothes and then rubbed her hands together and glanced around proudly, looking every bit like a doting grandmother sending her grandchildren off to school.

"So is this whole military setup just for going to war against the numa?" I asked Charlotte, who had come to stand next to me.

A fear had begun taking hold of my stomach, like a miniature anaconda squeezing my insides. I wasn't afraid for Vincent, doubting that in volant form he could be hurt by Lucien and his crew. But seeing the Kevlar vests and layers of protective clothing drove home the realization that my new friends were putting themselves in mortal danger.

"Look who's ready first. As usual," Charlotte called mockingly to Ambrose and Jules, and then turned to answer my question. "No, Kate. This isn't all about the numa. Saving lives doesn't just mean jumping in front of speeding bullets or pushing suicides out of the way of trains. We've been on SWAT teams, acted as bodyguards, served on antiterrorist squads. . . ." She laughed at my doubtful expression. "Yes, even me. I've made it to seventeen before, and makeup and the right haircut add years to my age."

Jules had strapped a crossbow and arrows into a large case and was overlaying them with daggers and swords. He looked up from his packing and, noticing my gaze, gave me a flirty wink.

"Why don't you guys just use guns?" I asked, amazed by their casual attitude.

"We use guns when we're expected to," answered Charlotte, "if we're fighting alongside humans in the cases I mentioned . . . bodyguarding and the like. But bullets don't kill revenants"—she paused—"or others like us."

Before I could ask her to clarify what she meant by "others," Ambrose, lacing up some massive steel-toed boots, yelled, "Plus, Katie-Lou, you've got to agree . . . hand-to-hand combat is way cooler." Despite myself, I laughed. He obviously loved a fight.

"How many times have you gone up against Lucien and his crew?" I asked.

"Uncountable. It's all part of a never-ending battle," Charlotte responded.

"Well, it must mean you're winning if you're all still around."

No one answered. And then Jules broke the silence. "Let's just say there used to be a lot more of us." The snake inside me constricted so tightly I couldn't breathe.

"There also used to be a lot more of them," called out Jean-Baptiste, who, with Gaspard, stepped down into the room. Charlotte, Ambrose, and Jules stood up, as if at attention, while Jean-Baptiste walked back and forth among them, carrying out an inspection of their body armor and weapons cases. "We've got everything," he said finally, nodding at the three of them approvingly.

He took two normal-looking canes out of an umbrella stand

and threw one to Gaspard. With a lightning-quick movement, Gaspard drew a sword forth from the cane and inspected its blade.

They certainly looked like a mini army, led by a fierce general. But individually, they could pass for musicians dressed for a gig—that is, if their band had a marked penchant for leather.

They led the way through double doors at the end of the gym, and up to the back courtyard where several cars, motorcycles, and scooters were parked. Jean-Baptiste climbed into a midnight blue sedan, while Jules and Charlotte took a dark-hued 4x4. Ambrose strapped his case to an enormous Ducati and started up the bike's engine with a roar.

As the other vehicles started their motors, I clutched my arms across my chest and clenched my teeth. *This isn't my fight,* I thought, *it's theirs.* But I couldn't help feeling helpless—like the damsel in distress that I never wanted to be.

I heard Vincent say, *When we're done, I'll come back to you.*

"Be careful," I murmured.

Nothing can happen to me, the words came. *My body is here with you.*

"Take care of the rest of them, then," I said.

Good-bye, Kate, mon ange.

The cars began backing up, and smoothly exiting one by one through the gates into the dark night beyond, they were gone.

THIRTY-SIX

GASPARD EXCUSED HIMSELF AND SAID HE WOULD be in the library, while Jeanne and I walked back up the stairs to the kitchen in silence. I watched her as she began cleaning up from the ad hoc meal. She must have seen so much over the years. And I needed a distraction. "Tell me about Vincent."

Jeanne tucked her towel into her apron. "Let me make you a coffee first," she said. "If you're going to be waiting up for them to get back, you'll need the stamina."

"That would be great, Jeanne. Thanks. Will you have one with me?"

"No, dear, I have to go home. My family's waiting for me."

She has a family, I thought, wondering why I was surprised. She too divided her time between the undead and the living. For the first time, I felt a bond with her.

She set my coffee on the table with a pitcher of milk and sat down next to me. "So. What can I tell you about Vincent?" she mused. "Well, I was sixteen when I started helping my mother here, doing the laundry and ironing. That would be about"—she did the math in her head—"thirty-nine years ago." She leaned back in her chair, squinting her eyes as if trying to see back that far. "Vincent was the same as he is today. Plus or minus a year. And they all follow the fashions of the time, of course, so as to not stand out. So his hair was a bit longer the first time I saw him. Oh, I thought he was so handsome."

She leaned toward me with a twinkle in her eye. "Still do. Even though he's a mere teenager and I'm now a grandmother of four." She sat back, smiling to herself.

"Anyway, there were more revenants then. They were scattered all over Paris in buildings that Jean-Baptiste's family owned. Now, of course, since there aren't many revenants left here in Paris, he rents out the places. Makes an absolute fortune off his real estate."

She sighed and paused for a moment. "Anyway, I've known Vincent since the 1970s and he's always been a . . . tortured kind of boy. I'm guessing he's told you about Hélène by now?"

I nodded, and she continued. "Well, following her death—and his own death, of course—he kind of closed down emotionally. After Jean-Baptiste found him, he took on the role of foot soldier. According to what I've heard, nothing was too dangerous for Vincent. He literally threw himself in harm's way. As if saving hundreds of strangers would make up for the one person he wasn't able to save. And it's continued like that. He's been like this avenging robot. A beautiful robot, mind you, but still . . ."

She blinked and looked pointedly at me. "A few months ago he came home with a spark of life in his eyes. I couldn't even imagine what had happened. And it was you." Jeanne leaned forward and brushed my cheek with the edge of her hand, smiling.

"You beautiful girl. You've given new life to my Vincent. He might be strong of spirit, but he's a tender soul. And you've touched him. For as long as I've known him, his only motivation has been vengeance and loyalty, which may be why he's one of the few survivors. But now he has . . ." She paused, thinking twice about what she was going to say, and settled for, "You."

Her smile was compassionate. "This won't be an easy relationship for you, dear Kate. But persevere. He's worth it."

Jeanne tucked her apron into the handle of the oven, kissed me, and began to gather her things. "I'll walk you out," I told her, all of a sudden realizing that I was going to be in that huge house with no one but a 150-year-old revenant and my boyfriend's dead body to keep me company.

"Are you going to be okay?" asked Jeanne.

"Yes," I lied. "No problem." We approached the granite fountain in the middle of the courtyard, and I sat down on its edge, waving good-bye as Jeanne bustled out through the front gate. It closed silently behind her. I gazed up at the statue in the fountain of the angel holding the woman.

The first time I had seen it, I had no idea what Vincent was. I had never heard of a revenant—either the murderous kind or the kind that spent their existence saving mankind. Even then, the fountain had already seemed truly creepy to me.

Now, when I looked at the ethereal beauty of the two connected figures—the handsome angel, with his hard, darkened
features focused on the woman cradled in his outstretched arms,
who was all softness and light—I couldn't miss the symbolism.
The angel was a revenant, but was he good or evil? And was the
woman in his arms sleeping or dead? I stepped closer.

The angel's expression seemed desperate. Obsessed, even.
But also tender. As if he was looking to the woman to save him,
and not vice versa. And all of a sudden, Vincent's name for me
popped into my mind: *mon ange*. My angel. I shivered, but not
from the cold.

Jeanne had said that meeting me had transformed Vincent.
I had given him "new life." But was he looking to me to save his
soul?

I looked at the woman. A noble strength radiated from her
features, and the light of the moon reflected off her skin onto
the angel's face. He seemed blinded by the light. I had seen the
angel's expression before: Its face was like Vincent's when he
looked at me.

I was overcome by a rush of emotions: amazement that Vincent
had found in me what he was looking for; fear of his expecta-
tions; concern that I wasn't strong enough to carry that burden.
Those were all there. But even stronger was the desire to give him
what he wanted. To be there for him. My destiny might include
helping Vincent to see that there could be more to his existence
than vengeance. There could be love.

* * *

I almost ran back to Vincent's room, pulling myself up on his bed until I was lying next to him. His cold features held no expression; his exquisite body was nothing but an empty shell.

I tried to imagine him as Jeanne had described . . . a violent, vengeful soldier. And though the picture that instinctively came to mind was the eyes-half-closed sexy smile he always gave me, I *was* able to imagine him as a furious avenger. There was something dangerous about him, as there was about all the revenants.

Just knowing that a fatal accident could be right around the corner must make humans more cautious, a trait that Vincent and his fellow revenants didn't possess. Their lack of fear of injury, or even death, gave them a reckless confidence that was both thrilling and terrifying.

I traced his features with my finger and thought about the first time I had seen him like this. His dead body had repelled me then, but now I felt a growing certainty that I could handle whatever was given me. To be with Vincent I would have to be strong. Courageous.

I heard my phone's text-message ring tone and jumped down off the bed to grab it. It was from Georgia:

Left party. I need to talk to you asap.

Me: Are you okay?

Georgia: No.

Me: Where are you?

Georgia: Outside Vincent's house.

Me: What??? How did you know I was here?

Georgia: You told me.

Me: No, I didn't.

Georgia: I need to see you. What's the digicode?

Why was she doing this? And what could I do? She obviously needed me, but I couldn't just give her the code.

Me: Can't give it out. Will come outside to talk.

The doorbell rang. I ran down the hallway to the front door and pressed the button on the videocam screen. The camera light went on, and looking up into the lens was my sister.

"Georgia!" I yelled into the microphone. "What are you doing here?"

When she heard my voice, she cried out, "Oh my God, Kate, I'm so, so sorry!"

"What happened?" I asked, panic rising in my voice as I saw the fear and anguish on her face.

"I'm sorry, I'm sorry," she wailed, raising her trembling hands to her mouth in terror.

"For what, Georgia? Tell me!" I yelled.

"For bringing me here," said a low voice, and Lucien stepped into the picture and put a knife to Georgia's throat.

"Open the gate or I'll kill her." The evil words affected me as much as if Lucien were standing next to me instead of across a courtyard behind a locked gate.

"I'm sorry, Katie," Georgia cried softly.

I lifted my finger to the button with a key symbol under it.

Gaspard began running down the stairs behind me. "Don't!" he cried.

"But he'll kill my sister!"

"I'll give you three seconds before I slit her throat," came Lucien's voice over the speakerphone. "Three . . ."

"I only have my swordstick . . . wait till I can get to the armory," yelled Gaspard, reaching the bottom of the staircase and hurtling toward me.

"Two . . ."

I looked back at Gaspard in desperation as I pushed the button. The gate unlocked.

"Lock the door behind me, Gaspard, and don't let him in. You have to protect Vincent!" I called. And then I leaped outside, slamming the door behind me, and turned to face the devil.

THIRTY-SEVEN

LUCIEN STOOD IN THE COURTYARD BEFORE ME, holding the knife to Georgia's back.

"Good evening, Kate," he said in a cold, even voice. His expression was murderous, and his enormous frame seemed twice as big now that he was looming over me. How Georgia could ever have seen anything seductive in this terrifying monster was beyond me.

"Now be a good girl and take me inside."

"I can't," I said. "It's locked. I can't do a thing for you now, so you can let Georgia go." I felt like I had won this round, but had no idea what would come next.

"Gaspard, I know you're in there," yelled Lucien. "Now come out or you'll have the blood of two humans on your hands."

Before he could finish, the door opened and Gaspard walked out, holding the cane-sword before him.

"No, don't, Gaspard!" I yelled. *What is he doing?* I thought wildly. He had to stay locked in the house, protecting Vincent. My sister was my responsibility alone.

Gaspard ignored me. Advancing, he said evenly, "Lucien, you vile leech. What brings your putrid corpse to our humble doorstep this fine evening?" He had recaptured the noble air he wore the day I saw him sparring with Vincent. The twitchy, stuttering poet had transformed into the formidable fighter.

Lucien stepped toward him, and I grabbed Georgia's arm and pulled her away. "Let's make a run for it," I whispered, keeping an eye on the men.

"You seem to be sorely lacking in weaponry tonight, you sad excuse for an immortal," Lucien growled.

"Mine seems a blade of equal merit to the bread knife you carry, you loathsome maggot," Gaspard said, and lunged at Lucien with the sword, making a clean slice across the giant's cheek.

Although a small trickle of blood ran from it, Lucien didn't even flinch. "Equal, perhaps, you farcical lifeguard-Lazarus, but that's why I brought backup." And he pulled a gun from under his coat and shot Gaspard point-blank between the eyes.

The older revenant staggered backward a couple of steps as his forehead absorbed the bullet. Then in slow motion it spit it back out and the bullet fell, clinking as it bounced against the pavement. Lucien used the couple of seconds that Gaspard was stunned to leap on him and push him to the ground.

I took Georgia's hand and began running with her toward the gate. "Stop right there or I'll shoot you both," Lucien said, pointing the gun in our direction as he straddled Gaspard's struggling body. We froze. "Now walk back here. You're coming with me." He watched, motionless, as we approached. "Closer," he commanded. Once we were within arm's reach, he replaced the gun in its holster.

Then, taking his massive knife, he swung it high in the air before bringing it down like a machete on Gaspard's neck. Georgia and I screamed as one, an earsplitting shriek, and we grabbed each other, tearfully hiding in each other's arms from the horror.

"A bit squeamish, are we, ladies? Well, there's more to come. Now inside, both of you," he said, pulling a handkerchief out of his pocket and wiping the blade before holding it out toward us.

I couldn't bear to look back at Gaspard as I walked obediently into the foyer. Lucien glanced quickly around. "Nice pad they've got here." His eyes flashed back to me with a piercing glare. "Now show me where he is."

"Who?" I asked, my voice trembling.

"Who do you think? Lover-boy," he sneered, stepping closer to me and pushing Georgia between us.

"He's—he's not here," I stammered.

"Aww, that's sweet. Trying to protect your zombie boyfriend. But I know you're lying, Kate. Charles told me he was dormant. And my colleague just told me that Jean-Baptiste and company, including Vincent's ghost, all showed up at my little get-together in the Catacombs. So let's just drop the games and get to business."

"I won't take you to him," I said, stepping backward to avoid Georgia, who he had pushed up against me.

"Oh yes, you will," Lucien said calmly, holding up the knife. Its blade sparkled in the light of the chandelier.

Georgia cried out, "Don't tell him, Kate. He said he was going to kill him."

"Bitch," Lucien growled and, grabbing Georgia by the hair, pulled her head back and held the knife to her throat.

I shook my head and whispered, "I would rather die than take you to Vincent." But seeing the panic in Georgia's eyes, I felt something slip inside me.

"Fine," said Lucien. "I was hoping to take Georgia safely along with me after paying you a visit, but I'm perfectly willing to accommodate a change in plans." The knife flashed as he drew it across Georgia's white neck. She screamed, but he didn't let go of her hair.

"Georgia!" I cried, horrified, as I saw drops of blood ooze out of the cut he had made.

"The longer you wait, the deeper I'll slice," he said. "That didn't hurt now, darling, did it?" he asked, leering at Georgia and giving her a peck on the cheek.

Her eyes spun wildly toward me, and I yelled, "Okay, okay. Just stop and I'll take you to him." Lucien nodded, waiting, but placed the knife firmly next to Georgia's straining neck.

My mind sped in a dozen different directions, grasping for ways to lead him astray. I could take him upstairs, or into one of the other rooms, but what would that do besides enrage him further?

"Move it!" Lucien demanded, and I headed through the door to the servants' hallway, my mind still searching for a way to buy time. I walked as slowly as I could, but couldn't come up with a plan that wouldn't end up with my sister's throat being slit, or more likely, both of us being killed. There was nothing I could do but plead silently with Vincent to come back, knowing that that was impossible: He was halfway across town helping his kindred.

I led them through the door into Vincent's room, and stepped aside to let Lucien pass. He released Georgia and paced quickly over to the bed, laughing as he approached it. "Ah, Vincent. You're looking better than ever," he said. "Love seems to suit you. Too bad it couldn't last." Glancing around the room, he fixed his eyes on the fireplace.

"Sit," he said to us, motioning with the knife to the couch. He began piling wood and kindling into the hearth and put a match to it.

With her face in her hands, my sister began weeping and lowered her head to my shoulder. "Kate, I'm sorry I didn't believe you."

"Shh. It doesn't matter now. Are you okay?" I whispered. "Let me see your neck."

She lifted her head, and I touched the knife wound. It wasn't much more than a scratch. "It's not that bad," I said, wiping a drop of blood away with my finger.

"Who cares about my cut?" she whispered. "We're never going to get out of here alive. We just saw him murder someone. What's wrong with Vincent, anyway? Why isn't he moving?"

"He's kind of . . . in a coma," I responded.

"What happened?" she asked, horrified.

"Georgia," I said, looking at her steadily, "Lucien didn't say anything when he brought you here? You don't know . . . what they are?"

She shook her head, confused.

There was no way I could avoid telling her. And seeing as we might not live through the evening, I didn't see the sense in hiding what should have been obvious by now. "Georgia, they're not human . . . Vincent and Lucien."

"What are they, then?"

"It's complicated," I began, and then, seeing tears of confusion begin to well up in her eyes, I took a breath and said, "They're called revenants. They're undead."

"I don't . . . I don't understand."

"It doesn't matter, Georgia," I insisted, grabbing her hands roughly and forcing her to look me in the eyes. I spoke the words slowly, as much for my benefit as for hers: "I don't care what Vincent is. We can't let Lucien destroy him."

Her eyes searched my face. For once I didn't regret being an open book. The bewilderment and fear left Georgia's face and were replaced by a look of pure determination. My sister had always been there for me, and she was here for me now. However insane the words coming out of my mouth sounded, she didn't doubt me for a second.

"What can we do?" she whispered. I shook my head and watched Lucien use a poker to move the logs around. The flames caught and shot up, exploding into a substantial blaze as the smell of wood fire flooded the room.

"He's going to try to burn Vincent's body," I whispered back. "We can't let him."

As if validating everything I had told her, Lucien turned. "It's such a pity to have to dispose of my old foe's body before giving him a chance to see me kill his girlfriend with his own eyes. It would be fitting vengeance for shooting my wife while I watched."

"Your going out with Georgia wasn't a coincidence, was it?" I asked, the realization suddenly shaking me.

"Of course not! There are no coincidences," he smirked, as Georgia's breath drew in sharply beside me. "I saw you girls together at the river a few months ago after Vincent saved that pitiful teenager who jumped from the bridge."

"You were the one who sped off in a car after almost knocking us over!" I gasped.

"Yours truly," Lucien leered and gave a bow. "So when I saw Vincent come swooping out of the Métro with you in his arms after the second suicide in a row that he ruined for me, I figured that you must be someone special to him. And it was so easy to find out everything about you afterward, including the fact that your party-girl sister was a regular patron at several of my nightclubs. Which isn't much of a coincidence either, since she isn't terribly discriminating about the places she frequents and the crowds she moves in."

I felt Georgia deflate at these words, and Lucien chuckled, enjoying her reaction. "You used me to get to Kate," she muttered, stunned by the revelation.

Lucien smiled and shrugged. "No offense, darlin'."

"But how did you know I was here tonight? How did you know to bring Georgia along as your human door pass?"

"I could tell that Charles was speaking to a human on the phone. What other human would answer Vincent's phone? Then I recognized your voice. And that gave me this wonderful idea!" He gestured to include the room and Vincent's body. "How do you think I became such a successful businessman if I didn't know how to grab an opportunity when it's sitting right in front of me?"

"Oh, I don't know," I said, disgusted by his flippancy. "Lying, cheating, murdering... That would have been my guess."

"Ah, flattery. It's like music to my ears." He cracked his knuckles loudly as he passed us on his way to the bed, and then, leaning over, picked up Vincent's stiff body in his arms and spoke to him as if he were there.

"Too bad you have to miss out on the bloodbath in your own bedroom. Reminds me of my own death. But since your spirit happens to be elsewhere, when I destroy your body you'll have the rest of eternity to float around and mull it over." Struggling slightly from the body's deadweight, he began walking toward the fireplace.

"No!" I screamed, jumping up and running over to position myself between Lucien and the fire.

"What are you going to do, little girl? Kick me in the shin?"

Georgia leaped from the couch and rushed up behind him, grasping at his arms. She let out a scream of pure rage as she clawed at him, merely managing to slow him down. I ran at him and tried to push him backward away from the blaze. But even

311

giving it all my strength, he didn't budge.

"Well, spit on my empty grave—if it ain't the attack of the Disney princesses!" he snarled, annoyed, and bending over to place Vincent's body on the rug, he whipped around and sent Georgia flying backward with a sweep of his powerful arm.

She landed against the side of the bed, her head cracking hard against the wood bed frame. He walked over to her and, pausing until she met his gaze, said, "I'm sorry to have to do this," and stepped on her hand. I heard the bones crunch sickeningly just before she screamed. "Actually, not that sorry," he said, tilting his head to the side as he watched her writhe. The pain must have been excruciating: Her eyes rolled upward and she slumped over, unconscious.

Picking up the heavy iron fire poker from next to the hearth, I ran over to where he stood and brought it down with all my force on his back.

"Damn it, girl, give that to me," he yelled, and yanked the weapon out of my hands, tossing it like a matchstick into a far corner. "If you want to bang on something, you can help me chop off lover-boy's head."

Reaching up, he pulled one of the swords from where it hung above the mantel. The second sword fell to the floor. I made a dash for it and picked it up by the hilt, staggering backward under its weight.

Lucien stood, holding his sword in one hand over Vincent's body, and watched me with an amused grin. I struggled to lift my blade and shakily pointed it at him.

"Don't get any closer to him," I said.

"Or what?" he spat. "If you wished to die before seeing your boyfriend decapitated, all you had to do was ask. But I hope you will allow me a little sport first. It's been ages since I've killed a woman with my own hands."

He lunged at me, grazing my right shoulder with his blade. A small spurt of blood spilled through the slice in my shirt and ran down my arm. I stared at it a second, feeling nauseated. And then I looked back down at Vincent's body, lying lifeless on the floor, and my strength returned. With all my force, I raised my sword.

"That's it," he said sarcastically. "You've got to put a little more muscle behind it." He was playing with me. I should be grateful—if he expended even a little effort, I would be dead. But instead of feeling intimidated, his condescension made me furious.

Fueled by my anger, I swung the massive weapon at him, and he stepped nimbly aside as the blade crashed against the terra-cotta floor tiles, breaking a couple in half and sending a large earthen chip flying through the air. His sword flashed in the firelight, and I felt a burning sting in my leg. I looked down and saw that my jeans were sliced open and a stream of blood flowed from a wound on my outer thigh, just below my hip.

"Now this is getting fun!" Lucien said with a glimmer in his eye. "You're even spunkier than your sister. I'd never have guessed. It would be a shame to kill you before I find out exactly how spunky you can get. You might just have to accompany me, and Vincent's head, of course, back to my home so we can have a little fun."

I tried to heft the sword back up, but faltered. My arms weren't working right. I had used all my energy on that one blow, and my muscles felt like rubber bands.

"This will all be over in just a second. If you move an inch, I'll put this sword through your pretty head," he warned, and then turned and began shifting Vincent's body around. Georgia began moaning from the other side of the room. Her eyes were half-open now, but she still lay motionless on the ground.

I fought against a wave of desperation and suddenly I realized I didn't care if he killed me. I would fight him even if it meant my own death, even if it didn't make one bit of difference in the end. Because it would be better to die fighting than to survive this nightmare and live a long, regretful life with only the memory of Vincent to hold on to. Calling on every last ounce of my strength, I lifted my sword.

All of a sudden I heard the crackling, static words: *I'm back.* My eyes widened as I looked around the room and reassured myself that the voice was coming from inside me. "Vincent," I whispered.

Quickly, Kate. Will you let me come in?

"Come in?" I puzzled frantically for a split second and then, realizing what he was asking, said, "Yes."

All of a sudden, my body was no longer my own. It felt like a door had opened in the back of my head, and a powerful surge of energy poured through it and ricocheted through me, filling me until I felt I was going to burst.

Although I was still aware, my limbs began to move without me willing them to, and I lifted the massive sword with ease, swinging it high with both hands in an elliptical curve. It remained poised there for a second, motionless in midair, until I brought it down with a powerful sweep, slicing cleanly into Lucien's left arm.

He roared with anger and dropped his sword, cupping the wound with his hand. Spinning on his heels, he stared at me in shock and then lunged at me, his wounded arm dangling by his side and spurting dark blood onto the tile floor.

I leaped aside, catlike, pulling the sword up into a vertical position, and crouched for a second before running toward Lucien, who had lurched back near the sword he had dropped on the ground. Bringing my weapon up, I swung again at his right side, underneath his outstretched arm. He let out a howl and swung around with sword in hand.

He stood for a second staring at me, uncomprehendingly, as blood gushed out of the wound in his side. Then with a staggering gait he charged at me, but wavered at the last second, thrown off balance as he tripped over Vincent's body.

I skipped to my right, away from him, and then, lunging again, took another swing at his head, missing as he ducked to avoid it. He leaped aside from his crouched position, squinting as he looked at me, and then all of a sudden his eyes widened in surprise. "Vincent. Are you in there?" he asked incredulously.

I felt myself laugh, and Vincent's words came out of my mouth, in my own voice. "Lucien. My old foe."

"No," Lucien said, shaking his head and holding the sword

up defensively with his good arm. "It's not possible. You're at the Catacombs."

"Looks like you're wrong there," Vincent said through me. "You never were the brightest zombie in the graveyard."

Lucien roared and charged at me, but I leaped nimbly to one side as he stumbled to stop himself from ramming into the bed.

"So what exactly were you trying to accomplish here?" my voice said smoothly. "Were you going to take my head back to Jean-Baptiste and then set to work slaying the rest of my kin?"

"I'm just finishing some old business," hissed Lucien. "I couldn't care less about your kinsmen, although now that you mention it, it might be fun to hold a little revenant barbecue once I kill Kate and bring your head back to use as kindling."

"It's the 'kill Kate' part that I think you might find difficult," I heard myself say, as I ran at him, feeling a strength coursing through my body that was several times my own. Lucien held up his sword to meet me, but I arrived faster than he could react.

"This is for all the innocents you betrayed to their death," I said, and cut deeply into his already wounded right side.

His sword went clattering to the floor, and he howled, lurching toward the fire. Blood dripped into the fire as he leaned over it, falling to his knees to grab the dagger he had set next to the fireplace. Then, with incredible speed, he jumped to his feet and threw the knife at my head. I jumped out of the way, but not quickly enough, and the blade sliced cleanly into my right shoulder.

I didn't scream. I didn't have time to. Transferring the sword to my right hand, I took my left and pulled the knife out of my shoulder. Then, without hesitating, I threw it back at him with superhuman force, knocking him back a step as the blade lodged deeply through his left eye into his brain. "And that's for all my kindred you destroyed," I heard myself say. Lucien's remaining eye rolled upward, and with mouth hanging open, he stumbled toward me, as if in slow motion.

I turned and leaped onto the coffee table. Holding the sword in both hands, I swung it high into the air and brought it down toward his neck with a powerful horizontal sweep. I felt the blade slice cleanly through, sending his head flying off in a bloody arc.

The headless body held its position for a couple of seconds before collapsing to the floor in a heap. "Burn in hell," Vincent said as I picked up the head by its hair and strode with it to the fireplace.

Just then the door flew open, and Ambrose burst through, yelling like a madman and swinging a battle-ax in one hand. His other arm was torn by a mean gash, and his shredded clothes were stained crimson. A rivulet of blood ran down his face from a scalp wound.

His crazed eyes fixed on Lucien's decapitated body and then swung toward Vincent's body, lying in a heap next to the fireplace. He looked at me, standing a few feet away, holding an enormous sword effortlessly in one hand and Lucien's head in the other. He nodded silently, and I nodded back. Turning to the roaring fire, I tossed the grotesque head into the flames.

"The body," I said, and grabbing Lucien's corpse by the arms and legs, Ambrose and I carried it to the fire, swinging it slightly backward before heaving it on top of the burning logs.

"Vincent, that you in there?" Ambrose said, stepping away and looking at me. My head nodded. "Well, it better be, because if that's you alone, Katie-Lou, I am officially afraid." I smiled at him, and he shook his head in disbelief.

"Come out of there, Vin, you're freaking me out," he said.

Ready? Vincent asked me.

"Yes," I replied, and immediately felt the whoosh of energy leaving through the back of my head. My body felt like a balloon deflating, and Ambrose stepped forward to catch me as I fell. He set me carefully on the ground.

Kate! Are you okay? came Vincent's words immediately.

I nodded. "I'm fine."

Your mind. No confusion? Panic?

"Vincent, I'm no different from before, except I don't think I'll be able to budge for a week, I'm so exhausted."

Amazing.

"Gaspard's body's outside," I said, turning to Ambrose.

"We saw. Jean-Baptiste's got him. He'll be okay."

"What about everyone else?" I asked, staring at the blood on his shirt.

He nodded. "We all made it back."

I breathed a sigh of relief. "And Charles?"

"We got his body," Ambrose responded, and then, gesturing toward the bed, asked, "What's your sister doing here?"

"Oh my God, Georgia!" I cried, and looked over at my sister.

I used the last bit of my strength to crawl over to her and touch her bloodless face.

"Are you okay?" I asked her.

"I think so. It just hurts to move," she replied, her voice weak.

"She needs help," I said urgently to Ambrose. "She might have a concussion—she really slammed her head hard and was unconscious for a while. And I'm pretty sure her hand is broken too."

Ambrose crouched over her and, being careful not to move her neck, pulled her out of her crumpled position and laid her flat on the ground.

"We need to get her to the hospital," I said.

"She's not the only one needing medical attention," Ambrose replied, pointing at my shoulder.

I looked down to see my shirt soaked in blood. Although I hadn't felt it before, a burning pain now raced through my arm, exploding as it reached the open gash. I grabbed my shoulder, and then just as quickly, wincing in pain, dropped my hand.

Hearing running footsteps in the hallway, I looked over to the door just as Jules burst through. "Kate?" he asked, panic in his voice.

"She's fine," called Ambrose. "Sliced up her shoulder and leg a bit, but she's alive."

Jules looked around the room wildly, and seeing Vincent's form near the fireplace, fell to his knees in relief. Holding his hands to his head, he said softly to the air, "Vince, oh man, I'm so glad you're still here."

A pungent, acrid smoke began to pour out of the chimney as Lucien's body caught fire. Looking in that direction, Ambrose said, "We should get out of here if we don't want to suffocate on the fumes."

Jules got to his feet, opened the windows, and then squatted down next to us. "How's she?" he asked, nodding in Georgia's direction.

"Alive," I said.

"And how about you?" he said, cradling my face in his hand.

Tears clouded my eyes. "I'm fine," I said, and quickly wiped them away.

"Oh, Kate," he said, and leaning toward me, wrapped me in his arms. It was exactly what I needed: human touch. Okay, not human, whatever. Since Vincent wasn't there to hold me, Jules made a more than adequate substitute.

"Thanks," I whispered.

"Hospital," Ambrose said simply, and stood to pull a phone out of his pocket. He walked to the other side of the room to make the call, and Jules released me to follow him.

I looked down at my sister. She seemed dazed. "We're going to a hospital. Everything's going to be okay."

"Where is he? Lucien?" she asked numbly.

"Dead," I said simply.

She looked at me and asked, "What happened?"

"How much did you see?" I asked her.

She gave me a weak smile and said, "Enough to know that my sister is one badass sword fighter."

THIRTY-EIGHT

THE OTHERS ARRIVED HOME JUST AS OUR AMBU-
lance pulled up. Ambrose had called their regular contact, who
agreed to take us to a private medical clinic without filing a police
report. The paramedics didn't want to move Georgia's head, so
she was fitted with a neck brace and carried to the ambulance on
a stretcher. After they put temporary wrappings on my wounds,
Jules and I climbed into the back, sitting next to her.

I had to wonder what the paramedics were thinking about us:
two fragile-looking teenage girls who looked like they had been in
a gang fight, and Jules dressed up like someone from *The Matrix*.
I was a hundred percent sure that if they hadn't been paid off, we
would be on our way to a police station to be questioned.

Even though I was dying to know what had happened at the
Catacombs, we didn't talk, since one of the paramedics was sitting in the back with us. He was obviously using discretion with
the questions he asked, and after glancing at Jules for approval, I

answered simply that Georgia had hit her head really hard on a wooden bedpost, and that someone had stepped on her hand. I told him that the cuts on my shoulder and leg were knife wounds. I hoped that providing him with basic information, no frills, would be enough, and judging from his satisfied nod, it was.

Once at the clinic, Georgia was inspected and judged to be fine, except for a few broken bones in her hand, which were set. My leg wound wasn't deep, but my shoulder required a dozen stitches. After testing my hand's mobility, the doctor said I was lucky that the blade hadn't touched any nerves.

He followed that with a regular checkup, light in the eyes, blood pressure, and the like. Finally he sighed and said, "Mademoiselle, it looks like you're suffering from extreme exhaustion. Your blood pressure is dangerously low. You're running a slight fever, your skin is ashen, and your pupils are dilated. Are you on any medication or taking any drugs?"

I shook my head.

"When you were hurt, had you been taking part in . . . intensive physical exercise?"

"Yes," I said, wondering what he would think if he knew exactly what type of physical exercise it had been.

"Do you feel faintness, fatigue, or nausea?"

I nodded.

Actually, since Vincent had left my body, I felt like a rag doll, with barely enough energy to walk. Knowing that the well-being of both my sister and myself depended on my being able to put one foot in front of the other was the only thing that had kept me going.

"You need to rest. Your body needs to recuperate from whatever it is that you've just been through. You and your friend"—he nodded at the bed Georgia was lying on—"have had quite an evening. Rest and recover, or you'll end up hurting yourself even worse."

He gestured toward Jules and lowered his voice. "You can answer me by nodding or shaking your head. Should I let you leave the clinic with this man?"

I realized how dangerous Jules appeared in his steel-toed boots, leather pants, and layers of black protective clothing. I whispered, "It wasn't him. He's a friend." The doctor looked me in the eye for another second, and, finally convinced, he nodded and let me step down from the table.

As Jules was talking to the doctor and handing him cash in exchange for the treatment, I whispered, "Vincent?"

Yes, came the immediate reply.

"Have you been here the whole time?"

How could I leave you at a time like this?

I closed my eyes and tried to imagine his arms around me.

We returned to a house that felt like a general's headquarters post-battle. There was a muffled movement from room to room as people visited one another and helped tend to the others' wounds.

I had explained to Georgia that we had to spend the night at Vincent's house. We couldn't go home like this. I led her up the stairs and helped her into Charlotte's bed, guessing that Lucien's body was still burning in Vincent's room. Even if it wasn't, I couldn't imagine going back to the scene of that gory bloodbath. Still mute from shock, Georgia was asleep by the time her head hit the pillow.

My shoulder was starting to burn again, now that the anesthetic used to stitch up my wound was wearing off. I headed downstairs to the kitchen for some water to swallow the pain pills I had been given.

Does it hurt? came Vincent's voice in my head.

"Not much," I lied.

Jules walked through the swinging doors, looking much more himself in torn jeans and a formfitting T-shirt. He flashed me a smile that conveyed both tenderness and respect. "House meeting," he said. "Jean-Baptiste wants you to be there."

"He does?" I said with surprise. Jules nodded and handed me a clean T-shirt. "I thought you might want to be a bit more presentable," he said, pointing to my blood-soaked clothes. He turned his back as I quickly changed and threw the ruined garment into the garbage can.

We walked together down the hallway and past the foyer into a massive room with high ceilings and two-story windows. A fug of old leather and wilting roses hung thickly in the air. A colony of leather couches and armchairs were arranged at the far end around a monumental fireplace.

Near the large fire burning in the hearth, I saw Charlotte lying down on a couch and Ambrose stretched out on the Persian carpet in front of the chimney. He had changed into a clean T-shirt and jeans, and though his wounds had been cleaned and there was no blood in sight, he had enough bandages on to qualify as a mummy. He saw me staring and said, "Don't worry, Katie-Lou, just a couple more weeks till dormancy and I'll be as good as new."

I nodded, trying hard to change my expression from freaked to reassured.

"Here they are," said Jean-Baptiste, who paced back and forth in front of the fire, holding a poker in one hand like a walking stick. "We waited for you and Vincent to get back before starting," he said, motioning me to a chair with his eyes. I sat down.

"There are some decisions that have to be made, and I need to hear what happened, in detail, from each of your perspectives. I'll start." He set the poker against the fireplace and stood with his hands behind his back, looking every bit like a general debriefing his troops.

Charlotte, Ambrose, and Jules began to recount their own parts of the story, with Jean-Baptiste "translating" for Vincent. The group, with Vincent's help, had recovered Charles's body before finding themselves trapped inside the Catacombs by a small army of numa. An army without a leader. It took a comment from one of their captors to alert them to what was happening: Lucien had forbidden the numa to kill any revenants until he returned with "the head." Suspecting that the head in question was his own, Vincent was off in a flash. The revenants took advantage of the numa's hesitation to kill them and fought their way out, then rushed back to assist Vincent.

"It doesn't seem we were followed," Jean-Baptiste concluded. "Kate"—he turned to me officiously—"would you kindly take over the narrative here?"

I told the group what had happened, starting with my sister's text messages, up to the moment where Vincent arrived and took over my body.

"Impossible!" Jean-Baptiste exclaimed.

I looked at him wryly. "Well, it sure wasn't me who chopped a giant numa's head off with a four-foot broadsword!"

"No, not impossible that he possessed you. Impossible that you survived with your sanity intact." Jean-Baptiste was silent for a second, and then nodded. "If you say so, Vincent, but I just don't see how it is possible for a human to experience that and come through it as untouched as Kate seems to be. Besides a few ancient and unfounded rumors, there is absolutely no precedent." He paused again, listening. "Just because you can communicate with her while volant doesn't mean that everything else is possible. Or safe," the older revenant scolded. "Yes, yes, I know . . . you had no other choice. It's true, if you hadn't you would both be gone." He sighed, and turned to me.

"So you killed Lucien?"

"Yes, I mean Vincent . . . um, the knife we threw lodged all the way through his eye, deep into his head. That one stroke must have killed him. At least, his face looked dead. Then we chopped his head off with the sword."

"And his body?"

"We burned it on the fire."

Ambrose spoke up. "I watched it after they left for the clinic. Nothing remains."

Jean-Baptiste relaxed visibly and stood immobile for a second, holding his forehead before looking back up at the group.

"It's clear, then, that the plan was to lure the rest of us, with Vincent volant, away from the house, clearing the way for Lucien to come here and dispose of his body. Knowing our old enemy, he probably planned to come back with the head to burn it in front of us before destroying us as well. That's the only reason I can think of that we weren't slaughtered as soon as we arrived in the Catacombs."

The room was silent.

"I would have preferred that Charles be here to join us for this conversation"—he paused, exhaling deeply—"but because of the circumstances I leave it up to you, Charlotte, to break the news to your brother that I have asked you both to leave."

THIRTY-NINE

EVERYONE LOOKED AT ONE ANOTHER IN SHOCK.

"What?" Charlotte murmured, shaking her head as if she didn't understand.

"This isn't a punishment," clarified Jean-Baptiste. "Charles needs to get out of here. Out of Paris. Out of this house. Away from me. He needs some time to get his head together. And Paris, in the wake of this battle, this"—he searched for the right term—"declaration of war, if that is what it turns out to be, is not a safe place for someone who doesn't yet know their mind."

"But . . . why me?" Charlotte said, shooting a quick, panicky look in Ambrose's direction.

"Can you live separated from your twin?"

She hung her head. "No."

"I thought not." His face softened as Charlotte began to cry. He walked over and sat next to her on the couch, displaying a tenderness that, in my limited experience of Jean-Baptiste, seemed completely out of character.

Holding her hand in his, he said, "Dear girl. It's just for a few months while we figure out what Lucien's clan will do without him. Will they attack us? Will their lack of a leader force them to go underground for a while? We just don't know. And having Charles around, confused and indecisive, will make us weaker when we need to be our strongest.

"I've got houses all over, you know. I'll let you choose where the two of you will go. And you will return. I promise."

Charlotte leaned forward and threw her arms around Jean-Baptiste's neck, sobbing. "Shhh," he said, patting her back.

Once she had quieted he stood again and, addressing Ambrose and Jules, said, "When Gaspard can communicate, I will confer with him as to our plans. We must invite others to replace Charlotte and Charles during this hazardous time. You are welcome to make suggestions.

"And as for you, Kate," Jean-Baptiste said, turning to me. I sat stiffly in my chair, not knowing what would come next but steeling myself for the worst. He couldn't banish me; I didn't live under his roof. And he couldn't stop me from seeing Vincent; I would refuse. Although I had never felt physically weaker in my life, my will had never been stronger.

"We owe you our gratitude. You protected one of our kindred at the risk of your own life."

I sat there, stunned, and finally said, "But . . . how could I have done otherwise?"

"You could have taken your sister and run. Vincent was the one Lucien was after."

I shook my head. No, I couldn't have. I would have preferred to die myself than leave Vincent to his destruction.

"You have earned my trust," Jean-Baptiste concluded formally. "Henceforth, you are welcome here."

Jules spoke up. "She was already welcome here." Ambrose nodded his agreement.

Jean-Baptiste looked at them mildly. "You both know how I struggle to protect our group. And though I trust you all, I don't always trust your decisions. Has anyone else been allowed to bring a human lover into this house?"

The room was quiet.

"Well, this one is now given my official welcome."

"And it only took hacking off an evil zombie's head to earn it," Ambrose mumbled sarcastically.

Jean-Baptiste ignored him and continued. "However, I would appreciate it if you would find some way of explaining this to your sister that would prevent her from having access to all our secrets. And if you have the slightest suspicion that she is in contact with any of Lucien's associates, I would ask you to tell me immediately. In any case, she will not be allowed within the house again, for the security of all of us. I realize it was against her will, but her presence permitted the only security breach we have ever experienced within our gates."

I nodded, thinking about how Georgia had almost been the end of the story for me and Vincent . . . for us all.

FORTY

"OLÉ!" PAPY SHOUTED, AS THE CORK LEFT THE bottle like a gunshot, causing all of us to jump and then cheer as he carefully poured the bubbly into tall, fluted glasses. He held his glass up in a toast, and the rest of us echoed his gesture.

"I would like to wish a happy seventeenth birthday to my princess, Kate. Here's hoping that seventeen will be a magic year for you!"

"Hear, hear!" piped up Mamie, clinking her glass against mine. "Oh, to be seventeen again," she sighed. "That was my age when I met your grandfather. Not that he seemed to pay any attention to me for the next year or so," she said in a manner that was almost flirty.

"It was all part of my plan," he retorted, winking at me. "And anyway, I've made up for lost time since then, haven't I?"

Mamie nodded and leaned over to give him an affectionate kiss before clinking his glass. I leaned over to touch glasses with

Papy, and then turned to Georgia, who held her drink in her left hand, since her right was still in a cast.

"Happy birthday, Katie-Bean," she said, smiling warmly at me, and then looked down at the table, as if embarrassed. Georgia hadn't been the same since "the accident," as my grandparents called it. Though my wounds were easily hidden under winter clothes, Georgia had to explain the cast on her hand.

As she told it, she had stepped into the middle of a fight at the nightclub and had been knocked down and trampled. Papy and Mamie were so horrified that they had forbidden her to go to any more bars or clubs. Funnily enough, she didn't seem to mind, and spent her nights now comparatively quietly, going to dinner parties or the cinema with a small number of friends. Since that night, she had sworn off men, vehemently vowing that she could no longer trust her instincts, but I knew that wouldn't last for long.

She had come to my room a few times late at night, awaking me either for a cry or to distract her from one of her frequent nightmares. She wanted to know everything about the revenants. And I told her. I didn't care about Jean-Baptiste's injunction—I knew I could trust her. Now that there were no secrets between us, Georgia treated me with a newfound respect and acted like Vincent had hung the moon.

"Here's to it being a happy year for both of us." I smiled at her, and then turned to Vincent, who was awaiting his turn. He had shown up that night wearing a vintage black tuxedo, and I had almost fainted when I opened the door.

"Um, did I forget to tell you that, for once, my family isn't wearing black tie to dinner?" I said, my sarcasm falling flat since I was bedazzled by his appearance. He looked like an old-fashioned movie star, his black hair flowing back in waves from his chiseled face. He just smiled mysteriously and refused to answer me.

Now our glasses touched, and he leaned over to give me a chaste peck on the lips, before saying, "Happy birthday, Kate." His eyes twinkled mischievously as he gazed at me with that look that always made me melt: as if I were edible and he could barely restrain himself from taking a bite.

"You kids better get going," said Mamie finally.

"Going where?" I asked, confused.

"Thanks for keeping my birthday plans a secret," Vincent addressed my family. Then, turning to me, he said, "You'll need this first," and pulled a large white box from under the table. Blushing, I unfastened the ribbon and opened the package to see, carefully couched inside layers of tissue, a midnight blue silk fabric embroidered in an Asian pattern with tiny silver and red flowers and vines. I gasped. "What is it?"

"Well, take it out!" Mamie said.

I pulled the fabric out to hold it up. It was a stunning sleeveless gown, floor-length, with an Empire waist and straps that tied behind the neck. I almost dropped it, it was so exquisite.

"Oh, Vincent. I've never owned anything nearly this beautiful. Thank you!" I kissed his cheek. "But when am I ever going to wear it?" I said, placing the dress carefully back into the box.

He beamed. "Well, tonight, for starters. Go ahead and change. Georgia told me your size, so it should fit."

Georgia had her smug grin back for once. It was good to see her looking like her old self, if just for a second. "I'll come with you," she said, and the two of us walked back to my room.

"When did he ask you about this?" I quizzed her as I pulled my clothes off and slipped the dress over my head.

Georgia buttoned the bodice up the back and tied the straps around my neck into a knot behind my hair. "Up, I think," she said, twisting my long hair and attaching it with clips behind my head into a simple but elegant updo.

"A week ago," she answered. "He called me from this really chichi new designer's studio and asked me for your size. Looks like I got it right," she said, appraising the dress with obvious envy. She touched the scar on my arm and disappeared into her room, coming back with a cobweb-thin shrug. "That hides it," she said, nodding with approval. "Holy cow, this thing is gorgeous." She ran her fingers down the silk as we gazed at my reflection in the mirror.

"Wow, with you looking like that, I can't believe you're the same girl who was doing a perfectly convincing Uma Thurman–*Kill Bill* imitation not even two weeks ago," she said. I hugged her as we left the room.

Vincent was waiting for me in the entranceway. The fire in his eyes when he saw me revealed exactly how I looked to him.

"Oh, darling, aren't you stunning!" exclaimed Mamie, beaming as she handed me a long black hooded coat. "You'll need this to keep warm. It's always been too big for me but should fit you perfectly," she murmured.

"You're beautiful, just like your mom was," whispered Papy emotionally, kissing my cheeks and telling us to have a good time. Georgia waved us off, and closing the door, we walked down the staircase.

Once we stepped outside into the nippy air, I was happy for Mamie's coat, which was so well insulated that I was able to leave it open, showing off the dress. Halfway down the block, Vincent stopped, turned toward me, and whispered, "Kate, I feel so"—he paused, seeming lost for words—"so honored to be with you. So lucky. Thank you."

"What?" I replied incredulously. He leaned in to kiss me, and I lifted my mouth to meet his.

As our lips met, my body molded itself to his. I felt his heartbeat next to my own, and a luscious heat rose inside me as I responded to his kiss. Vincent held my face gently as his lips pressed more insistently against my own. The warmth inside me transformed into a flow of lava.

Finally breaking our connection, he gathered me into his arms. "More. Later," he promised. "When we're not standing in the middle of a city street." He looked at me as if I were his own personal miracle and, wrapping his arm around my shoulders, pulled me tight as we walked toward the river.

Once there, we headed down the long flight of stairs to the quay. I laughed when I spotted a familiar figure standing a few yards away. "What are you doing here, Ambrose, in the middle of my birthday date?"

"Just part of the plan, Katie-Lou. Just part of the plan," he said as he bent down to kiss my cheeks. "Let's see you, now." He stepped back and gave a low whistle as I let the coat fall halfway down my arms to show off the dress.

"Vin, you are one lucky man," he said, giving Vincent a playful but painful-looking punch on the shoulder. Vincent rubbed the spot, laughing, and said, "Thanks. Just what I need, bodily injury while I'm trying to impress my girlfriend."

"Oh, you're going to be impressed." Ambrose smiled. "You'd better be!" He motioned to the water with one hand. "Look at what I've been babysitting for you for the last hour and a half."

A small rowboat, painted bright red, rocked gently in the waves of the river.

"What is this?" I gasped.

Vincent just smiled and said, "Normally I would say, 'Ladies first,' but in this case . . ." He climbed down the steep stone steps in the side of the quay and leaped nimbly into the boat. Ambrose helped me down halfway, and then Vincent grasped my hand and I stepped carefully into the rocking craft.

Ambrose gave us a salute before walking away. "Text me when you need me, man," he called behind him, as he made his way up the steps to street level.

Vincent unlatched the oars and rowed west, toward the glimmering lights of the Musée d'Orsay. "Take a blanket," he said, gesturing to a pile of throws and furry coverlets spread across the bottom of the boat. He had thought of everything.

"How—how did you get this boat? Is this even legal?" I stammered.

Vincent nodded. "As legal as any of Jean-Baptiste's dealings. But to answer your question, yes, the boat is registered with the city of Paris. We won't be getting pulled over by any river cops." He laughed under his breath and then said, "So when do you want your presents?"

"Are you kidding, Vincent? I don't need any more presents. This is the most incredible present anyone's ever given me. A boat ride on the Seine? In an amazing silk ball gown? I've got to be dreaming!" I watched the lights shimmering in the Tuileries Gardens as we made our way past a monumental Greek-columned edifice looming over the left bank. Enormous statues of gods and goddesses flanked the building. I felt like tonight, with Vincent by my side, I belonged right up there in their midst.

"Open your presents," he urged with a sexy smile. "They're under the blankets." He took his heavy coat off and continued rowing. I fished under the covers and retrieved two packages wrapped in silver paper.

"Open the big one first," Vincent replied smoothly. He wasn't even winded by the rowing.

Gingerly I opened it and saw, nestled within layers of tissue, a tiny handbag made of an Asian-patterned silk matching my own dress, attached on each side to a long, waist-length chain. The clasp was made of two metal flowers enameled in red and silver, matching those on the fabric. "Oh my God, Vincent, it's gorgeous," I breathed, running my fingers over it.

"Open it," he said. The sparkle in his eye told me he was enjoying this as much as I was. Maybe more.

I carefully pushed the two flowers apart to pop the bag open and pulled out a small pile of tickets. Holding them up to the light cast by the streetlamps at the river's edge, I saw the Opéra Garnier's logo.

I looked at Vincent questioningly, and he said, "You told me you liked dance. They're season tickets to the Opéra Garnier, where all the ballets and contemporary dance events are held. I reserved a private box that's ours for the season. That's what the dress is for, but since the first ballet is still a couple of weeks away, I didn't want you to have to wait to wear it."

I didn't know what to say. My eyes filled with tears.

Vincent stopped rowing. "What, Kate? Are you upset? You said you wanted to go on some normal human dates, so I thought this was a good idea."

Finally finding my tongue, I said, "There's nothing normal about season tickets and a private box at the Opéra Garnier. Or ordering a custom-made dress for me to wear to it. No, Vincent," I shook my head. "'Normal' would not be the word."

His features softened as he realized that I wasn't upset—just overwhelmed. "So what would the word be? Abnormal?"

"Exceptional. Extraordinary. The polar opposite of normal."

"Well, darling Kate, as I once explained to you, I am asking you to trade a normal life for something extraordinary. So I want to make it up to you in an extraordinary way."

"You're doing a good job," I breathed.

"You've got another one left," he said, nodding at the remaining box.

I opened the paper and drew out a hinged jewelry box—the size that would fit a bracelet or necklace. I glanced up at him, alarmed. "Vincent, it's way too early for something like this," I said uncomfortably.

"I would hope I know you a bit by now," he said, obviously enjoying my discomfort. "You think I'd scare you off by giving you jewelry so soon? Trust me, it's not what you think."

I opened the box slowly. Inside was a card. In tiny, ancient-looking script was written: *For Kate Beaumont Mercier, fencing lessons given by my own person, Gaspard Louis-Marie Tabard. Number of lessons specified by V. Delacroix: as many as you can handle.*

"Oh, Vincent!" I cried, lunging forward to hug him, almost capsizing the boat in the process. "This is perfect." I sat back down and shook my head at him in amazement, as he laughed and righted the boat. "*You're* perfect," I sighed, and he gave me one of his dreamy smiles that just about knocked me over the edge of the boat into the water.

"That gift is more a thank-you for saving me from floating around as a disembodied ghost for the rest of eternity," he explained.

"But you're the one who did all the work," I protested.

"We couldn't have done it together if you hadn't had such a strong will. Now you'll have the skills to go with it. I'm hoping you won't ever have to use them in a real-life situation, but since you've agreed to share at least a little part of my life"—he flashed me a cautious smile—"I would feel better if you were equipped to handle anything that might come your way."

The tears I had been holding back began to course down my cheeks. "Kate! You're not supposed to cry," he said, locking the oars into their rings. He slipped forward off his bench to sit on the floor of the boat in front of me.

We floated under the Alexandre III Bridge, the most beautiful bridge in Paris, with stone garlands draped across its arch and bronze-and-glass lamps gleaming across the top. But I could barely see its opulent beauty as it engulfed and then released us from its shelter on the other side. Because the boy sitting in front of me was all I could focus on. I closed my eyes for fear of being swept away by my emotions.

He wanted to be with me. Enough to change his life for me. Enough to launch upon an unknown, uncharted future. For me.

I love him. I had been keeping those three words stuffed deep inside me, for my own protection. But I was done with self-preservation and my heart was open. I had feared that love would make me vulnerable. Instead I felt empowered.

"Kate, are you okay?" He brushed the tears off my face.

Carefully pulling the dress up to my knees, I eased myself down to sit in front of him. He took my ankles in his hands and wrapped my legs around his hips until I was sitting snugly between his legs, our faces inches away from each other.

As he took me in his arms, I lay my head on his shoulder and closed my eyes. I let the knowledge that I loved him mount until it suffused me with a heat that set the entire surface of my skin aflame.

Our boat bobbed around a corner of the quay, and I opened my eyes to see the Eiffel Tower, just downriver from us, decked in a million tiny lights and sparkling like a Christmas tree. Its reflection on the surface of the water glimmered like a universe of tiny crystals. "Oh, Vincent, look!" I exclaimed.

He smiled and nodded, not needing to turn since he saw the reflection in my eyes. "Your last present," he said. "That's what we came to see. Happy birthday, Kate. *Mon ange.*" And in a whisper so light I wasn't sure I hadn't imagined it, he breathed, "My love."

Though I was sitting in a boat on the Seine, floating in the middle of a million points of light, holding the first boy I had ever loved, I couldn't help but think about our chances.

Luck, normalcy, fate . . . none of those seemed to be on our side. Our very being together went against all the odds. All I knew was that something good had begun. A flame had been lit. And the whole universe was watching to see if it would be blown out.

All I could do was hold my breath. And wait.

ACKNOWLEDGMENTS

THERE ARE SO MANY PEOPLE WHO HELPED ME get here. I would like to thank just a few.

For the enthusiasm, trust, and know-how that turned my story into a book, I am profoundly grateful to my editors Tara Weikum and Catherine Onder. They patiently guided *Die for Me* into its finished form, and I am truly lucky to have worked with both of them.

I owe an enormous debt of gratitude to my superhuman agent, Stacey Glick, who stirred up an interest for *Die for Me* that surpassed my every hope. Thanks, Stacey, for believing in me from the very beginning. Thank you to Miriam Goderich for not clicking "delete" when she found my query letter in her inbox. And to Lauren E. Abramo for selling a slew of foreign rights long before the book was even published. Dystel & Goderich rocks!

My friends Mags Harnett and Nathalie Cousin listened to my initial idea and used superhuman self-control not to show their true feelings when I said I wanted to write a zombie love story. Thank you both.

Infinite love and gratefulness to Saint Laurent of the Bleeding Ears, aka my enormously supportive husband, who let me read the very first draft to him every day over lunch and tried to hide his disappointment that the bad guys didn't show up in speedboats at the end. Thank you for having faith in me, *mon amour*.

Also up for canonization: my friend Claudia Depkin, who went above and beyond what I would have ever dared ask, enthusiastically volunteering to read draft after draft of the manuscript. Her daily comments were invaluable and her unflagging encouragement helped me persevere.

Thank you to those friends who let me hide out in their vacant homes for precious writing time: Nicolas Mercier and Paul Krieger for their beach apartment in Trouville and castle in Saintes; Cassi Bryn Michalik for her rooftops-view apartment in Paris; Guy for his home in the Loire; and my father-in-law, Jean-Pierre, and Christiane for their home-five-minutes-away-from-home.

Remerciements to my friend Mags Harnett for the several read-throughs and invaluable comments. Also to my sister Gretchen Scoleri, my friends Kim Lennert, James Kidd, and Sandrine Hosti, and my cousin Diana Canfield for their thoughts on the manuscript. My veteran-writer cousin-in-law Matthew Randazzo V, was of immense help with fellow-author counsel on getting published. His advice and long-distance hand-holding was much appreciated. And much thanks to my childhood friend Lou

Anders, editor of Pyr Books, for his enthusiasm and for looking over my "revenant rules" to verify that my monsters made sense.

Thanks to Terry Jones for legal advice. Bill Braine for brainstorming. "Olivia" for making her opinion known and for being the book's first true fan. Melissa Randazzo for leading my own personal cheering section. And my mother-in-law, Jeannine, for being so certain that one day I would be published.

And finally, but not least importantly, thank you to the faithful readers of Chitlins And Camembert. Your constant support and enthusiasm about my writing gave me confidence that I had stories worth telling.

DIE FOR ME

Letters from the Author:
Amy Plum shares her thoughts on the City of Light
and how the revenants came to be

Kate's Tips for Living *La Belle Vie*

Immortal Inquiries: A *Die for Me* discussion guide

Sneak Peek:
An excerpt from *Until I Die*, the sequel to *Die for Me*

Letters from the Author: Amy Plum shares her thoughts on the City of Light and how the revenants came to be

Amy Plum on Paris

Writing about Paris is like writing a love letter. I am passionately in love with the city. So when I set out to write a romance, Paris was the obvious setting. It is the most romantic place I know, so what better place for Kate to meet Vincent? Sparks were sure to fly.

In writing *Die for Me*, I wanted you, the reader, to be right there with Kate, experiencing the city in all of its cultural wealth. Kate has been coming to France since she was a baby, but she is still an outsider and doesn't take the city for granted. She still sees Paris with a fresh eye, like I did when I lived there.

I moved to Paris when I was twenty-three and stayed for five years. I had an office job that I commuted to every day, taxes to pay, food to make, nights to sleep—a completely normal existence. But every single morning of those five years I stepped out my front door and experienced a frisson of wonder as I beheld the city around me.

As I still do, even though I've spent a quarter of my life in France. I now live three hours south of the city in the Loire Valley. But as soon as I get off the train and step into Paris, it's like I've been filled with helium. I am floating and giddy when I am there. Even though it's not all beautiful, it is all pure magic to me. (Especially the not-so-beautiful parts.) I hoped that my love of the city and its joys and idiosyncrasies could be translated to you through Kate and her story.

During my five years in Paris, I accumulated some amazing experiences. So while writing *Die for Me*, I tapped these memories and wove some of them into Kate's tale. I didn't meet any revenants (as far as I know), but I did ride on a scooter through the streets of Paris behind a handsome artist. I kissed someone on the Pont des Arts. And I held hands with a devastatingly gorgeous boy on the quai of the Île Saint-Louis. (That one became my husband.)

I also tapped my memories for the locations in *Die for Me*. Jules's art studio is my old apartment—so my "front porch" was the steps of the Église Saint-Paul, where I sat and imagined the jousts that had taken place there. I browsed the Village Saint-Paul for vintage and antique treasures. I went to an underground club like Lucien's. And the museums and restaurants and cafés are places that I frequented.

Kate's grandparents' building actually stands a few blocks away from the park that I have placed it next to on rue du Bac. Jean-Baptiste's house has been taken over by a museum (how dare they!), and I borrowed its courtyard from an *hôtel particulier* a few blocks away.

So all the locations in this book actually exist—except for the Café Sainte-Lucie, which I had to make up because there wasn't the perfect café standing where I wanted, near the Métro and both Kate's and Vincent's homes.

But besides my nostalgia and an abundance of romantic locations, Paris holds another element that made it the ideal place to situate *Die for Me*: The city is ancient. Paris is relatively small, so every inch of it is steeped in history. And when you are there, its millions of ghosts are constantly pulling on the edge of your consciousness.

It's the macabre aspect—all the beheadings, murders, and war crimes that happened there—that lends to its being the perfect setting for a supernatural war between good and evil. Although revenants live everywhere in the world, Paris's history made it the perfect place to introduce them to you.

Paris is undoubtedly one of the main characters of *Die for Me*. In my mind, the city is a sentient being. She's a woman . . . of course! And Paris as a woman is incredibly sexy in a sophisticated way. She is extremely cool. She is bemused by her occupants but likes to toy with them, sometimes in a slightly sadistic manner. If you lose your heart to Paris, you will never regain it completely. She will hold your heart hostage until you come back to her.

If you haven't already met her, I hope you soon will.

Amy Plum on revenants

When I began writing *Die for Me* I used the word "zombie," but it quickly became obvious that I needed to find a new term. Besides their undead state, the beings I envisioned had nothing in common with zombies. Would you kiss a zombie? Would you trust a zombie with your life? About halfway through, the French word "revenant," which literally means "one who comes back," sprang to mind, so I asked my French husband what it meant to him. He said that it was a ghost or spirit that came back after death.

Perfect, I thought. I had found my word. Not only do my revenants animate three days after their death, but they reanimate repeatedly, making them "ones who come back . . . again and again."

Since finishing the book, I have come across references to revenants in both English-language and French fiction. However, there seems to be no consensus between authors as to exactly what a revenant is. As I had already concocted a complex mythology for my characters, I decided to appropriate the term and cast the revenants as historical creatures that were as old and venerable as vampires, zombies, and werewolves.

Kate's Tips for Living *La Belle Vie*

Kate's 10 Favorite Places in Paris to Kiss

1. On the steps of Sacré-Coeur, overlooking the city, at either sunset or sunrise.
2. On one of the bridges (preferably Pont des Arts, but any will do) . . . at night.
3. On the Champs-Élysées at Christmas, all of the trees sparkling with lights.
4. On a Bateau Mouche, one of the tour boats going up and down the Seine.
5. On the Champ de Mars, behind the Eiffel Tower during the Bastille Day fireworks.
6. During a picnic in the Buttes Chaumont park.
7. On a rooftop, overlooking the city. (Most buildings have roof access if you look hard enough!)
8. In the back row of one of the many cinemas that show old movies.
9. Down by the river on one of the quais. (I like the Île Saint-Louis, personally!)
10. In a museum, standing in front of a painting by Modigliani, whose models often look like they've just been kissed.

Kate's Top 10 Etiquette Tips for Paris

1. Parisians have a flair for style, and if you want to fit in, make sure you do too! Your Paris visit is an excuse to play dress up. Save the casual wear and sweatpants for jogging and glam it up as you stroll by the Seine.
2. You can write a five-hundred-page manuscript or read an entire book at a café table and no one will bat an eye—as long as you order some food or drink once

an hour. Consider it renting your own office space—an office with an unparalleled view: While reading and writing you get to watch cute Parisians saunter by!

3. Cheek kisses, or *bises*, can be confusing. In parts of France you give two, others three, and some southerners give four! But when you meet someone in Paris, give them one kiss on each cheek when you first see them and the same when you say good-bye. Follow that rule and you'll never go wrong.

4. When you enter a shop or boutique, it's like you are walking into the shopkeeper's home or their personal space. So always remember to say *"Bonjour, Madame"* or *"Bonjour, Monsieur"* to whoever's behind the counter when you walk in, and *"Merci, au revoir"* when you leave. You'll be surprised by the difference that little gesture makes!

5. If you want to exude Parisian sophistication, don't stroll the sidewalks or ride the Métro with a toothy grin on your face. Think coy. Think *Mona Lisa*. Generations of Frenchmen have been dying to discover just what's behind her secretive smile. Intrigue them with your own mystique.

6. What goes on a table in France that doesn't in America? Your hands and your slice of baguette. The "hands" rule is opposite ours: They're supposed to rest on the table at all times, not on your lap. And unless you're at a restaurant that gives you a separate bread plate, you are expected to set the bread on the table next to your plate.

7. Although it's frowned upon to ask for a doggie bag in restaurants, you might find yourself sitting next to an actual canine in some cafés. Dogs are still allowed in

many establishments, and owners can ask for plates to give their dogs under-the-table treats from their own meal. The message: Leftovers are for the dogs!

8. Although Paris is known for being steamy, the food and drink is not. Since extremes are thought to distract the palate, you won't find anything piping hot, freezing cold, or extra spicy. Don't ask for extra ice cubes or for something to be heated up: Instead, see if your taste buds agree with the French.

9. If it seems like salespeople are treating you like the Invisible Man, try using this magic formula I discovered. Just say, "I am so sorry for bothering you. But I could really use your help. Could you please . . ." and then ask them for what you want. Shopkeepers will instantly jump to your assistance. Who knows why it works? The important thing is, it does!

10. Want to make a Frenchman (or woman) swoon? Learn a few words in French and make an effort with the accent. People will love it and try their English out on you right away. Even if you feel silly, nine times out of ten, the person will come back with, "Oh, I love American accents. It sounds so . . . Hollywood!"

Immortal Inquiries:
A *Die for Me* discussion guide

1. Have you lost a family member or someone close to
    you? Did you find Kate's and Georgia's reactions to their
    parents' death to be realistic?
2. Do you think that the city of Paris was important to the
    story, or could it have been set somewhere else?
3. One of the novel's themes is the risk of investing oneself
    in a relationship that could prove painful. From marrying
    a spouse who is in active duty in the military (or another
    potentially dangerous profession) to committing to
    someone from a completely different background, there
    are many concessions people make to be with the one
    they love. Have you ever had to step out of your own
    comfort zone or face difficult challenges in order to be
    with the one you love?
4. Kate says, "The old dictum was backward. It should be
    'Better not to have loved at all than to love and have
    lost.'" Has there ever been a time in your life where you
    would agree?
5. Georgia and Kate have a very close relationship.
    Do you think this is a realistic portrayal of teenage
    sisterhood?
6. When Georgia and Kate saw Vincent dive off the
    Carrousel Bridge and were told by Ambrose that the
    sword fight was police/gang activity, they tried to come
    up with theories of what could have been taking place.
    What was your own theory at this point in the story?
7. When Kate sees Vincent for the first time at the café, she
    makes the comment: "I had the strangest feeling that
    I knew the guy. I'd felt that way with strangers before,

where it seemed like I'd spent hours, weeks, even years with the person." Have you ever had this sensation?

8. Both Kate and Vincent have struggled with the loss of loved ones in their pasts. How do you think this shared experience influences their relationship?

9. What would be your dream date with Vincent? How about Jules or Ambrose? Or Kate or Georgia? What is it about each of them that would convince you to accept a date?

10. If you could create your own revenant character, which period in history and location in the world would you choose for them?

11. If you could control each of the characters' destinies, what would you have happen to them?

12. What figures from history can you imagine becoming numa?

13. The sisters leave their old life in Brooklyn behind when they move to Paris to live with their grandparents. What advantages and disadvantages do you see in starting life in a new place after a tragedy?

14. Do you think that Kate should tell Papy and Mamie about what Vincent really is? How do you think they would respond?

15. In your point of view, what are the challenges that lie ahead for Kate and Vincent?

UNTIL I DIE

I LEAPT, DRAWING MY FEET UP BENEATH ME, AS the seven-foot quarterstaff smashed into the flagstones where I had been standing a half second before. Landing in a crouch, I sprang back up, groaning with the effort, and swung my own weapon over my head. Sweat dripped into my eye, blinding me for one stinging second before my reflexes took over and forced me into motion.

A shaft of light from a window far overhead illuminated the oaken staff as I arced it down toward my enemy's legs. He swept sideways, sending my weapon flying through the air. It crashed with a wooden clang against the stone wall behind me.

Defenseless, I scrambled for a sword that lay a few feet away. But before I could grab it, I was snatched off my feet in a powerful grasp and crushed against my assailant's chest. He held me a few inches off the ground as I kicked and flailed, adrenaline pumping like quicksilver through my body.

"Don't be such a sore loser, Kate," chided Vincent. Leaning forward, he gave me a firm kiss on the lips.

The fact that he was shirtless was quickly eroding my hard-won concentration. And the warmth from his bare chest and arms was turning my fight-tensed muscles to buttery goo. Struggling to maintain my resolve, I growled, "That is totally cheating," and managed to work my hand free enough to punch him in the arm. "Now let me go."

"If you promise not to kick or bite." He laughed and set me on the ground. Sea blue eyes flashed with humor from under the waves of black hair that fell around his face.

He grinned and touched my cheek, with an expression like he was seeing me for the first time. Like he couldn't believe that I was standing there with him in all my 3-D humanness. An expression that said he thought *he* was the lucky one.

I rearranged my smile into the best glare I could muster. "I'm making no promises," I said, wiping the hair that had escaped my ponytail out of my eyes. "You would deserve a bite for beating me again."

"That was much better, Kate," came a voice from behind me. Gaspard handed me my fallen staff. "But you need to be a bit more flexible with your hold. When Vincent's staff hits yours, roll with the movement." He demonstrated, using Vincent's weapon. "If you're stiff, the staff will go flying." We walked through the steps in slow motion.

When he saw that I had mastered the sequence, my teacher straightened. "Well, that's good enough for sword and quarterstaff today. Do you want to move on to something less strenuous? Throwing stars, perhaps?"

I held my hands up in surrender, still panting from the exercise. "That's enough fight training for today. Thanks, Gaspard."

"As you wish, my dear." He pulled a rubber band from behind his head, releasing his porcupine hair, which sprang back into its normal state of disarray. "You definitely have natural talent," he continued, as he returned the weapons to their hooks on the walls of the underground gym-slash-armory, "since you're doing this well after just a few lessons. But you do need to work on your stamina."

"Um, yeah. I guess lying around reading books all day doesn't do much for physical endurance," I said, leaning forward to catch my breath with my hands on my knees.

"Natural talent," crowed Vincent, sweeping my sweaty self up into his arms and pacing across the room, holding me like a trophy. "Of course my girlfriend's got it. In truckloads! How else could she have slain a giant evil zombie, single-handedly saving my undead body?"

I laughed as he set me down in front of the freestanding shower and adjoining sauna. "I don't mind taking all the glory, but I think the fact that your volant spirit was possessing me had just a tiny bit to do with it."

"Here you go." Vincent handed me a towel and kissed the top of my head. "Not that I don't think you're totally hot when you're dripping with sweat," he whispered, giving me a flirty wink. Those butterflies that suddenly sprang into action in my chest? I was beginning to consider them permanent residents.

"In the meantime, I'll finish your job and take out that pesky nineteenth-century weapons master. *En garde!*" he yelled, as he flicked a sword from off the wall and turned.

Gaspard was already waiting for him with a giant spiked mace. "You'll have to do better than that measly steel blade to make a dent in me," he quipped, waving Vincent forward with two fingertips.

I closed the shower door behind me, turned the lever to start the water, and watched as the powerful streams spat forth from the showerhead, sending a cloud of steam up around me. My aches and pains flew away under the steady pressure of the hot water.

Incredible, I thought for the thousandth time, as I considered this parallel world I was moving in. A few Paris blocks away I led a completely normal life with my sister and grandparents. And here I was sword fighting with dead guys—okay, "revenants," so not really dead. Since I'd moved to Paris, this was the only place I felt I fit in.

I listened to the noises of the fight coming from outside my pinewood haven and thought of the reason I was here. Vincent.

I had met him last summer. And fallen hard. But after discovering what he was, and that being a revenant meant dying over and over again, I had turned my back on him. After my own parents' death the year before, being alone seemed safer than having a constant reminder of that pain.

But Vincent made me an offer I couldn't refuse. He promised not to die. At least, not on purpose. Which goes against every fiber of his un-being. Revenants' compulsion to die when saving their precious human "rescues" is more enticing and powerful than a drug addiction. But Vincent thinks he can hold out. For me.

And I, for one, hope he can. I don't want to cause him pain, but I know my own limitations. Rather than grieve his loss over and over again, I would leave. Walk away. We both know it. And, though Vincent is technically dead, I'll venture to say that this is the only solution we can both live with.

THE STORY
CONTINUES...

Romance with a revenant was never going to be easy.
Even after they've defeated Lucien, Kate and Vincent must
face new challenges. Can Vincent maintain his immortality?
Can Kate and Vincent make their love immortal? Find out in
this second book of Amy Plum's rich and romantic trilogy.